T0265526

LIKE IT
NEVER
HAPPENED

Also available by Jeff Hoffmann

Other People's Children

LIKE IT NEVER HAPPENED

A NOVEL

JEFF HOFFMANN

CROOKED
LANE

NEW YORK

Published in the United States by Crooked Lane Books, an imprint of The Quick Brown Fox & Company LLC.

Crooked Lane Books and its logo are trademarks of The Quick Brown Fox & Company LLC.

Library of Congress Catalog-in-Publication data available upon request.

ISBN (hardcover): 978-1-63910-699-8
ISBN (ebook): 978-1-63910-700-1

Cover design by Heather VenHuizen

Printed in the United States.

www.crookedlanebooks.com

Crooked Lane Books
34 West 27th St., 10th Floor
New York, NY 10001

First Edition: March 2024

10 9 8 7 6 5 4 3 2 1

For Dad

CHAPTER

1

Milwaukee

WHEN TOMMY SEES Kevin's obituary, that dark puddle of blood from thirty years ago springs to his mind even before he can remember what Kevin looked like. He remembers it black, darker than the asphalt of the Burger King parking lot, but it must have been red that night. It happened so long ago it's hard to be sure. He had gone back to look at that puddle several days later, to convince himself that it had all really happened, that it wasn't some terrible fever dream. By then it was black for sure, just another stain—like motor oil or transmission fluid. Tommy doesn't really care that he can't remember the color of the blood, but it troubles him deeply that it takes so long and so much effort to summon the memory of Kevin's face.

"Hey, Dad? Can I borrow your truck?"

Tommy drops the newspaper to his lap and looks up at the door of the den. His daughter Sophie is wearing her coat, too much mascara, and a blank expression.

"Where you going?"

"To the library? Got a test tomorrow. Physics."

Tommy glances at his watch. "Mom will be home in ten minutes. We'll eat in twenty."

Sophie's eyes flicker toward the front door. "I'm not hungry. I had soup."

Tommy knows that she isn't going to the library, that the library is just the excuse most likely to spring her on a Wednesday night without an argument. She's probably headed to her boyfriend's basement to vape and make out. He knows what Maggie will say about that when she gets home, but he decides to argue with Maggie tonight rather than Sophie.

"Be home by nine thirty."

"Fine."

Sophie disappears, and a moment later the front door slams.

Tommy pushes up from the couch to get dinner ready. When Maggie's gearing up for a case, he's in charge of food, and Tommy can't stomach another pizza, so that morning he made stew in the Crock-Pot. He lifts the lid and inhales the scent as he stirs.

He knows that if his mom were still alive, she'd remember exactly what Kevin looked like. Her mind was sharp right up until the end, even as her eyesight failed. She lived with them her last six months, and every night when Tommy came home from work, she'd ask him to read her the obits so she could track the passing of her friends, her acquaintances, and her enemies. She'd sit in the recliner over by the fireplace, and Tommy would settle onto their old green couch. He read names until she recognized one.

Eight months ago, Tommy's mom's name appeared on that page with her own too-small paragraph that failed to describe a life well lived. After she was gone, Tommy kept reading the roll call. He occasionally recognizes a name—one of his mom's friends, somebody from church. He spotted the name of a friend's daughter on that page, and for more than a week he was paralyzed by the idea that Emma could die in some other place, that he'd miss the notice, and that nobody would tell him she was gone.

If his mom heard him read Kevin McNamara's name, she'd remind Tommy of that first day Kevin came over, the summer after kindergarten, and she would say that he never really left until that summer after high school. She'd talk about the peanut butter and jelly sandwiches she made for them after their mornings building the tree fort in the woods, or the hot cocoa after an afternoon of sledding down by the creek. She'd complain about all those sleepovers when Kevin's mom was out on a date or just out. And then she'd ask Tommy yet again why he and Kevin McNamara weren't friends anymore.

* * *

Maggie squeezes the steering wheel so hard her knuckles hurt. The anger knots her shoulders like it always does after a day like today. Sometimes the drive is enough. The jazz that trickles from the radio relaxes her breathing and allows her to unclench by the time she arrives home. Tonight, the drive won't suffice. Tonight, she'll need Tommy to wrap her in his strong arms. Maybe later, after dinner, he'll dig his thumbs into her shoulders, knead the day away. When she pulls into the empty driveway, she wonders for a moment where Tommy is. But then she realizes that Sophie probably took the truck, and she thinks of Sophie's boyfriend, and the vise squeezing her temples cranks just a bit tighter.

Maggie trudges up the front steps of their modest brick two-story and wonders whether to order pizza or Chinese. When she opens the front door, the thick, swampy smell of beef stew hits her, and she thanks the universe for Crock-Pots and for Tommy. She sets her purse on the kitchen table and lets her eyes linger on Tommy's broad back as he leans over dinner, stirring. He's a mountain of a man. He's solid, and not just his tall, thick body. Tommy, if nobody else, she can count on. The knot in her shoulder eases just a little.

"How was the day?" he asks without turning, in that gentle way of his. It was his voice more than anything that first piqued Maggie's interest. It doesn't fit this strong bear of a man, and that disconnect caught and held her attention. It still does.

Maggie takes off her glasses, rubs the bridge of her nose. "Leonard fucked me."

Tommy puts down the spoon, turns, and wraps her in a hug. Maggie lets herself disappear into his embrace. "What'd he do this time?"

"Remember that drug dealer? The one they caught with nine kilos of heroin?"

"Yeah?"

"Rock-solid case, and Leonard forced a plea deal on me. Six months in county rather than the decade in Stanley that he deserved."

"Why?"

"Leonard went to law school with the defense attorney."

Tommy rests his chin on the top of her head, and she presses her face into his chest. His shirt smells of engine grease and tacos and Old Spice and Tommy. He squeezes her tightly, and her jaw slackens. Her fists become a bit more like hands.

"Did she call today?" Maggie murmurs into his shirt.

"No," he says, and he doesn't ask who *she* is. Since that day in January when the dorm supervisor down at Marquette called to say that she was missing, Emma became that pronoun. When the police told them that her boyfriend was gone too, their worst fears eased, but Emma lingers in their thoughts all day, every day. In February, when Emma finally called Tommy to let him know that she was all right, the police traced the number to a prepaid cell phone.

Maggie slips from the hug, puts her glasses back on, and walks to the sink to wash her hands. "How was your day?"

Tommy goes back to stirring the stew. He shrugs. "HVAC in the science building went out."

"Any snowflakes melt?"

At this Tommy grunts a laugh. "No. We got it back up in two hours. Everyone survived."

"At least it wasn't a dorm." Tommy is the senior building engineer, and Maggie knows that when something breaks down in a dorm, parents start calling, and if those parents are alumni or donors, things can get complicated. "Where's Sophie?"

Tommy puts the lid back on the pot and opens the cabinet for the plates. "Library."

Maggie leans back against the counter. She wants to accept the testimony. She tries not to cross-examine. "How do you know she's at the library?"

Tommy sets the plates on the table before he answers. "I don't."

He leaves it at that, and Maggie doesn't have the energy to press the point. "Jeremy?"

"Locked in his bedroom. Doing his math homework or jacking off into a gym sock."

"Stop."

"Just sayin'. He's thirteen."

Maggie smiles, maybe for the first time today. "He's still my little boy."

Tommy unplugs the Crock-Pot and carries it to the table. "Dinner!" he shouts up the stairs.

They sit down to wait for Jeremy. "I've got a wake on Friday," Tommy says.

"Who died?"

"A guy from high school."

"I've got nothing on Friday night," Maggie says. "Want me to go with?"

"Nah." Tommy looks down at his hands, scrapes grease from under a thumbnail. "He was just a guy I used to know."

* * *

After he finishes the dishes, Tommy climbs down the wooden steps to the rec room. He built out the basement shortly after Jeremy was born, when the girls were still little. The shelves he built for the kids' toys now sit mostly empty, their contents given away or sold at long-ago garage sales. It used to smell like popcorn, Play-Doh, and finger paint. Now, it mostly sits quiet and dark unless Tommy's paying bills or Maggie's throwing clay.

He sits down at the particleboard table in the corner and shakes the mouse. The monitor flickers to life, and he clicks open the web browser. He starts by reading Kevin's obituary again. It's brief, but it's him. Forty-nine years old. Killed in a motorcycle accident. Survived by his loving sister, Susan, and his wife, Naomi. Preceded to God's kingdom by his mother. Like every obituary, it leaves out so much. It doesn't mention where he worked or where in Milwaukee he lived. It doesn't speak of his empathy or his quirky sense of humor.

And it doesn't describe what a self-righteous ass he could be when he thought he was right.

Tommy types Kevin's name into Google and finds a metric ton of Kevin McNamaras that aren't Kevin. He's done this every few years since the internet became a thing. He scoured AOL and MySpace and Facebook and LinkedIn and Instagram, but he never found Kevin. Tommy heard that he lived down in Chicago and was trying to make it as a sculptor, and then that he had drifted north to Fond du Lac to build furniture. The latest rumors placed Kevin back in Milwaukee, making ends meet as a handyman. He'd never heard about a wedding. Kevin didn't scatter breadcrumbs. His obituary is the only morsel that the internet coughs up.

Malcolm proves a lot easier to find. He can't, in fact, be avoided. Fifty lawyers under fifty. Quotes during mergers. Comments after acquisitions. Pictures at charity balls. Profiles in *Forbes*, *Chicago Magazine*, and the *Northwestern Law Review*. Tommy clicks on a random link and finds Malcolm staring at him from the lobby of the Chicago Hilton. He stands next to his wife, her long, dark hair hanging over bare tan shoulders. Her prominent Roman nose makes her face distinctive rather than just beautiful. She's a bit taller than Malcolm, who seems to be straining to his full height. His smile is gone, along with the long hair from high school—now trimmed to the corporate spec. He's still got those eyelashes that the girls loved and that so embarrassed him. Malcolm's suit probably cost more than Tommy's truck. He wonders if he and Malcolm would still be friends if they never pulled into that parking lot, if the shit never hit the fan, but it's hard to imagine having anything in common with the tight-lipped lawyer in the photo. He searches for a home address or a phone number but finds nothing. No Facebook, and Malcolm's LinkedIn account doesn't allow messages. He clicks through to his firm's website and writes down the main number. Malcolm will have to wait until tomorrow.

He also finds Henry easily. Rocky Mountain Tissue Solutions in Denver. An altruistic Henry proves even more difficult to square than a driven Malcolm. Henry grew up with little—his dad worked maintenance at the parish— and Henry always talked about owning his own business or becoming a management consultant or an investment banker. He finds no home listing for Henry either, but when he clicks through to his company website, he's surprised to find Henry's email and cell phone number under his profile picture. The years have been good to Henry. His forehead hasn't expanded, and his hair remains so blond that Tommy wonders if he dyes it. His crow's-feet make him seem happy rather than old. Tommy punches the number into his phone, and it rings only twice.

"This is Henry."

Hearing Henry's voice, all grown up and confident but with that same rumble it always held, sends Tommy reeling back decades, like hearing an old song that he forgot he knew.

"Hey. This is Tommy."

Henry says nothing for a long moment, and Tommy tries to imagine what his own voice must be doing to the other man.

"Hey, Tommy." His words come even, calm, as if they had talked last week. "What's up?"

"Kevin died."

Another silence. Longer this time. Tommy imagines Henry soaking in *that* news, measuring the implications. "How?"

"Motorcycle accident. All I know is what I read in the obituaries."

"We're forty-nine. Aren't you a bit young for the obituaries?"

Tommy almost tells him about his mom and the obits, but knows how that will sound. "Wake's on Friday. Thought you might want to know."

"Yeah," Henry says. "Yeah. I'm glad you called."

Tommy doesn't know what else to say. He didn't consider anything past telling Henry about Kevin. He thinks to ask about kids, whether he's still married to Alice, how he likes Denver, but Kevin's death and that long-ago night hang between them.

"Did you call Malcolm?" Henry asks.

"Not yet. All I could find was a work number. I'll call him tomorrow."

"I'll have to see about Friday," Henry says after another awkward silence. "I'll have to check with Alice."

"Yeah. Okay."

"Did you ever tell anybody?" Henry blurts. "About . . . you know."

"No," Tommy says, and he thinks about Maggie.

Tommy hears Henry breathing into the phone. When he speaks again, his voice is softer, less confident, younger. "I bet Kevin did."

2

Denver

THE AIR AT altitude is cold after dark, but Alice is layered for it. Henry used to argue against her running at night, especially after they moved up into the foothills with their narrow, serpentine roads. She'd tell him not to worry, that the dark was actually safer. The headlights warn her of cars approaching from behind or about to speed around a curve in front of her. The concern that caused Henry to complain about her nighttime runs used to warm Alice even as she ignored him, but it's been years since he's brought it up.

As she settles into her pace, she drinks in the lights of the city below her. The grid glows with geometric predictability in the center, but the lines of light snake toward twists and turns in the suburbs. The jagged skyline lurches up from the southeast. The darkness and the glow below help her savor the burn in her thighs and calves. Her lungs push air in and out like a bellows, and all of it allows her to think.

She needs the run tonight. She needs the night and the sweat and the lights to clear her mind. She had three closings in the last two days, and one was a disaster. She put the Jacobsens' house on the market more than eight months ago, and they insisted on listing it for two and a half million dollars, which Alice knew was too much. They refused four reasonable offers before Alice finally found fools from the East Coast willing to offer the ask. Problem is that those fools from the East Coast are also a pain in the ass. After the inspection, they started asking about radon and complaining about holes in screen doors and the depth of the footings for the deck. At first, the Jacobsens refused to consider any of it, so Alice had to call back and forth, negotiating common ground. The buyer finally shut up about the screens. She convinced the Jacobsens to drop five grand from the price for the footings that didn't meet code and to place another ten in escrow for radon remediation in the unlikely event it was necessary. Mostly, though, she played marriage counselor. She helped both sides realize that they really didn't want the whole thing to fall apart.

Alice takes a left at the fork in the road, toward the mountains, because she needs a long run today and she wants the climb. The wind is in her face now, but her legs feel strong. Her breath comes easy given her pace and the steep slope. Her mind is starting to clear of the messy, meaningless details, allowing her to focus on what she plans to say to Henry.

Marriage counseling. She saw the parallels with her job when she and Henry went through couple's therapy two years ago. After he screwed his personal trainer. Henry's transgression flayed Alice. The fact that he betrayed her in such a trite, clichéd way ground salt into the wound. The way she found out, though, was by far the worst part. Trish, someone Alice didn't even know that well, told her after hot yoga while they toweled themselves off on the bench outside the studio. Trish's face was drenched with sweat and pity, and her words came in a halting whisper. *"I know it's none of my business,"* and *"I've heard it from multiple people,"* and *"I just thought that you should know."* Trish didn't even know Henry or his personal trainer. *Multiple people.* Alice has no idea how many women had fingered Henry's dirty laundry before passing it along to the next, until Trish, of all people, finally felt compelled to show it to her.

Alice's watch taps her wrist at three miles, and she turns back toward home. Six miles will be just about right tonight. She's facing the lights again now, and the wind is at her back. It took half a year and a couple dozen therapy sessions to unpack all of her anger, disappointment, and disgust, examine it all, and then pack it away again. It helped that she believed Henry when he told her that the affair was his first and promised that it would be his last. He said he was sorry with words and flowers and random acts of kindness like doing the laundry and the dishes and even scooping the cat box. It helped that they had a good therapist, who encouraged both of them to examine what had happened but also what they'd had before and what remained. She helped them catalog what they still valued about their relationship—their shared love of good books, bad jokes, long vacations, and great sex. The therapist tried to help Henry explain why he did what he did, but she never managed to pry a meaningful answer from him. After a month of sessions, Alice finally concluded that Henry really didn't know why he cheated on her. He'd spent his entire adult life creating and maintaining emotional distance from ugly things, so he was well practiced. It took her six months to decide that she didn't want to blow it all up, and now, sweat trickling down her back and her pulse pounding in her ears, she feels like an idiot for that too.

Alice comes around a corner, and she sees the back of their house above her, third one from the main road, clinging to the side of the mountain. Most of the lights are on. The pine ceilings gleam gold, and the light through the windows glows warm. She slows to a walk for the last stretch. The view from those windows sold her on the house. She wonders whether she or Henry will keep it. She doubts that Henry will fight her on much of anything, but Alice can't decide if she wants to live with all those memories. There are other houses. Other views.

Six miles always leaves her feeling alive, but tonight, it's more than just the run. She's felt tall and strong and free since she made her decision. She's been mentally packing her things for the last week, stripping the list down to the essential. As she separated the wants from the needs, and ignored everything that she never wanted anyway, her list became short. As her belongings fall away, Alice feels almost weightless. She imagines a new home in Albuquerque or Santa Monica. Barcelona, even—although she'd have to brush up on her Spanish.

For the longest time, their childlessness left Alice empty in a way that was difficult to talk about. It wasn't one decision, but many. She had to decide in her twenties when Henry started talking about kids. It seems like her thirties were filled with constant deciding. That was the decade when everyone she met—friends, clients, coworkers—asked her how many children she had, and then studied her with naked curiosity when she said that she had none.

Many assumed fertility issues and talked about the latest technology for making babies. When she told people that she didn't want children, that her life was full without them, they must have read something on her face, because as her thirties dwindled, a startling number of people gave themselves the permission to tell her, with pity in their voice, how much time she still had left. Everyone seemed to think she was eyeing her biological clock, weighing the future. Only Henry knew that the past kept its heavy thumb on the scale.

But that was all put to bed years ago. Once she turned forty, people stopped asking, even Henry. And now she knows the void that always makes her chest ache a little will make everything simpler, cleaner. She only has to worry about herself, and this time she'll make the decision with a clear head and on her own terms. Her cat won't mind the changes.

Alice steps from the shoulder of the road onto the sidewalk of their little development. Ridgeline Drive. Just six houses carved out of the hillside and the forest. She has them pegged between two and four million dollars each, based on proximity to the city, square footage, aesthetics, and the view. She'll miss their friends, especially the Wesolowskis and the Kopecs, but she knows she'll miss them whether she moves to Barcelona or stays on Ridgeline Drive. Everything will change. Those late summer nights on the Kopecs' deck drinking expensive cabernet, the long weekends at Vail, their dinners in the city—all require an even number, pairs, couples. Everything will change. Of course, everything's already changed, hasn't it?

It changed a month ago. That's when the sex stopped, like a spigot turned. Henry stopped visiting her side of the bed, stopped nibbling her ear, just like the last time. Henry seldom went more than a few days without rolling across, never a week, and a month was out of the question. Last time, it puzzled her, but this time she doesn't have to wait for Trish or somebody else to tell her why she isn't getting laid anymore. She spent that first week in denial, but then she raced through the remaining stages of grief like running a 5K at sea level.

Alice opens the door and steps from the brisk cold into the cozy warmth. She hears the fireplace crackle and smells burning juniper. Her face goes flush, and pins and needles stab her neck and back. She tugs off her gloves and stops her watch. She removes the hair tie, slips it onto her wrist, and lets her long blond hair fall loose. She wriggles out of her shoes, and she peels layers as she walks down the front hall. The slate floor feels cool, even through her socks. By the time she makes the great room, she's down to just her tights and a sports bra. The walk settled her breathing and her heart rate, but she's still slick with sweat.

Henry perches on a stool at the kitchen island, peering at his laptop. Alice takes the opportunity to study him one last time before she tells him what she's decided, and everything changes. He looks an awful lot like he did when they started dating their freshman year of high school. Not a hint of gray in his blond hair, and his blue eyes still move quickly, taking everything in. But creases claw at the corners of his eyes, his chin doubles up when he's looking down, and a slight paunch bulges when he's sitting. He only works out occasionally now. No more personal trainer—just a treadmill in the basement.

Tonight is the night. She's promised herself. As soon as she showers, she'll tell him. Last time she confronted him as soon as she got home from yoga, and she was a sweaty,

blubbering, hysterical mess. It will be different this time—
on her terms.

"How was the run?" he asks.

"It was good," she says, because it was. "Dark. Cold."

Henry looks up, and his mouth is pinched in that way it
gets when he's deciding how to say something. "I'm booking
a flight to Milwaukee."

Alice walks to the stove and grabs a dish towel from
where it hangs on the handle. She wipes the sweat from her
face and her neck. She knows Henry hates when she does
this, and that's half the reason she's doing it. "For when?"

"Friday morning."

A trip to Milwaukee works well. She can pack her things
while he's gone. "Why?"

"Kevin died."

The sweat on her back goes instantly cold. Goose
bumps dimple her arms. "McNamara?" she asks, as if there's
another Kevin in Milwaukee.

"Yeah," Henry says. "Motorcycle accident."

"Oh," Alice manages. "Oh, fuck." And she realizes that,
in a way, she's been waiting to hear Kevin's name for the
last thirty years. The way Henry blinks tells Alice that he,
too, is thinking about that parking lot and the aftermath.
"How'd you find out?"

"Tommy called."

"Of course. Tommy."

Alice wants to tell Henry what she's decided. She wants
to tell him right then, half-dressed, standing in the kitchen.
It isn't the sag on his face that stops her. She's past worrying
about that, but her mind snags on what Kevin said that last
time Henry saw him. *"We're all gonna regret this,"* he said.
"In the end the truth's gonna come out." Even all those years

ago, the way Henry described it made it seem more like a threat than a prediction. She stands in the kitchen, with her decision on her tongue, even as she tries to sort out if she's still part of that *we*. Finally, she hangs the towel around her neck and wanders toward the bedroom. All she wanted from the day was to end her marriage. Kevin ruined even that.

"Book me a ticket too," she says over her shoulder. "I'm going with you."

CHAPTER

3

Chicago

ELENA PUSHES HER sleeves up to her elbows and reaches into the bowl. Her hands churn the eggs and flour, slowly squeezing. The eggs are cold and runny, the flour warm and dry, and as they mix, they change each other. Together they become something different. As the dough forms, she kneads it gently, like her mom taught her. Up and down and over, slowly. There's nothing special about the ingredients of ravioli dough, but her mom taught her that you can't rush it. Time and care are the special ingredients.

While she kneads, her mind churns the call that she got from her lawyer a few hours ago. Malcolm wants Kinsey to stay with him every other weekend and two weeks a year. Elena laughed when he told her, but her lawyer didn't. There's no way in hell that's going to happen. On the face of it, it doesn't seem like a lot to ask. If she were divorcing a different man, she'd use every other weekend to restart her life. She would take improv classes or fly to cities like Seattle and Asheville, simply because she'd never been there before. She would meet a strange man in a strange bar and drive all night to see the sun rise over Niagara Falls because it seems like everyone should do that at least once. But she's divorcing Malcolm. Malcolm, who, when he's not traveling, seldom leaves work before nine at night. Malcolm, who works most weekends. Malcolm, who probably couldn't name one of Kinsey's friends, much less surface a number to call one of their parents to set up a hangout. Does he plan to leave her alone in that downtown condo? Would he hire a babysitter for a thirteen-year-old? Elena doesn't even have to ask Kinsey what she thinks. She would set fires or file for emancipation or parachute from the roof of his building if she had to stay with Malcolm every other weekend.

When the dough forms enough, she takes it out of the bowl and presses it to the board, turning it slowly, putting her weight into it. When it feels right, she slips it back into the bowl, covers it with Saran Wrap, and sets it in the fridge. She washes her hands and then walks around the enormous kitchen, gathering what she needs: another egg, two bowls, forks, spoons, the fluted pastry cutter, and her mom's favorite rolling pin.

When Malcolm first showed her the blueprints for the house, back when they talked through their plans, she just laughed at what she saw. She could tell, even on paper, that it was way too big, that it would feel more like a barn than a kitchen. At the time, she had given Malcom credit for good intentions—he knew that she loves cooking, and he wanted the best for her. But she couldn't make him understand what *she* had in mind: a cozy kitchen like her mom's in that bungalow on Cass. Everything in that kitchen was one step away, two at the most. When Elena cooked with her mom, they couldn't help but bump elbows. Add a drunk aunt or three, turn on the oven, and that kitchen became as warm as the laughter that filled it. She tried to hint at it—then she scribbled all over the blueprints, cutting the size of everything in half, and finally they argued. But Malcolm doesn't like to lose arguments, so the granite island that she's working on seems just a little bit larger than her parents' entire house.

Every time they moved—from their first apartment in Wicker Park, to the house in Lakeview, and finally to Winnetka—everything got bigger. More rooms, more square feet in every room. This house could shelter a small South American village. It took most of the first six months for Elena to buy enough furniture to keep the echoes at bay. A few of the couches she has yet to sit upon.

As the homes grew larger, Malcolm's time in them contracted, until seeing him at home felt like spotting a snow leopard or a snipe. He had always been driven, but when they first started dating, while he was in law school, there had been room for Elena alongside his ambition. He took her to concerts. She showed him the Art Institute. He laughed at her jokes. He listened to her back then. He talked to her. They even cooked together when she asked him to.

When he started working at the firm, when he started slicing his time into fifteen-minute morsels, the firm ate most of them. Elena tried to satisfy herself with the scraps. She reminded herself that she'd known about Malcolm's work ethic up front. She was there for all those long nights studying for exams and the bar. Truth in labeling and all that, but it got lonely fast. Malcolm made partner in record time, and for a while that success helped him settle. He eased back just a bit, and Elena pried her way back into his life. She gorged herself on the time Malcolm spent with her, and she deluded herself that it would last, that making partner could allow him to relax back into their marriage.

After Kinsey was born, he dialed it back even further. Those first few years, he was almost like a regular dad. He woke with Kinsey on weekend mornings. He put her to bed whenever he was home on time. He read *Go, Dog. Go!* as if he were memorizing a case from a law school textbook. But when Kinsey was almost two, when she started walking and talking, when she was finally edging out of the *pet* phase of child development into the *person* phase, the Cellutec deal hit. That was the biggest of his career up to that point, and he let himself be drawn back into the thick of it. After that, he never really came back.

Elena beats another egg with which to seal the pasta, and then takes the dough out of the fridge. She's rolling the first strip when she hears the front door open and close. She glances at the clock. Kinsey—home from school. She flips the strip over and pats some flour onto the other side. As she rolls, she deftly shifts the pressure on the rolling pin to keep the thickness of the dough consistent. Back when she was learning, if the dough wasn't perfectly even, her mom would scoop it up and wad it into a ball, Elena would cry, and they'd start again. Elena taught her daughter the same way, but of course Kinsey never cried. If the dough isn't even, the pasta ruptures at the thin spots when the water boils. The filling spills out and makes a mess of everything. In the end, making pasta from scratch depends on smoothing things just right. It takes patience and consistency and steadiness to keep everything from exploding into a terrible mess.

Elena hears Kinsey's sneakers squeak across the hardwood into the kitchen.

"Hey, girl. How was school?"

Kinsey drops her backpack on the island and washes her hands. "Fine."

"Fine like almost crappy or fine like sublime?"

Kinsey says nothing.

"Fine like so thin that it's hard to see with the naked eye?"

Still nothing.

"Did you have to pay a fine?"

Not even a whisper of a smile. Kinsey was never one to spend unnecessary words. Puberty made her even more frugal, but since Malcolm moved out, she's become downright stingy. Elena still works to goad them from her, though. She steals a look at her daughter. She's wearing her Sacred Heart plaid skirt, knee socks rolled down to her ankles. Her legs are scrawny like Elena's used to be, and she's got Elena's long dark hair. Her enormous eyes, that nose, and her high cheekbones sometimes make Elena feel like she's looking in a mirror, but Kinsey carries herself more like Malcolm, with a quiet self-assurance that Elena was never able to manage at that age.

Kinsey glances at the board. "Ravioli?"

"I'll make an Italian out of you yet." Elena starts on the second strip of dough, dusts it with flour. She moves the pin. She keeps it even. "Can you make the filling before you practice?"

Elena hears the fridge open behind her and takes that as Kinsey's answer. Kinsey likes to spend an hour with her mandolin after school, and she's been practicing more with the concert coming up, but Elena can still sometimes coax her into helping. It takes two trips to the fridge for the ricotta, the parmesan, the spinach, and the mushrooms.

Kinsey piles it all right next to Elena, and that makes Elena smile. A quarter acre of countertop, but Kinsey still chooses to work elbow to elbow with Elena.

"I've got parent–teacher conferences tomorrow," Elena says. She's been teaching half-day kindergarten for the last four years. It helps her feel useful and allows her to escape the big empty house for the morning, but she's home most days when Kinsey arrives. "I won't be home until about seven."

Kinsey just nods. She minces the spinach. Her knife makes quick, clean work of it, and she starts in on the mushrooms.

"And we're going to Milwaukee this Saturday," Elena says.

"What for?"

"Mia's birthday." Kinsey's cousin is just a year and a half older, and she and Kinsey have always been two peas in a pod.

Kinsey mixes the mushrooms, spinach, and cheese. She puts the bowl on the board. "What time?"

Elena hands a spoon to Kinsey. "Probably leave around nine. Why?"

Kinsey takes a long time to answer. They both spoon the filling into clumps on separate strips of dough. "Reza has a sleepover."

"We should be back by then."

"The sleepover's on Friday."

They both dip their fingers into the bowl and wipe the egg along the edge of the dough. They fold it over the filling and press the seam with a fork to seal it. Elena knows that Kinsey remembers, but she reminds her anyway. "You have dinner with your dad on Friday night."

Kinsey's fork stops for a moment, and then it starts moving again. "You're finally making the right amount," she says.

Elena smiles up at Kinsey, but Kinsey's hair is hanging over her face. "I always make enough."

Kinsey finishes sealing her strip of dough and then drops the fork into the sink. "That's not what I mean. When Dad still lived here, you always made too much. He never came home for dinner, but you always made enough for him too."

Elena bites her cheek and picks up the pastry cutter. She locks her eyes on the board. She carves the ravioli from the strip of dough. Kinsey pinches the seal on each and gently places them in the bowl. Kinsey's right, of course. Elena always knew that he wouldn't show, but the Italian grandma at her core always hoped that Malcolm would surprise them, and she didn't want to be caught with too little. But he usually ate takeout at the office when he didn't have a business dinner. Mostly, she put the leftovers down the garbage disposal when they finished eating, but sometimes she packed them into Tupperware and stored them in the enormous Sub-Zero for a few days before she washed it all down the sink. Tonight, she's making just eight ravioli— four each—the right amount.

"I don't want to go to dinner with him," Kinsey says quietly.

Elena looks up at her, and Kinsey meets her gaze. She's waiting to see how Elena will react. She has that gift of stillness, of waiting, that comes from Malcolm. The older she gets, the longer she can wait, and the more it unsettles Elena. Elena wants to tell Kinsey to go to the sleepover, that she'll handle Malcolm, but that call from her lawyer nags. She knows that Malcolm's dreading that dinner more than

Kinsey. She suspects that dinner is probably related to that call from her lawyer, Malcolm trying to pretend that he still knows how to act like a dad, that he hasn't evaporated from Kinsey's life entirely. Not yet. But the last thing she needs right now is a pissing contest with Malcolm about a freaking dinner. "I know, honey, but—"

"No. You don't know." Kinsey's eyes harden. Her voice is matter-of-fact, but with an edge to it, like Malcolm's when their paths crossed long enough to argue. "He won't know what to talk about, and I have nothing to say to him. We'll just stare at our food until it's gone, and then we'll stare at the other people in the restaurant until the bill comes."

Elena wants to wrap Kinsey in a hug. She wants to tell her that she doesn't have to go. But even as she wants to capitulate, she wants to scream at that cold, stubborn part of her daughter that reminds her of Malcolm, because although she works hard not to admit it to herself, she hates that part of Kinsey.

"It's like having dinner with a stranger, Mom."

During the day, Elena's been able to hold everything at a distance—the divorce, the disintegration of their family, the overwhelming loneliness. She's been able to deal with the lawyer as if it was all just a transaction, like selling a car or a house. She's been able to laugh about it with her neighbor, Holly, because prying a serious conversation from Holly is like trying to warm your hands with ice. She's only allowed herself to cry at night, lying alone on her side of the too-big bed in the too-big bedroom. But now a big fat tear rolls from the corner of her eye down to the tip of her nose. Her hands are covered in dough and flour, so she lets it settle there, quivering. Finally, two more tears roll down her nose and they fall as one onto one of their eight perfect ravioli. She has no idea what to say to Kinsey. She has no idea what will happen next or what she should do or how she'll manage to keep all of this from bursting open into a terrible mess that they'll all regret. Kinsey pushes away from the counter and grabs her backpack from the island.

"It doesn't matter," she says as she walks across the enormous kitchen toward the cavernous living room. "He'll probably cancel anyway."

* * *

Malcolm stares straight ahead as he plunges toward the lobby. The two associates in the elevator car are working for him on the McGregor deal, but he doesn't know their names. And they have the common sense not to attempt small talk. That would only draw attention to the fact that they're either leaving too early or squandering billable minutes to sneak out for a double latte.

When the doors open, he glances at his watch. 6:52. He left his office one minute early. It takes just seven minutes to walk to his condo building and ride the elevator to the thirty-ninth floor. He pushes through the revolving doors, turns left, and walks briskly toward the lake. He doesn't notice the warm spring breeze that ruffles his hair, or the men and women walking head-down and fast in the other direction, toward the late train. He certainly doesn't notice the panhandler sitting on his haunches, leaning against the building at the corner of Madison and Wabash, shaking the coins in his McDonald's cup, trying to compete with the rumble of the L train passing overhead. Instead, he sorts through the loan covenants for the mezzanine financing for the McGregor deal. He has a meeting with the banks for that layer of debt tomorrow morning. They threw in the kitchen sink, like they always do, and he evaluates which two or three covenants their loan committees really need. He crafts the arguments that will shred the rest.

Malcolm strides past the black leather chairs and across the marble lobby of his building to Security. He glances at his phone, sees nothing urgent, and then looks up at the kid behind the desk.

"Name's O'Donnell," he says. "I'm on thirty-nine. I've got a visitor arriving shortly. A Ms. Bradford. Send her up."

He turns before the boy can respond. He steps into the elevator and slips his keycard into the slot. The door closes, and thirty seconds later it opens again in his living room—the room that will become his living room, anyway. Malcolm walks across the empty space and stops at the floor-to-ceiling windows. He finished with the loan covenants during the elevator ride, but he doesn't really notice the first sailboats of the season, bobbing at their moorings, or the way the evening sun filters between the buildings to the west, or the gulls' effortless rise on the updraft between his building and the next. His eyes linger for a moment on the young couple in the building across from him. They're sitting close to each other on the couch, folding their laundry. He forces himself to look away—back out at the lake.

He's got dinner tonight with the managing partner of the firm, and they'll discuss how to position themselves for the ElekTek IPO. He thinks again about the dossiers that his assistant prepared on the CEO and CFO. ElekTek, if he lands it, will be his biggest deal by far. He reviews from memory the alma maters and personality profiles and the web of connections through colleagues, boards, and clubs, probing for the shared soft spot that will serve as the beachhead upon which he'll mount his assault. ElekTek would be huge. ElekTek would get his name on the door.

The elevator chimes softly and slides open. Malcolm turns to find a slight older woman with an enormous canvas bag over her shoulder. Her straight gray hair and tan face remind Malcolm of his mother when she returned from spending the winter in Alabama, but his mother would never dress so fashionably.

The woman pulls a notebook and pen from her bag, sets the bag on the ground next to the elevator, and joins Malcolm at the window. Her eyes flick from him to the view of the lake and back. "I'm Evelyn," she says, extending her hand.

"Malcolm." He takes her hand, and it feels fragile, like a baby bird.

"What a beautiful space," she says. "You have the whole floor."

It's not a question, so Malcolm doesn't answer. Evelyn walks toward the kitchen, glances in at the empty countertops, turns back to him. "'Bout seven thousand square feet?"

"Something like that."

"My initial consultation usually takes about two hours," she says, looking around the wide expanse of the living room. "But we might need a bit more than that."

Malcolm looks at his watch. "I've got seventeen minutes."

Evelyn coughs a laugh. "Right. I need to unpack your expectations. I need to understand your style and the mood you're hoping to create. We'll develop a preliminary color palette. We'll discuss how you anticipate moving through the space, your entertainment needs, how you live. And the budget, of course."

This all makes Malcolm smile. "Listen. Now I've got sixteen minutes. My expectations are easy to unpack—I expect you to fill this place up with furniture and make it look nice."

"But—"

"Fifteen and a half. I don't really care about the budget, but if I'm not out the door by 7:22, then I'll find another designer."

Evelyn blinks and her mouth works, but Malcolm can see the words *"I don't really care about the budget"* work their magic and settle her lips toward stillness. She looks at her own watch and then back up at Malcolm. "I'll need to stay for a couple of hours to measure and imagine."

"That's fine."

"And we'll need to walk through so that I know what room's what."

Malcolm knew that she'd see it his way. "We've got fourteen minutes," he says without looking at his watch.

Malcolm blurts decisions as they circle the condo: *living room, dining room, office, guest bedroom, exercise room, guest bedroom.* Evelyn scribbles notes and sketches as they walk. She lingers at the doorway of the master bedroom. Malcolm watches as she takes in the mattress on the floor, neatly made, and the open closet full of suits and shirts and shoes.

"How long have you lived here?"

"Three weeks."

He sees her digest that and weave a narrative in her mind that's probably pretty accurate in its broad strokes, even if it's impossible for her to imagine the details. She finally looks back down at her notebook and scribbles a short paragraph before following him to the last bedroom, the one that faces Navy Pier.

"This will be my daughter's room," he says, his mouth suddenly dry. "When she's here."

"How often will she be with you?" Evelyn asks quietly.

Malcolm looks at the Ferris wheel, its lights on now, turning so slowly but never stopping. "We're still working that out."

Evelyn steps into the room, moves to the window. "How old is she?" she asks.

"Thirteen."

"What does she like?"

Malcolm finds the question slippery, hard to hold much less answer. He tries to think about Kinsey's room in Winnetka, but he was only ever in there after she was asleep, so all he can summon is the smell of it, like persimmons and plastic. Worse, when he tries to picture Kinsey, even though it's only been three weeks since he's seen her, the image is already starting to blur. A thickness that Malcolm fails to recognize as terror fills his throat. He wants to say that she likes whatever it is that thirteen-year-old girls like, but he knows how that will sound.

"Hobbies?" Evelyn asks the window. "Interests?"

He wants to say *Austin & Ally* and American Girl dolls and Harry Potter, but he knows those were all years ago. He wants to ask for more time to answer the question, because that's all he needs, really, is more time. He looks past Evelyn, past the Ferris wheel, past the lighthouse, but the vast, darkening expanse of Lake Michigan holds no answers.

"I don't really know," he finally admits with a whisper.

Evelyn turns and their eyes lock. Hers leak pity, and Malcolm hates her for it.

4

The Wake

TOMMY SITS IN a chair in the corner of the room farthest from the casket. He leans forward, elbows on
his knees and his eyes on the patterns in the maroon carpet. His shoulders strain against his sport coat when he sits,
and because he only wears his wingtips to funerals, his feet
hurt when he stands. He looks up each time someone new
enters, and the room is starting to fill with a strange mix.
A few seem like relatives, mostly old and frail. More than
half are hipsters with too-tight clothes, absurd facial hair,
and glasses with thick, black frames. Hard-looking men
wearing jeans with creases and starched flannel shirts make
up the balance. Nobody from high school. Nobody that
Tommy knows. Just family and people from the second half
of Kevin's life.

Tommy works hard to ignore the smell of the flowers.
There aren't many, just a few small arrangements huddled
behind the casket, but he gags on their stench. He knows
that the flowers are supposed to smother the smell of a dead

body, but since his mom's funeral, for Tommy, flowers *are* the smell of death. He avoids looking at the casket, and he certainly doesn't look at the terrifying woman standing next to it.

Tommy's been to this funeral home recently. He can't remember who died, but he remembers the intricate gold and red pattern of the wallpaper, like a brothel in a western, and he remembers the slant and the creak of the floors. Tommy always goes to funerals, and he isn't sure why. He concluded long ago that the steady stream of strangers and semi-strangers does little for the family of the deceased. It usually saps what little strength they have. Most of the time, they'd rather huddle with those closest to them and cry in private. And it's been many years since he's said a prayer when he bows his head in front of the casket. He certainly doesn't go to funerals for himself. He always leaves feeling exhausted, a lot closer to death than when he arrived. Catholic obligation is the only explanation, a sense of duty pounded into him by his parents and then the nuns in elementary school and the brothers in high school.

Earlier, when he reached the front of the receiving line, he was confronted first by Susan, Kevin's sister. Her close-set eyes and the dissatisfied slant to her mouth were immediately recognizable, even after thirty years. They shook hands, and she squinted at him as if trying to make out something in the distance.

"Tommy Rizzo," Tommy said. "I was a friend of your brother's in high school."

"I thought I recognized you," she said, her voice neutral, devoid of surprise or even interest.

"I'm sorry for your loss," Tommy said, because that's what Tommy always says.

Susan's head twitched to the side, as if she was about to shrug but managed not to. "Thank you," she said after an awkward pause. Then she leaned in and spoke quietly. "Of course, with Kevin, something like this was bound to happen."

Tommy was trying to formulate a response to *that* when the woman next to the casket seized his hand and shook it. "You're Tommy," she said. Not a question. An accusation. Her jet-black hair was cut painfully short, and her face was pale and smooth, like porcelain. She was pretty in a fierce way, like a hawk.

"I am. I'm a friend of Kevin's from high school," Tommy said.

"I know," she said. She stared at him intently, as if trying to divine what he was thinking or to memorize his features for the sketch artist. "He talked about you often. I'm Naomi. Kevin's wife."

Tommy tried to free his hand, but Naomi wouldn't let go. "I'm terribly sorry for your loss," he said, because that's what he always says.

She blinked rapidly, and for a moment, Tommy thought she might cry. But then a smile whispered across her lips, and when she spoke, her voice was steady. "Yes," she said. "I'm sure that you are."

*   *   *

Tommy glances at his watch. Quarter 'til seven. He feels the heat of Naomi's gaze on him, or imagines it anyway, but he keeps his own eyes pinned to the floor. He tries to decide how much longer to wait. There's no reason to think that Henry or Malcolm will come. Henry never called him back. It took a day and a half to get past Malcolm's assistant, and when he finally got through, the conversation was short. Malcolm made it very clear that Kevin's death held no interest for him. The cold, clipped way that Malcolm spoke before he hung up told Tommy how much he resented the past's intrusion on his present. And Tommy still isn't sure that he wants to see them. He's hungry, and he's tired. It's probably Naomi's words that keep him sitting there. *"He talked about you often."* Tommy knows that it wasn't the sleepovers or the sledding or that fort that they built in the woods that Kevin told her about. Her hard eyes and the way her lips twitched told him that she knows too much.

Tommy checks his phone again, but there are no new messages, no emails, no calls from Emma. Emma hasn't called in over two weeks—she's due—so Tommy checks his phone often. And every time that he checks it and sees that she hasn't called, his throat goes tight because he worries that something might have happened to her or, worse, that she's decided to stop calling for good.

Her absence was difficult enough when she moved into the dorms at the beginning of her sophomore year. He worked hard to stay connected. He met her for lunch every week or so. They even shared a few beers down at Caffrey's once. Tommy ignored the fake ID, and he never told Maggie about that, of course. There has always been friction between Emma and Maggie, and the gears seemed to lose their grease when Emma hit puberty. From then on, most of their conversations sounded like metal on metal. Tommy blames Maggie for Emma's disappearance—there's no way around that—but he tries not to hate her for it.

Tommy stands up to leave. Malcolm and Henry aren't coming, and he knows that he should go home, but when he looks up at the door, the past nearly flattens him. Henry and Alice. And it's like they just stepped out of the pages of the St. Pius yearbook. They look around the room but don't spot Tommy in his dark corner, so they drift to the end of the receiving line. Tommy sits back down and tries to decide what in the hell he'll say to them.

The website didn't lie. Henry wears a charcoal suit, but he's still the power forward with the perfect hair and the strong chin. He's gained a few pounds, but he still moves with confidence, and his blue eyes still dart about. And Alice, wearing a simple black dress, looks even stronger and leaner than she did in high school. He forgot how tall she was. She used to slouch a bit back then, as if trying to make herself shorter, but now she stands ramrod straight. Her eyes look gray, even though Tommy remembers them as blue. Her hair is still blond and straight, although she's let it grow long. Most importantly, they are together. That was the thing about Henry and Alice—they were always glued to each other. Henry leans toward Alice to whisper something in her ear. Alice rests her palm on his forearm while they talk to Susan. They fit each other. Even after thirty years, Tommy can see that they each still define the other.

They make it past Naomi and spend their obligatory moment, heads bowed, in front of the casket. Tommy wonders if Henry finds it easier to look at Kevin's body than Tommy did. When Tommy stood there an hour ago, for a long time he stared at Kevin's hands. They were folded neatly over his stomach, with a rosary wrapped around them. He finally allowed his gaze to drift to Kevin's face, and of course, it looked nothing like Kevin. Tommy holds a dim view of morticians' abilities and ambitions. At every funeral, someone will claim otherwise, probably to make the family feel better, but in Tommy's opinion, corpses never resemble the people they used to be. When Tommy first saw his mom lying in her coffin, he thought for sure that there had been a mistake, that they were showing him someone else's mother.

Tommy hasn't seen Kevin in so long that he really wasn't in any position to judge, but the shock of graying hair and the creased face failed to match any version of Kevin that Tommy remembered from childhood or that he'd invented during the decades since. He was surprised by the smile, though. Morticians never allow a smile. They always sew the lips into a grim straight line, as if even the corpse should look miserable at a funeral. But the mouth turned subtly upward at the corners. And it was Kevin's smile—the way the right side crimped a bit higher than the left, delivering a slice of the irony that was pure Kevin. Maybe this mortician knew Kevin, or maybe he was an exception, an artist. Or maybe Kevin's lips are straining against the stitches, rebelling right up until the very end, refusing to give up that smile.

When Henry and Alice turn from the casket, they look dazed and disoriented. Tommy stands and walks toward them, and Henry catches sight of him before Alice. Tommy watches as Henry's face ripples with recognition. He leans close to Alice and whispers in her ear, and her expression shifts too. They both settle on smiles that are equal parts uncomfortable and wary. They meet in the center of the room, and none of them seem to know how to greet each other. Finally, Alice gives Tommy a hug that lasts barely a second, and he smells sage or hemp. When she pulls away, Tommy and Henry hesitate and then shake hands— something that they've probably never done before.

"It's good to see you," Henry says. He sounds like he means it. "Good thing somebody reads the obituaries."

"I thought that you might want to know," Tommy says.

"It's been a long time," Alice says.

"Yeah," Tommy says. "Almost thirty years."

This wedges an awkward silence between the three of them. How do you resume a conversation that was interrupted so long ago? What questions do you ask? What do you share? Where do you even start?

"I've thought about reaching out," Henry says. Alice looks at him, surprised.

"Me too," Tommy says, realizing it's true even as the words leave his lips.

"I guess it might be a little bit easier now," Henry says, nodding toward the casket. "Without him around to throw gas on the fire."

In those weeks after Burger King, they all argued, they all said things that couldn't be unsaid. But whenever the heat began to settle, Kevin supplied the accelerant that fueled the next raging argument.

"Did you find Malcolm?" Alice asks.

"Yeah," Tommy says. "He . . . let's just say that I doubt we'll see him."

"That's what I figured," Henry says. He looks up at the coffin and then back at Tommy. "Motorcycle into the side of a truck. Doesn't sound very accidental."

The same thought had whispered through Tommy's mind as he waited—probably because of what Kevin's sister said. Tommy glances toward Naomi and then back at Henry. "What do you make of her?"

"The ice queen?" Henry looks over his shoulder again. His eyes linger on Kevin's wife, and then he turns back. "I'd maybe drive into the side of the truck too if I woke up next to *that* every day."

"She knows," Alice says.

The cold, hard certainty in Alice's voice confirms what Tommy suspected. "Yeah," he says. "I think she does."

Henry touches the small of Alice's back with his hand. Alice tucks her hair behind her ear. Tommy tugs at his collar.

"You were wrong," Henry says as he waves toward the door. "Gordon Gecko is in the house."

Tommy turns to find Malcolm standing in the doorway, wearing a suit and that same blank stare from the photo at the Hilton. He scans the room, and when he sees them, he doesn't wave, he doesn't blink, his expression doesn't change. He just stares at them.

* * *

Malcolm walks through the door of the funeral home a little after seven. If he makes this fast, he can get back to Chicago by nine thirty. Ten at the latest. He needs to read the redline of the purchase agreement for the McGregor deal before he goes to bed, because he has a conference call with the executive team at nine tomorrow morning. He's already thinking about that call, so it takes him a moment to realize that the man in the center of the room is waving at him, and another to recognize that the man is Henry. Tommy and Alice stand next to him. He was expecting to see Tommy, but not Henry. He didn't give a thought to Alice, but she's married to Henry, isn't she? He looks at the casket, and then back at the three of them. Malcolm always makes a point of tackling the most unpleasant task first, so he walks toward his high school friends. They shake hands all around and murmur hellos.

"It's good to see you," Henry says, but his words sounds more like a question than a statement.

"I didn't think you were coming," Tommy said.

Malcolm shrugs. "I had a meeting in Milwaukee this afternoon," he says. "I was in town."

This is a lie of course, but Malcolm would be hard-pressed to explain the truth. He usually makes decisions only when he knows exactly why he's making them. But this didn't feel much like a decision—he just found himself driving north on the Edens Expressway after his last meeting was cancelled. If he had examined his motivations, he would have denied that he was curious to see Tommy or Henry. He wouldn't have admitted to himself that a funeral in Milwaukee provided a perfect excuse to cancel dinner with Kinsey, sparing himself the long, painful silences. And it would have felt wrong to acknowledge that he wanted to see Kevin's body for himself. But if he *had* asked himself why he drove north, he might have found all of those reasons woven into the truth.

They talk for several minutes about the usual topics—jobs and kids and homes and dead parents. They don't talk about the man who will be buried tomorrow. They don't talk about the secret that they are all hoping will be buried with him. Malcolm doesn't listen too closely, because he'll never see these people again, but the basics seep through. Tommy has three kids, and he's some sort of janitor at Marquette. Alice and Henry live in Denver. No kids. A realtor and a tissue broker, whatever the hell that means. For his part, Malcolm says he's married with a thirteen-year-old daughter and a house in Winnetka—all of it true, if not all of the truth.

While they talk, Malcolm works to match the people in front of him with the people that he knew in high school. Tommy's hair is still clipped short, but there's more salt than pepper now. He still has that enormous chin that makes him look a bit like a comic book hero. He's every bit as big as Malcolm remembers, but none of it has softened to fat. As a teenager Tommy seemed uncomfortable in that body, clumsy, as if he were wearing his older brother's shoes. Now, he seems to have mastered it. The settled way he stands tells Malcolm that he's become accustomed to its power.

Henry hasn't changed a bit, still trying to wedge a joke wherever one might fit, and Alice's long, graceful body remains muscled and sinewy in a way that only childless women seem to manage. She smiles at something that Tommy says, and her perfect teeth are still that unreasonable shade of white that nobody could ignore back then. But their way of being together seems subtly different. In high school, they were always touching one another. They still touch a lot, her hip against his, his hand on the small of her back, but it seems different somehow, as if the contact is the product of repetition, part of a routine, a performance even.

Alice is saying something about their house, its elevation, its distance from central Denver. Malcolm's eyes drift across the room and land on the casket. They still haven't talked about Kevin, which suits him just fine. If he's lucky, he can escape without discussing the dead man at all. He surveys the reception line, estimates how long it will take him to get through. He looks to the front of the line. The woman next to the casket is looking over the shoulder of the man in front of her. Right at Malcolm. She doesn't look away when their eyes meet, and her gaze is greedy.

"Who's that?" Malcolm asks. The rest of their heads swivel toward the woman. Malcolm looks away before she does. "The woman next to the coffin."

"That's Naomi," Tommy says. "Kevin's wife."

"I didn't know he was married." The implications of this unfold in Malcolm's mind and stomach simultaneously, but he's careful not to let anything show in his face.

"She knows," Alice says. "I can tell that she knows."

They are all quiet for a long moment, taking that in. Finally, Tommy starts talking again. He's telling them something about his oldest daughter, but then he stops mid-sentence. Malcolm turns to see Kevin's wife walking toward them. In spite of her boyish build, there's something feline in the way that she walks. When she gets close, Malcolm sees that she's wearing no makeup, that her face really is that white. Her gaze fastens on him and won't let go.

"You're Malcolm," she says, as if she's serving a warrant.

"And you're Naomi," he says, to knock her back a bit, if gently.

A slight nod. A pause. "Elena couldn't make it?"

Malcolm struggles to keep his own face steady, even as he studies hers for irony or malice, but he finds nothing but that stare. "My condolences," he says instead of answering the question.

This earns him another little dip of the head. The silence hangs heavy between them, and Malcolm refuses to say anything more.

"I'm glad you could all be here," she says. She keeps looking at him, as if he's the spokesman.

"I'm glad I could make it," he lies, because there's really nothing else to say. He's intentional about the pronoun, because he refuses to speak for the others.

"Kevin's will is being read tomorrow," she says.

Tommy and Henry stir. Malcolm is careful to keep his face neutral. He sorts through the reasons that she might say this. She's doesn't seem the type to blurt random facts.

It's unlikely that she's looking for free legal advice. Malcolm's mind refuses to examine any other possibilities.

"That's quick," he says, because he can sense that Henry, Tommy, and Alice will say nothing. In spite of his best intentions, he has become the spokesman. "They usually don't read the will so soon."

"The lawyer said that Kevin wanted it that way." Her slate-colored eyes flick to Tommy and Henry, then back to Malcolm. She holds out a business card, but Malcolm refuses to take it from her. "Here's the address," she says. "It starts at noon. The lawyer said that Kevin left something for the three of you."

* * *

Henry sits on the barstool next to Tommy, feeling small. The bartender sets two beers in front of them without either of them asking, and Tommy thanks her by name. Alice went back to the hotel when they left the funeral home, which was just as well. Malcolm looked baffled when Tommy asked if he wanted to join them for a beer. He just shook his head and walked to his car.

The Club is a dump, just a long wooden bar and a few scattered tables. Bucks and Brewers jerseys hang in between beer mirrors. A shuffleboard table lines the back wall. A scruffy collection of regulars nodded to Tommy on the way in. But the mugs are chilled, at least. And Johnny Cash is playing on the jukebox. "Fancy," Henry says.

Tommy shrugs. "It's on the way home."

Henry studies Tommy in the mirror behind the bar. It's strange to be sitting next to him after so long, gulping a High Life as if nothing happened. So familiar, but skewed, as if he's wearing new contacts or recovering from a concussion. Tommy looks about the same as he did in high school, just a bit of gray at the temples and his share of the wrinkles that they've all earned. Tommy takes a long drink, killing half the mug. He sets his beer carefully back on the square cardboard coaster.

"That was fucking weird," he says.

"You're a savant when it comes to understatement," Henry says. "I was expecting a wake, not a summons."

"What the hell could he possibly leave us that we'd want?"

Henry laughs. "She never said that we'd *want* it."

"So, you think it has to do with—"

"What else?" Henry turns to look at him. "His class ring? Some Waterford that his mom gave him? Of course that's what it's about."

Henry sips from his own beer and tries not to think about that night and what came after it. In the beginning that was all he could think about, but he managed to shove it into a corner of his brain, and he seldom pokes at it. He sometimes goes months, even years without thinking about that night, but Tommy's call nudged him toward that musty mess.

"They could have just left," Tommy says. "We would have let them just walk away."

Henry's fingers tighten around the handle of the mug. This is not why he came to the bar. He thought that maybe he could reconnect with Tommy, relive some old memories, try to remember why they used to be friends. But Henry can tell that the memory of that night looms too large for Tommy to see around it. He knows that if he tries to talk about the past, Tommy will keep drifting toward that parking lot. "Let's not do that tonight," Henry says. "Things will get complicated enough tomorrow."

Tommy opens his mouth as if to argue, but then he closes it without speaking. He nods. He finishes his beer and motions to the bartender for another with a twitch of his fingers.

"Kevin looked like shit," Henry says, to change the subject. "I know he's dead, but Jesus. Promise me. If you come to my funeral, shut the goddamn lid."

A smile tugs at Tommy's lips. "What did you make of Malcolm?"

"Dude could crack walnuts with his ass."

Tommy finally shows his teeth. "Yeah. He's wound a little tight."

"Wound a little tight? You think? Dude didn't even comb his hair or tie his shoes back in high school."

"I guess it makes him good at what he does." Tommy looks sideways at Henry. "What about you? How the hell did you, of all people, end up working for a nonprofit?"

That question used to bother Henry. Most people make the same assumption. Early on, he'd deflect it with a joke and change the subject to something else. But when people found out—and they always found out—they'd stare at him in a way that told him that they considered lying about his job almost as bad as the job itself. "Actually, we're for-profit."

Henry watches Tommy in the mirror as the big man takes that in. He blinks. His hand hitches a bit as he hoists the beer to his mouth. He places his mug carefully back down on the cardboard square.

"I thought you worked at an organ bank."

"Nope. Tissue broker."

"Which means?"

For a moment, Henry considers telling Tommy exactly what that means, but he'd rather not see Tommy's face drift toward disgust, so he sticks with his usual spiel. "Surgeons need to train on the latest equipment, and they need cadavers for that. If it wasn't for what I do, that outpatient surgery that your mom probably had would still require forty stitches and three nights in the hospital. Sometimes the good walks hand in hand with the ugly."

"My mom died six months back," Tommy says.

Shit. "I'm sorry. I didn't know."

"She was old," Tommy says quietly. "It was time."

Tommy's finger twitches again, and the bartender brings Tommy's third and Henry's second. They both take a drink, and for a long time they're silent. Henry manages not to think of his own parents' funerals. He's about to ask about Tommy's wife, but Tommy speaks first. "It was good to see Alice," Tommy says.

Henry just nods.

"You two still look like your prom picture. It's like nothing changed."

"Yeah," Henry says. "Not so much."

"How so?"

"It's complicated."

"Complicated like how?"

Henry takes another drink of his beer and stares at himself in the mirror. The High Life makes him want to talk, and of course Tommy will listen. He wants to tell Tommy about that thing with Lyla a couple years ago, when he almost fucked up everything. He wants to tell him about the deep well of generosity that allowed Alice to forgive him and about the debt he incurred when she did. He wants to say that his marriage is exquisite and deeply flawed, and that both can be true at once. But mostly he wants to tell Tommy how he was flattened by that call last month. He wants to tell him about the test and the follow-up test and the knowing for sure. He wants to tell Tommy that he still hasn't told Alice yet, and he wants to explain why he hasn't told her, so that he can try to make sense of it. But telling Tommy before Alice seems like one betrayal too many. He tears the cardboard coaster in half before he speaks.

"Let's just say that sometimes the good walks hand in hand with the ugly."

5

The Phone Call

TOMMY IS WATCHING golf when Emma calls. When he was younger, before kids, he might spend an entire hungover Sunday watching golf, drifting in and out of sleep, never really missing much. Now, Tommy watches golf only when there's no other sports on TV, and he usually only watches a hole or two, just twenty, maybe thirty minutes, until he decides what he's going to fix or build or clean. But when he's got something on his mind, he'll let the holes drift past as he sorts things out—the gentle lilt of the announcer's voice calms him without distracting him. Rickie Fowler is making a run at Spieth today, while Tommy tries to sort out the funeral and works to imagine what will happen later.

When the phone rings, Maggie is downstairs throwing mud, which is good. Jeremy is in his room, as usual. Who knows where Sophie went. Tommy has never seen the number before, but the insistence of the ring and the way his stomach tightens tell him that it isn't a telemarketer.

"Hello?"

"Hey, Dad." Her voice sounds small. Far away.

"How are you, sweetheart?"

"I'm okay?"

Tommy hears that question mark, and it terrifies him. When Sophie hit puberty, she adopted that annoying habit of tilting the end of every statement as if she's uncertain of everything. Emma, though, always spoke in a firm, declarative way. The first two times that she called him, she was skittish, but he could hear the excitement in her voice—the way she talked fast and laughed when he wasn't expecting it. The third time, she sounded normal, almost bored. Today, though, she speaks quietly, like she doesn't want Kyle to hear. Tommy chooses his words carefully, determined to move slowly, as if trying not to frighten a wild animal—a deer or a rabbit.

"How's Kyle?" he asks.

She hesitates. "We're both kinda stressed out."

"What're you doing for money?" Tommy asks. He's been wondering this for the last month or so. They both emptied their savings accounts, but it was just thousands of dollars—birthday gifts and babysitting money in Emma's case. Kyle used to sell weed, and Tommy worries that he knows exactly what they're doing for money.

"Kyle's got a job," she says quietly.

"Doing what?" Tommy asks.

"We're fine, Dad."

Suspicion confirmed.

"Can I send you some money?" Tommy asks softly. He glances at the basement door. The first thing Maggie said when Emma called that first time, after she stopped shouting and crying: *"Don't give her any money."*

"We're okay," she says. "For now."

Tommy licks his lips and asks the next question as delicately as possible. "Are you nearby, Emma?"

"Not really."

"Are you in Wisconsin?"

Very long pause. "Yeah," she says quietly.

"Can I come see you? Meet you somewhere?"

Even longer pause. "Maybe," she says. "But just you. Not Mom."

It's Tommy's turn to hesitate. "Okay," he finally says. "Just me."

"I need to think about it," she says. The phone on Emma's end rustles. "I gotta go."

"Emma," Tommy says too loudly, "I love you."

For a moment he thinks that she's hung up, but then he hears Kyle's voice rumbling in the background.

"Me too," she whispers, and then the line goes dead.

Tommy stares at the TV. A long Rory McIlroy putt falls far short. And then he looks at the basement door and tries to figure out how much he's going to tell Maggie. He's always helped bridge the gap between Emma and Maggie, but before, it was easy. Just helping them understand each other, translating the miscommunications, prodding Emma to apologize when it came to that. The last few years, though, it's like he's wedged between them, like a fender between a dock and a boat when a storm hits. And worse than that, there are two Maggies: Maggie the lawyer and Maggie the mother. The lawyer knows that Emma is nineteen. She knows that Emma's an adult, whether she's fully formed or not. She knows that Emma has every right to leave home, and she doesn't have to talk to them if she doesn't want to. It's a lot harder for Maggie the mother.

She wants to send Emma to her room and ground her from the car. She wants to file a missing person report. Tommy knows that even as he mediates between his wife and his daughter, he's also wedged between those two Maggies. He turns off the television and heaves himself from the couch. He walks to the basement door—but walks slowly because he still doesn't know what he's going to say.

*   *   *

Maggie sits between her kiln and her wheel. She's baking three mugs that she threw last week. On the wheel she's forming what will probably be a vase, but if it starts to sag in the wrong places, she might just make a bowl instead. The heat on her back feels good and contrasts nicely with the cool, wet mud slipping through and past her fingers.

She knows that she's not much of a potter. Fran, her friend from work, dragged her to a class a decade back after a particularly stressful case. After two classes she bought her own wheel. After the third class she bought a second-hand kiln. Tommy pulled up the carpet in a corner of the rec room and replaced it with tile. He installed a utility sink in the corner and built walls of shelves to frame out a little room. The calming whir of the wheel and the hypnotic shape of the mud as it spins bring her heart rate down. And the feel of the mud transports her back to that creek that ran through her grandfather's land out past Kewaskum. She and her brothers would form pies and crude animals out of the mud at the bend of the creek, under the maple tree. That mud smelled like fish and rot, but it felt the same against her fingers. The mud rewards her for patience. It's become her way to center herself, her therapy. And although she knows that she'll never make anything brilliant, she makes something. If she hates it, she can crush it back into a lump, but when she throws something she likes, she can bake it toward a satisfying hardness that won't change. Unless she drops it, and it shatters.

Maggie hears someone on the stairs, and after several footfalls she knows that it's Tommy. Only Tommy's big enough to make the stairs groan like that. He almost never comes downstairs while she's throwing, so she thinks that she knows why he's coming. She keeps her eyes on what she hopes will be a vase, keeps her fingers on the mud, and tries not to hope that he's heard from Emma.

Maggie leans into the glimpses of her daughter through Tommy. In a way, her relationship with Emma has been filtered through Tommy for years. When Emma became a teenager, they began to rub each other the wrong way. Maybe it was because Emma was the oldest, and Maggie expected the most from her. Maybe Maggie was overprotective. Maybe she kept the leash pulled too tight because of everything she saw at work—the drugs, the perverts, all the young adults making bad decisions. Probably, Emma was just a little bit too much like Maggie.

Tommy threads his way through the basement and stops in the gap between the shelves that serves as a door to her makeshift studio. Maggie doesn't look up because if she looks up, she'll ruin the vase for sure, and she'll read too much on Tommy's face. She's thinning the neck, the delicate part. It changes the balance of the spinning mud, but if she does it slowly, carefully, barely moving her fingers, the piece will find its own shape. Tommy looms in the doorway, though, not speaking, just watching, and that makes it difficult to keep her hands steady.

"What's up?" she asks.

"Emma called."

Maggie's fingers quiver a bit, and the smooth outline of the spinning vase bends. She tries to compensate, and the neck of the vase becomes a bit thinner than she intended, but she manages to stabilize it. "How is she?"

"I'm not sure. She seems a little bit off."

"Off in what way?"

He shrugs. "It's hard to tell. I wonder if she and Kyle are getting along."

Maggie tries not to feel it, is ashamed that she feels it, but something swells in her chest that's far too close to joy. She spent eighteen years celebrating her daughter's happiness, doing whatever she could to smooth her path. Now, she wants to see Emma so badly that she's reduced to reveling in Emma's pain. The neck of the vase wobbles, like an ice dancer coming out of a spin, an elbow protruding. "What makes you say that?"

"I don't know," Tommy says. "Something about the way that she answered when I asked about Kyle. And she practically hung up on me when Kyle came into the room."

The ice dancer's knees are now spilling from the spin too. Although Maggie tries to keep her fingers steady, tries to let the wheel do the work like all of the YouTube videos tell her, she can't help but apply a little pressure, which only seems to make things worse. "Did she say where they are?"

Tommy shifts his weight and hesitates just a moment before answering. "No," he says.

Maggie knows lies. Twenty-five years trying criminal cases have shown her so many lies that she doesn't even have to look at Tommy, doesn't even really need to hear that pause to know that he's lying. The air changes just a little, and she feels the lie. The ice dancer feels it too, and she wobbles uncertainly, as if she might fall. Whenever Emma calls, Maggie asks Tommy an open-ended question—just like she does at the end of any interrogation or deposition. That's probably why Tommy's still standing in the gap between the shelves, but she isn't sure what she'll do, what she'll say if he tells her another lie, so she says nothing. Instead, Maggie takes her hands from the mud and watches as the vase collapses. She clicks the wheel off with her toe, and it spins slower and slower until it stops. She doesn't look up at Tommy. She kneads the clay that was going to be a vase and churns it into a shapeless lump so that she doesn't have to think about what it was supposed to become.

"I've gotta go to work," Tommy says. "Transformer blew at the business school."

"Okay," Maggie murmurs.

Tommy waits for her to say more, to look up maybe. Finally, he turns and goes. The stairs complain again as he climbs them. Maggie dips her hands in a bowl of water, and then works the wet into the lifeless lump of clay, trying to decide what she will make of it now.

6

The Will

THE THREE MEN sit quietly in the waiting room of the lawyer's office. They all arrived before noon, and now it's almost quarter after, but they don't talk. Maybe it's the receptionist that keeps them from talking, but they probably wouldn't have spoken if her desk sat empty. Malcolm texted Tommy for the address at eleven thirty, which surprised Tommy. Henry, on the other hand, fully expected Malcolm to show. Malcolm decides that the office, with its threadbare gray carpet, cut-rate chairs, and a sliding glass window between the receptionist and the waiting room must have been converted from a dentist office. Henry wishes that he had taken some Tylenol, and he wishes that he quit drinking a few beers before he finally stopped. Tommy's not hungover, but the lie he told Maggie in order to slip away on a Saturday roils his gut.

Tommy wonders whether Naomi is already in with the lawyer. She wasn't in the waiting room when he arrived ten minutes early. Surely she isn't fifteen minutes late for this.

Malcolm thinks about the McGregor call that he took from the car. He prioritizes all the follow-ups that he committed to, arranging them and rearranging them in his mind. It helps him to ignore what his research assistant told him about Naomi. Henry wonders yet again why he came and wonders if it's too late to leave.

When the door opens, all three men expect to see the lawyer, but it's Naomi. She's wearing a different silk blouse, gray this time, and black pants that flare at the bottom to cover her shoes. Malcolm tries to read the pale mask of her face, but he comes away with nothing. Henry finds it hard to look at her. Tommy can't take his eyes off the envelope in her hand.

"Thank you for coming," she says. Her voice is cold and harsh, the aural equivalent of fluorescent lights. She holds the envelope out to Malcolm. "Kevin left this for the three of you."

At first Malcolm doesn't budge. He's never been to a will reading before, but he can't imagine that this is how it's done. He thinks to ask to see the lawyer, but that won't change Naomi's profession, and it won't change the contents of the envelope. He knows that Tommy and Henry won't make a move, so finally he reaches out and takes it from her. Their names are typed on the front. It's not sealed, which means that Naomi has read it, of course. He feels her eyes on him as he pulls the sheet of paper from the envelope, and he feels Tommy and Henry shift in their seats. He unfolds it and finds six words: *Tyler Greavy is at Linden Glen.* He stares at those words, sorts through everything they might mean, and then hands the paper to Tommy.

* * *

The three men file out of the lawyer's office onto the strip mall sidewalk. They blink into the Saturday afternoon sun. They stare out at the street. The cars rushing past punctuate their stunned silence. They all recognized the name on that sheet of paper. They read that name in the newspaper the morning after that night in the parking lot—right next to the name of the boy who died. They pieced together which name matched which boy as they huddled in Tommy's basement, sorting out what they had done.

"What in God's name was *that*?" Tommy finally murmurs toward the street.

Henry and Malcolm say nothing because both men know that the question is rhetorical, and they all know the answer. That was Kevin reaching out from the grave and pressing "Play" on the argument they had paused three decades ago.

"And what the hell is Linden Glen?" Henry asks.

Tommy and Henry have never heard of Linden Glen, but Malcolm has. Malcolm has written a check to Linden Glen every three months for the last eight years. When he learned about the shithole that the state of Wisconsin had dumped Tyler into, when he learned that Tyler had no family left, he arranged the move.

"It's a long-term care facility," Malcolm says quietly.

The other two men turn toward Malcolm, but they find no answers on his face as he stares blankly out at the traffic. Tommy can think of no way that Malcolm would know this. Henry's mind churns through the possibilities, and right at the edge of those possibilities, he begins to guess at the truth. All three men poke at the next question, the question that matters. Tommy forms it into words first.

"What the hell are we supposed to do now?"

"I'm not sure about you, but I'm supposed to be on a seven o'clock flight," Henry says. "And nothing on that piece of paper is going to change that."

Tommy thinks about Maggie. He thinks about how awkward this will be for her at work, but that worry melts as he imagines the look on her face when she learns his secret, his enormous lie of omission. Henry is thinking about Alice, but he's thinking of another secret altogether. Malcolm's mind is an unaccustomed jumble as he considers ethics committees and termination agreements and his law license. He tries to find a gentle way to tell them, although it's been so long since he's spoken gently that he doesn't think in quite those terms. It doesn't matter anyway, because there's no gentle way to say it.

"We're supposed to go visit him," he says quietly. "Naomi's a reporter. From the *Milwaukee Journal Sentinel*."

7

Cheese Castle

KINSEY'S BEEN YAMMERING like an auctioneer since they left Milwaukee, about her cousins and her cousins' friends and her cousins' friends' friends. Dom's three-bed-room split-level was clogged with relatives and friends and noise and joy. As they drive past Sturtevant, she tells Elena a convoluted story about Snapchat and a trashcan and some boy that Mia likes from school. It's not the stories she tells, but the way she tells them that makes Elena smile.

"You had fun today," Elena says.

"Milwaukee's so different," Kinsey says.

The older Kinsey grows, the harder it has become to ignore the difference between how she acts in Milwaukee compared to Winnetka. "You think?"

"People say what they mean. And they laugh more."

She heard Kinsey laughing today, and she didn't even know that it was her daughter. Elena was leaning against the kitchen doorway, hoping that nobody would ask why Mal-colm hadn't come. She stood next to her brother, listening to Uncle Frank tell that ice-fishing story that he always tells. He droned on about the pickup truck that plunged through the ice in Door County, when laughter burst loud from the den behind Elena. Dom glanced toward the den and then leaned in close to Elena and whispered, "Somebody's enjoying herself."

When Elena turned, she saw Kinsey kneeling on the carpet in a circle of Mia's friends. She was leaning back and laughing—cackling, really. She laughed so loud and so long that Elena blinked and looked more closely, to make sure that it really was Kinsey.

She looks at Kinsey now. "What can I say? We're Italian. We tell you what we think whether you want to hear it or not."

But Kinsey isn't having it. She stares hard through the windshield. "Even Mia's friends that aren't Italian. They seem to like me, and they don't seem to fake it. They all talked to me and they listened to me when *I* talked. Nobody told me what their dad does for a living, and nobody asked about mine."

The mention of Malcolm drops a curtain of silence between them. Elena thinks about her own childhood, the summers running feral on Cass with Dom, Tony, and a pack of kids that were either family or friends who seemed like family. Her dad was an electrician, but she can't remember anybody ever asking about that. Maybe they already knew. Certainly they didn't care. She tries to chart a line from her own childhood to Kinsey's but fails. The girls that Kinsey runs with are aloof at best, absolute bitches at their worst. Even Reza, Kinsey's supposed best friend, ghosts her for weeks at a time for no reason that Kinsey can articulate. Whenever Elena sees Kinsey with her friends, she always

feels like they're older than thirteen. They seem discon-
nected in some fundamental way, leaning away from each
other just a little, as if they all have chronic halitosis. But
in Milwaukee, Kinsey just seems like a thirteen-year-old.
Elena tries to convince herself that she's succumbing to nostalgia about her own childhood, or that being a kid is different now. But every time they visit Milwaukee, she sees
it—that connection, that leaning in.

"Yeah," Elena finally says. "Milwaukee's different."

"Grandpa seems so sad," Kinsey says.

"He is," Elena says. "Maw Maw was everything to him."

When Elena wasn't in the kitchen making fun of her
brothers or Uncle Frank, she sat on the couch with her
dad. They watched the Brewers game around the legs of
partygoers streaming through the room to the food. The
wrinkles were etched more deeply around his mouth. His
face was gray, like gunpowder or a storm cloud. When he
managed a smile, usually when one of his grandchildren
came near, it seemed forced. He didn't talk about Elena's
mom. He just complained about the pitching staff and the
left side of the infield. Elena didn't say anything about her
mom either, because the few times she had tried to in the
past, her father's face closed up tight, and Elena had wept.
In so many ways, Maw Maw was everything to Elena too.

Elena's mom had been at the center of so much—their
family, their block, their parish. Everyone reached toward
her when the joyful, the confusing, or the tragic happened.
They called for advice, and they sat at her kitchen table to
tell stories and cackle. She was essential to so many people,
but whenever Elena called, her mom made her feel like she
was the only one that mattered. When she died, Elena and
so many others lost the most important person in their lives.

Elena can't stop thinking about the way her own life com-
pares to her mom's. She keeps feeling all the empty spaces.
She can't help but think how nonessential *she* has become.

When they pass the Mars Cheese Castle, Kinsey shifts
in her seat and leans her forehead against the passenger window. She's quiet and still for a long time. Elena grips the
leather steering wheel of her too-big Mercedes and resists
the urge to ask Kinsey what's wrong. She doesn't need to ask
because she feels it herself. The Mars Cheese Castle sits just
north of the Illinois border, and it tells them both that they
are nearing that big empty house in Winnetka.

"They probably have mandolin teachers in Milwaukee,"
Kinsey says, apropos of nothing.

Elena looks at her, back at the road, and then back at
Kinsey. Her daughter has been with the same instructor
down at the Old Town School of Folk Music for more than
four years, and she loves him. "Nothing more to learn from
Chris?"

Kinsey turns from the window. "We should move
there," she says quietly. "To Milwaukee."

Elena laughs, but Kinsey doesn't. Elena takes her eyes
from the road to look at Kinsey again. "Sure. Right. We'll
just pack a few suitcases and move to Milwaukee."

Even as she dismisses the idea, she feels herself lean
toward it. She imagines beers with Dom and Tony, wine
with her brothers' wives, Brewers games with her dad. Her
best friends from high school all still live within ten miles of
where they grew up. She imagines neighbors that aren't jack-
asses, a kitchen where she fits, a new start. It's impossible,
of course—thirteen-year-old thinking. But as she assembles
the list of reasons that prevent them from pulling up stakes
and heading to Milwaukee, she finds it surprisingly short.

"Why not?" Kinsey asks.

"Your friends, for one."

"My friends are all assholes," Kinsey says in her Malcolm voice. "They're not really friends. They're just kids I know."

This is true, of course. Elena surveys Kinsey's class for the nice kid every year, the kid that reminds her of the friends that she grew up with, but she always sees more assholes. And the women that she knows in Winnetka are mostly assholes too. She always calls them that—*women that she knows*—not friends.

"And then, of course, there's school."

"They have schools in Milwaukee," Kinsey says too quickly, as if she's been planning this conversation for a while. "For me *and* for you."

"You're serious, aren't you?"

Kinsey considers the road—or maybe she's looking past that—and then turns in her seat to face Elena. When she starts making her case, she's jabbing her finger south toward Winnetka. There's a quiver of emotion in her voice—not her Malcolm voice at all. "We don't have family there. You don't like the people any more than I do. Our house is too big. And we don't have to be near Dad's job because he's not even part of our family anymore."

Elena opens her mouth to argue, because that's what responsible adults do when thirteen-year-olds come up with hairbrained schemes without thinking them through. But she finds Kinsey's case remarkably tight, and she struggles to marshal arguments against it. The longer the silence stretches, the more Milwaukee and her father and the rest of her family tug at her. Her mom tugs at her. More than anything, the person she once was tugs at her. Kinsey has wrapped words around an urge that Elena didn't even know that she was feeling. The question slips out before Elena can consider all its implications. "You really want to do this?"

"More than anything," Kinsey says.

She says it in her not-Malcolm voice, the voice that Elena knows comes from her heart, not her head. But she says it with a settled certainty that tells Elena that she's been waiting for the right time to bring it up. And then Elena's mind starts to race, sorting through all the things she'd have to do—the selling, the packing, the giving away. She'd have to find a new job and a place to live. She'd have to make new friends and reconnect with old ones. She'd have to start over. And then her mind slows and starts to wrap itself around those ideas, and they become not tasks to be accomplished, but opportunities to savor. And she thinks about that smile she saw on her daughter's face that afternoon, that laugh she never hears in Winnetka, and more than anything, she wants to give this to Kinsey.

"I'll think about it," Elena says.

"Thank you," Kinsey says.

Elena laughs. "I only said that I'll think about it."

"I know," Kinsey says. "But that's what you always say right before you give in."

CHAPTER

8

Lou's

TOMMY OFFERED TO give Henry a ride back to the hotel,
but Henry told him he'd take an Uber. But an Uber
ride wouldn't give him enough time to sort everything out,
so he's walking. His route through downtown Milwaukee
is littered with familiar restaurants and bars that should fill
Henry with nostalgia, but he doesn't see any of them. He's
still trying to sort through what the hell happened at the
lawyer's office and at lunch after that.

They ate at a diner in a strip mall. The word *diner* is generous. It was just a long room with tables that wobbled, hard
chairs, and too little on the walls. It was the kind of place that
fries the shrimp, the chicken tenders, and the French fries in
the same oil, so that they all taste like something in between.
The kind of place where you can get a patty melt and sal-
monella for less than seven dollars. It was called Mel's or
Lou's—something like that. Henry can't remember because
as they settled in, and while they pretended to study their
menus in order to keep from looking at one another, he was

too pissed off to notice. He's still angry. He's angry at Tommy for calling him. He's angry at Malcolm for what he didn't tell them and for what he probably still hasn't told them. He's angry at Naomi and Kevin and Tyler Greavy. But more than anything, he's angry at himself for getting on the goddamn plane, for answering Tommy's call in the first place.

After the waitress took their order—a salad for Malcolm, a club sandwich for Henry, a Rueben for Tommy—Henry picked up his paper napkin and started to polish his spoon. "How'd you find out she was a reporter?" he asked without looking up.

"My firm has people who do research," Malcolm said.

"Research." Henry switched to the fork, rubbing the tines. Goddamn things were filthy. "These people that do research. Did they come up with any good reason that we should go visit Greavy?"

"They didn't," Malcolm said. "But she's a reporter."

Henry started in on the knife. "You already said that."

"And she knows what Kevin knew," Malcolm said.

"Fuck Kevin," Henry said.

"Henry," Tommy said sharply. He looked down at the table, straightened his own silverware. "Kevin's dead."

"Exactly," Henry said. "Safely in the ground. And he sends this pile of shit for *us* to deal with. Fucking coward."

Tommy took a deep breath as he looked up, his nostrils flaring. "Listen—"

"No, Tommy," Henry said. "*You* listen. Kevin was always full of shit. All that talk about doing the right thing was bullshit. He knew that we'd never let him do it. He just liked to hear himself say it."

Tommy folded his napkin in half, folded it again, and then looked up at Malcolm. "How is he?"

"Not good," Malcolm said.

"Of course, he's not good," Henry said. "He hit the side of a goddamn truck."

Malcolm takes in a deep breath and lets it out slowly. "I think that Tommy was talking about Tyler."

That fucking name. Henry never wanted to hear it again. "How in the hell do you know how he's doing?" he demanded.

"They send me reports," Malcolm said quietly. "I don't ask for them, but because I pay, they think I want to know."

Henry finally put the silverware down and stared at Malcolm. "Why the hell would you—"

"That's beside the point," Malcolm said. He held up the envelope that Naomi foisted on them. "We need to deal with this."

Henry looked from Malcolm to Tommy, then back at Malcolm. They were actually considering this insanity. "So—what? We're supposed to go on some goddamn scavenger hunt because a dead man wants to fuck with us?"

"She's a reporter," Malcolm said for the third goddamn time. "She knows what we did."

"What we did was defend ourselves," Henry said.

Both of the other men shifted in their seats. "That might have been a useful argument thirty years ago," Malcolm said.

"And what about what Tyler Greavy did?" Henry demanded. "They could have just left. Tommy, you said so yourself last night. They could have just left, and nothing would have happened."

"But they didn't," Malcolm said. "And then we did what we did."

"Bullshit," Henry said, glaring at Malcolm. "*You* did what *you* did."

The table grew quiet. Malcolm's eyes drew to slits, and his mouth tightened. Henry could feel that argument in Tommy's basement edging toward the surface, and he could tell that they felt it too. The waitress waded into the silence with their lunches. When she left, they all stared at their food for a long moment before anyone spoke.

"We were all there," Tommy said. "We were all part of it."

Henry wanted to argue the point, but instead he leaned toward Malcolm. "We go to that place, it's like pleading guilty."

"If we don't," Malcolm said, "she'll publish an article with what she knows, which we have to assume includes everything that Kevin knew."

"She'll publish it anyway," Henry said.

"Maybe," Malcolm allowed. "But visiting Greavy might buy us some time."

"Time for what?" Henry demanded. "To go cut the fucking grass around Hoyer's headstone?"

The dead boy's name quieted them all. Malcolm picked at his salad. Tommy stirred his ketchup with a French fry. Henry ate one of his own fries, and it did indeed taste like shrimp.

"Time to gather some leverage of our own," Malcolm finally said.

"What the hell does that mean?"

"I've got a guy," Malcolm said quietly.

"What kind of guy?"

"He digs up compromising information. When it becomes necessary."

Henry laughed acidly. "What is this, a fucking Grisham novel?"

Henry looked from Tommy to Malcolm, but both of them had their eyes fixed on their plates. They were really going to do this. "And what if there's no dirt?" Henry said. "What if she's clean?"

Malcolm shrugged. "Then he'll look at her family, and after that he'll look at her friends. Sometimes it takes a while, but there's always something."

"So, until then, when she says dance, we just dance?"

Tommy stared at Malcolm. Henry stared at Malcolm. Malcolm didn't look up from his plate; he just nodded. "Until we gain leverage, we don't have a choice."

*   *   *

Alice checks the Uber app again. Her driver stopped four blocks away for some unknown reason, and it's been ten minutes since the car moved. She stares out the window at the stunted Milwaukee skyline and considers canceling her ride and requesting a new one, but the fleet seems thin tonight. She looks at her watch and gets even more pissed off. She's angry at the Uber driver because she wants to be gone before Henry gets back. She's angry at Kevin for pulling that bullshit about the will. She's mad at herself for moving her flight to the evening when Henry changed his. But mostly she's pissed that she came to Milwaukee in the first place.

It wasn't sympathy that made her come—she isn't sorry in the least that Kevin is dead. And it wasn't nostalgia—she harbors no desire to reconnect with Malcolm or Tommy. The only reason that has any meat on the bone is a misplaced sense that she was part of that thing that happened at Burger King. But she wasn't even there. She was only part of the endless, pointless arguments that came after.

She knew none of them before St. Pius. Henry was her lab partner in freshman biology, and everything changed during that first experiment about osmosis. His hand brushed hers when he reached for the petri dish, and the hairs on her arm stood on end. They kissed for the first time, at a dance in the Pius gym, while the chaperones and Henry's friends weren't looking. Several weeks later, when her parents were out, they started to explore each other's bodies, struggling against too many layers of clothing. For many years, the words *mitosis* and *cell membrane* made her horny.

She didn't meet his friends for another month. She saw them, of course—in the cafeteria, in the hallways, in the parking lot—but what little Henry said about them, and everything that he didn't say, told Alice to tread lightly. They seemed to know about her, although none of them directly acknowledged it. Tommy and Kevin studied her with what looked like curiosity, but Malcolm stared at her with hostility. When Henry finally brought her to Tommy's basement that first time, it was clear to Alice that if she was going to date Henry, to a certain degree she was entering a relationship with all of them.

She made Kevin laugh. She argued basketball with Malcolm. Tommy seemed to like her from the start simply because she made Henry happy. During those first few months, she gently embedded herself into their friendship, even as she and Henry became inseparable. By the time Henry did what he did in that Burger King parking lot, their lives had become intertwined, like the roots of two trees planted too close together. She was there for so many of those arguments about what to do, because by then, whatever happened to Henry happened to both of them.

Henry didn't tell her that Kevin was married—she's still not sure that he knew—but when she saw how Naomi stared at Henry in the receiving line, she knew that everything was about to go sideways. For the last thirty years Alice has been waiting for the past to catch up with them, waiting for Kevin's threat to distill itself into fact. But when it came, when Naomi told them about the will, Alice felt detached from the whole thing in a way that she hadn't expected. Henry had taken a chainsaw to their relationship, poisoning their common roots. It doesn't have anything to do with her anymore. The past didn't come for *them*—it came for *him*.

Alice checks her phone again, and the car has finally started moving. She's glad that Henry's not back, that he won't make the flight. She can try to relax on the plane, and she can start to pack when she gets home. She can get used to the idea of a new life without Henry. But then she hears a keycard in the door, and her stomach sinks. Henry barges into the room, red and rumpled, smelling of sweat. The door swings shut, and he looks from the suitcase to Alice, to his watch.

"How was lunch?" she asks indifferently.

"It was—" His mouth works as he searches for words. "It was really fucked up."

Alice knows that he wants her to ask about what happened, but she manages not to.

"Those morons want me to stay," he says.

Henry's voice tells Alice that whatever happened at the lawyer's office has Henry angry or scared or both. It tells her that he wants Alice to ask him questions, help him sort it out. He wants her to tell him that it's all right to go home. Her phone vibrates. Her ride is arriving. "Whatever you want," she says.

"They want to go visit Tyler Greavy at the facility he's in."

The name means little at first, a collection of sounds that she's long ago forgotten to attach meaning to, like the name of a second-tier Civil War general or a South American capital. But then she remembers the article in the paper with that name and the endless arguments about that name. And she almost asks why, but she stops herself because it's no longer her job.

"I'm leaving," she says instead.

Henry's forehead rumples like it always does when he's unsettled. "Tonight?"

The pleading tone in his voice makes her hesitate for just a moment, but she looks at her phone and sees that her Uber is in front of the hotel. "Yes," she says. "I'm leaving tonight." Alice finally decides that it's time. Past time. "And I'm leaving you. For good."

Henry goes very still. "What . . .?" But he struggles to form more words. And Alice regrets saying anything. Not because of Henry's distress, but because her car is waiting, and she wants to eat something at the airport before her flight. "Why?" he finally manages.

Alice hoists her purse higher onto her shoulder. "We both know why," she says. "Is it Lyla again, or have you found someone else to screw?"

"But I didn't—I haven't."

He answers so quickly, so convincingly, that if Alice hadn't fallen for his lies before, it would give her pause. "Bullshit. We both know that you can't keep your dick in your pants."

"But, Alice," he says, "that's not—"

"I have to go. I have a flight to catch."

She steps around him and grabs the door handle.

"I have HIV," he blurts. "I didn't know how to . . . once I found out . . . I couldn't . . ."

He stops talking, and her hand stops, and her heart stops, and for one long moment everything stops.

9

Sienna Grill

MALCOLM SIPS FROM a glass of seltzer while Kinsey studies the menu. The restaurant is crowded for a Sunday—Malcolm had to call in a favor to get a table near the window. He wishes he had a Maker's and Coke in his hand instead of the seltzer, but it's been decades since he's allowed himself that. He knew that he'd have the risotto even before he arrived. He always has the risotto. Kinsey probably knows what she wants too, but she's holding the menu in front of her face so that she doesn't have to talk to him.

When Malcolm called Elena to reschedule for Sunday night, he suggested Avli in Winnetka, but Elena said that Kinsey wanted to meet him in River North instead. She said that Kinsey had really enjoyed the Sienna Grill when the two of them had gone to see *Hamilton*. Malcolm knows the real reason: Kinsey wants to avoid Avli because she might see people that she knows—she might be seen with him. He tries to tell himself that he doesn't care. He reminds himself that Sienna, just a short walk from his condo, saves him more than an hour in the car. Besides, he didn't have much leverage given his late cancellation on Friday. If there's one thing that Malcolm understands at a visceral level, it's leverage.

Malcolm glances at his watch. "Did you decide?"

"I think that I'll have the risotto," Kinsey says.

She puts the menu down, looks out the window, and Malcolm studies her. In so many ways she's a miniature of her mother—the long dark hair, the eyelashes, that nose, the skin like weak coffee. He misses that face terribly. Before he moved out, he'd sneak into Kinsey's room every night, after she was asleep. He started so many years ago, during the Cellutec deal. She sleeps with a nightlight on—even now—so that face was the last clear image he saw every night. Some nights he just sat in the chair and watched her breathe. Others, he'd whisper details of his day to his sleeping daughter, because he'd long ago forgotten how to have a proper conversation with her when she was awake.

Malcolm signals for the waiter, and while they order, he tries to think of something to talk about. He considers asking about the banjo, but he isn't entirely sure that she still plays. He tries to remember the name of one of her friends, but he fails. He's about to ask about school when Kinsey pushes her chair out and stands.

"I have to go to the bathroom."

Malcolm swallows more seltzer along with his relief. His phone, sitting on the table next to his plate, vibrates with a text. It's from his assistant. The visit to Linden Glen is locked in for Tuesday. He'll text Tommy and Henry after dinner and let them know. Malcolm chews an ice cube and wonders how much Naomi knows about Greavy's situation. Probably everything.

Whenever Malcolm thinks of Naomi, the base of his skull tingles in that way that he's learned to associate with lack of control. Naomi is running the show. She knows everything, and she's working them like puppets, making them dance—just like Henry said. Henry's also right about what comes next, after they visit Linden Glen. She'll pull the strings again, and if Yuri still hasn't found some leverage by then, they'll dance some more. That or she'll make them all famous.

That article will destroy Malcolm. There will be repercussions for Henry and Tommy, to be sure, but Malcolm has the most at stake. It happened thirty years ago, so it would probably only garner a few paragraphs, but that would be enough. If his name is mentioned in those paragraphs, it could cost him his job, his reputation, his law license. A criminal investigation would cost him much, much more.

Kinsey sits back down, but this time she looks right at Malcolm and waits. Her eyes set her apart from her mother. Elena can't hold Malcolm's gaze—she always looks away first. Kinsey only looks away when she wants to. Malcolm knows that it's Kinsey's stare that unsettles him the most, but he has no idea how much it mirrors his own.

"How's school?" he asks.

Her lips wriggle, probably because of the predictable nature of the question. "It's fine. How's work?"

Malcolm's own mouth twitches. *Touché.* But Malcolm never minds talking about work. It's a safe subject. The safest. "It's good," he says. "Did I tell you about the McGregor deal?"

Kinsey shrugs.

"It's a big one. Telecommunications. The whole thing's worth almost two and a half billion."

Malcolm watches as Kinsey arranges her features into an expression approximating interest. "What do they do?"

"They build infrastructure mostly. Cell towers. Large antennae. That sort of thing. They're buying their largest rival. They're calling it a merger of equals, but it's never a merger of equals."

"I know," Kinsey says. Her face remains expressionless, but her eyes remain locked on his. "Somebody's always gotta call the shots."

Kinsey takes a drink from her water glass and looks out the window again, up at the Wrigley Building. Malcolm signals the waiter for a refill and wishes yet again that he was drinking Maker's. He looks out the window and attempts to distract himself from Kinsey's last comment by trying to see the city through her eyes. People rush past the window. Cars crawl down Michigan. Lights glitter and glare.

"What're you doing on the seventeenth?" Kinsey asks.

She's arranging her silverware now. She's suddenly skittish, and he can tell that she's pretending not to care about his answer to her question. He shrugs. "I have no idea. Why?"

"I got a concert. You could come if you want."

For a moment Malcolm says nothing, stunned by the invitation. It feels like a lifeline, and he wants to lunge for it, even though he's grown unaccustomed to lunging. He picks up his phone and hopes with an unfamiliar urgency that he's free, and he finds that he is. "What time?"

"Seven thirty."

"That should work." He thumbs a reminder into his calendar. "Where at?"

"Old Town. I got asked to play with the String Masters," she says, and the way she says it tells him that he's supposed to know who the String Masters are.

"Wow. That's great." Her faces flushes, and he's grateful for that warmth, astonished that he caused it. "So you'll play banjo for them?"

Her face hardens, and she looks down at her plate. "It's a mandolin," she says through her teeth.

Has she always played mandolin? Did she play banjo before she played the mandolin? What the hell is a mandolin anyway? As he eats his risotto and she picks at hers, he manages to surface a few of her friends' names and asks about them, but she rewards his efforts with one-word answers. Desperate to break the silence, he asks, "How's your mother?"

Kinsey moves her risotto from one side of her plate to the other. She looks back out the window, at the people this time, eyes darting from one to another. "You should probably ask her that."

Malcolm knows that he should give up, that he should just fold his tent and call it a night, but for once, he can't help himself. "How do you want your room decorated?"

"What room?" Kinsey asks, still looking out the window.

"Your room at my condo."

She looks back at Malcolm, confused. "Why would I need a room at your condo?"

"You'll be staying with me every other weekend."

Kinsey looks as if she's been slapped. "Why?"

"Because you're my daughter," he says.

"No," Kinsey says. "I mean why would I want to?"

Malcolm scowls at the table. His chest swells in that way he hasn't allowed in so long. He swallows the words that struggle against his lips. The waiter brings the dessert menu, and although neither of them order anything, the interruption is enough to allow Malcolm to ignore her question.

"You talked to Mom about this?" Kinsey asks when the waiter leaves to get the check.

"No," Malcolm says. "The lawyers talked about it."

"We're moving to Milwaukee."

Malcolm's pulse slows. Without realizing it, he leans slightly forward, the same way he does when he threatens someone in a conference room. "No," he says. "You're not."

Kinsey leans forward too, her jaw jutting, her eyes flashing. "We are," she says. "We already decided."

10

Coffee

"HAVE YOU CREATED a Tinder profile yet?" Holly asks.

Elena regrets yet again telling Holly about the divorce, but she felt like she had to tell someone. Holly's sitting at the island while Elena makes coffee. Her auburn hair hangs around her face as she scrolls through her Facebook feed. She's dressed in yoga pants and a tight yellow work-out shirt that she undoubtedly chose to best showcase her fake breasts. She works out every afternoon—yoga or Pilates or Pure Barre or FitRX. She hops aboard every fit-ness bandwagon that pulls through town, stretching and burning and toning and melting in studios cranked hot enough to cook a turkey. Elena sometimes wonders if she's tightening things up for her current husband or her next one.

"No," Elena says. "I'm working through the stages of grief, but I haven't quite gotten to the 'screw-random-strangers' stage."

Holly makes a face like she swallowed plastic. "It's not like that. It's how people meet now. It's like TGI Fridays in the nineties, but without the suspenders."

Elena laughs. "I thought you were trying to talk me *into* Tinder."

"You're such a prude."

"Maybe I should get some flair."

Holly goes back to her feed, and Elena pours cream into her coffee. Holly's been badgering Elena to sign up for Tinder for the last couple of years, ever since she made the mistake of complaining about Malcolm's absence, about her loneliness. Holly is five years into her third marriage, and she seems as happy as she ever gets, but she still has Tinder on her phone, and she sometimes thumbs through it while sipping coffee. *"It's nice to know there are options,"* she said when Elena asked her why.

"At least tell me that you called Luther."

"Yes. I called Luther."

Luther handled both of Holly's divorces, and she swears by him. Holly was almost giddy when Elena asked her for his number.

"Malcolm is a fucking idiot," Holly says. "Rule number one: leave the house, lose the house."

Elena sits down with two mugs and slides one over to Holly. She steals a glance at the clock on the microwave. She knows that Holly probably has a litany of rules for a lucrative divorce, and on a different day she'd find them funny, but not today. "What time's your workout?"

"Hatha yoga at one thirty," she says. "But they have the same class at two thirty and four thirty."

Elena takes a sip of coffee. Three or four times a week, Holly stops by after Elena gets home from school, but before

Kinsey arrives. She doesn't knock; she just walks in the back door and yells Elena's name to announce her arrival. Sometimes she stays fifteen minutes, other times, three hours. The most blatant hints roll off her like water—Elena has to kick her out as often as not. She'll miss Holly when she moves to Milwaukee—one of the few people from Winnetka that she'll miss. Truth be told, Holly's just like the rest of the women Elena knows. She and Holly have nothing in common except the fence between their yards, but she was the first person Elena met when they moved in, so Elena's got a soft spot for her.

"You should go to Miami with us," Holly says. "You look like you could use it."

Elena would rather poke herself in the eye with a pencil than fly to South Beach with Holly, but she knows that it's easier to play along.

"I would, but work."

"We're going in June."

"Who's going?"

"Same crew as always. Hillary and Hannah."

Hillary, Hannah, and Holly. None of them seem to find the alliteration ridiculous—or that their handbags are all the same brand, or that their highlights match the exact same Pantone color. Elena's not sure that they even notice.

Elena has learned not to argue with Holly. It's like arguing with a toddler—she's more relentless than logical. "Did Hannah find a new supplier yet?" Elena asks, so that she doesn't have to say no to Miami. Hannah was gobbling her Xanax too fast, and her doctor refused to up the ante.

"Yeah. She has to drive to Oakbrook, though."

"Wow," Elena says. "That must be hard."

Holly came over with a plate of store-bought cookies the day after the O'Donnells moved in, and she never really left. She told Elena which restaurants to try and which dentists to avoid. She invited Elena into her playgroup with Hillary and Hannah and a handful of other women who have since drifted off or moved away. That first time, Holly's nanny took all the kids downstairs to the basement, leaving the women to drink mimosas, gossip about people who weren't there, and ask each other prying questions so that they'd have new gossip for happy hour. All of them seemed to know where Malcolm worked, although Elena had told nobody. And they all wanted to know how big her house was. *"How many square feet?"* each of them asked.

"You look like shit, by the way," Holly says. "We need to get you to my Botox guy before Miami."

"I was thinking about eating bad salmon," Elena says. "I prefer to ingest my botulism."

Holly looks up from her phone, takes a sip of her coffee, studies Elena closely. "Seriously," she says. "You look exhausted."

"I haven't been sleeping well," Elena says. "It's been a long month."

Elena knows that Holly is about to start in about Tinder again and that then she'll lurch into a rant about the regenerative effects of orgasms. Elena's formulating a lie about a doctor's appointment when the doorbell rings. She sets her mug on the counter. "Be right back."

She expects to find the UPS man when she opens the door, but instead she finds Malcolm. He's wearing a gray suit and a blank expression that tells her nothing. It feels strange to answer the door and find her husband standing on the front step—familiar but off-kilter—like when her dad shaved his beard. She can tell by the long pause before Malcolm says anything that he finds it awkward too.

"Do you have time to talk?" he asks.

For the briefest moment, Elena thinks about using Holly as an excuse. But it's Monday afternoon, and Malcolm has left the office to talk to her, so it must be something important. "Sure," she says. "Come in."

Malcolm hesitates for just a moment before stepping into the house. Elena closes the door, and they stand awkwardly in the entry foyer. He glances up the stairs and down the hall to the family room. They can't just stand in the foyer or sit down in the living room like he's a salesperson. Besides, whatever he wants to talk about, she probably wants to be in her kitchen when she hears it. One o'clock on a Monday. Malcolm handles pedestrian matters with a curt phone call or an email, usually sent by his assistant. Finally, Elena says, "Wait here. I need to get rid of Holly."

* * *

Malcolm settles onto a stool while Elena pours him coffee. She steals a glance at him, but he's looking down at his hands, and he's hard to read. She considers the possible agendas for this meeting, because it's definitely a meeting, and Malcolm always has an agenda. Maybe he's come to negotiate the divorce, but that doesn't seem right—lawyers always say, *"Leave it to the lawyers."* And he's not here to sort out who gets the photo albums or the china or Kinsey's baby shoes. It suddenly occurs to her that maybe he's come to try to patch things up, to say he's sorry, to reconcile. But sorry won't be enough. If he's come to fight his way back into his home, he'll get a fight, because when he left last month, they skipped that part.

Elena planned to fight. In a lot of ways, she's been building toward that fight for a decade. For a while, Kinsey filled the void left by Malcolm, but she eventually went to school, of course. It didn't take long for Elena to realize that the PTA was more for the mothers than the children, so she went back to teaching. Those first few years back in the classroom had distracted her from the fact that her husband was MIA. It probably would have continued to distract her if her mom hadn't gotten sick.

Malcolm never once asked Elena how her mom was responding to the chemo. He never visited her in the hospital and was seldom home when Elena returned from her own visits, drained by the effort of not crying while she was with her mom, and exhausted from all the tears on the drive home. He visited her mom just once—when she was in hospice. That's when Elena realized that she needed more than to fill her time. She didn't need distractions. She needed a husband, and she was ready to fight for one.

She was like Perry Mason or Atticus Finch as she prepared for that fight—rehearsing her opening statement, imagining his objections, practicing her rebuttals, but she was also like Mike Tyson, ready to pummel him, bite off a chunk of his ear if necessary. She wouldn't let him bob and weave. She'd force him toward the center of the ring, and she would shout and cry and throw objects if she had to. She was ready for everything except for what happened.

It was after eleven that night when she heard the door to the garage close and his feet on the stairs. He slipped into the room and undressed without turning the lights on, just like he always did. She heard him hanging his suit and shirt, because he's become so damn anal that he even hangs his clothes before he sends them to the drycleaner. When he finally climbed into bed, she rolled over to face him. She could see the silhouette of his face against the curtains, staring at the ceiling.

"Nice that you could make it," she said.

Malcolm didn't say anything. He didn't move.

"The front desk expected you later."

Still nothing.

"Because you act like this is a hotel or a fucking bed and breakfast."

Stillness.

"Hello? Are you there, Mr. O'Donnell?"

She could see the shadow of his lips part, but they pursed shut again.

"I know that you're busy at work, but the staff would like a word with you."

Nothing.

"You might have noticed a teenage girl around the facility. It's been a while since you had a real conversation with her, but she's your daughter. I was going to put a picture of you in her room, but I worried that a photo of a stranger might creep her out."

Silence.

"Do you give a shit about us at all?" Elena demanded. She said it too loudly and her voice cracked, but he still said nothing. "Maybe when you get your name on the door of that goddamn firm, you can have a bed installed. It would save you some driving."

Elena waited. She was determined to wait him out for once. She was determined to goad him into a meaningful discussion about the state of things, about the frayed remnants of their family. It was a long time before he spoke, and she didn't get her argument.

"It sounds like you want a divorce," he said quietly.

"No! I don't want a goddamn divorce!" She squeezed her eyes shut, and she wanted to punch him and pull his hair and shove him off the bed. But when she opened her mouth, she only managed one rasping sentence. "I just want my husband back."

Malcolm climbed out of bed, and Elena heard him pad down the hall. She heard the door of the guest bedroom click shut. For the next three days, he arrived home after she was in bed, and he left before dawn. He slipped into their bedroom every morning to get fresh clothes, and Elena pretended to be asleep. On Thursday morning, she felt him pause next to her side of the bed. She opened her eyes to find him standing there like a golem.

"You should get yourself a lawyer," he said, his voice almost tender. He laid a card on her bedside table. "Here's the number for mine."

And then he walked out.

*   *   *

Elena sets the two cups of coffee on the island and settles onto a stool opposite Malcolm. For once she's happy that her kitchen is so damn big. She has no desire to sit elbow to elbow with him. She knows that there will be shouting, but she still doesn't know what she'll shout about or how that might end, because she has no idea what she even wants anymore. Malcolm stares at her over the rim of his mug as he sips. He swallows and puts the mug back down, but he never takes his eyes off her. Elena knows from experience that she can't outstare Malcolm, and she doesn't have the patience to outwait him.

"So," she says. "I don't think I saw your meeting request. What's this about?"

"I thought that we should keep the lines of communication open."

Elena snorts a laugh. Like he's on a conference call. "*Keep the lines of communication open*? Should we try to align our goals, maybe take a deep dive? Or should we just see what bubbles up, and circle back to the low hanging fruit?"

"I think that it's important we stay on the same page," Malcolm says.

He can't help himself. That's really how he talks now. Elena leans back on her stool and crosses her arms. She studies Malcolm. He's still handsome: those same full lips, that nose that's only a bit too small, those eyelashes. The same face that she fell in love with so long ago, but all the expressiveness of those early years has leaked away. When they first met—all through law school, really—she knew what he was thinking before he said it. Their friends joked that some couples are able to complete each other's sentences but that Elena could start Malcolm's. Those law school friends are long gone, though. And he disciplined himself—not just for the long hours and the punishing work. He trained himself to banish any trace of emotion, anything that might cost him something in a negotiation, any flash of anger that might trip up his march toward partner. And he spends so much time at the firm that it's like discipline has become his default setting—maybe his only setting.

"It's been a long time since we've been on the same page," Elena finally says. If he wants to claw his way back, he's going to have to do a lot better than that.

"Kinsey told me about Milwaukee last night," he says.

Bile rises in Elena's throat as she absorbs his words. She squeezes her mug so tightly that she's afraid it might shatter in her hand. *That* explains why Kinsey went straight to her room after the Uber dropped her off last night, why she was more quiet than usual this morning. She didn't even think to tell Kinsey to keep her mouth shut, because she only said *maybe*, and she thought for sure that Kinsey knew better. She struggles to keep her face arranged, to keep what she's thinking from Malcolm, but of course, he sees it. And all the while, his face remains an impassive blank slate. Elena wants to walk around the island and slap him, force him to feel something. Instead, she drinks a gulp of scalding hot coffee to rinse the awful taste from her mouth.

"When do you plan to move?" Malcolm asks mildly.

"Nothing's certain," Elena says.

"Kinsey seemed pretty certain last night."

"Maybe you should have your lawyer call mine," Elena says.

This draws a tiny smile from Malcolm. "But I'm trying to save you some money. Give you some free legal advice."

Elena grips the mug with both hands. He's decided to threaten *and* humiliate her. "Always trying to save money . . ."

"And I'm trying to keep you from confusing our daughter."

Our daughter. That pronoun suddenly sets her off. "You have one dinner with Kinsey, and now *you* want to tell *me* about *my* daughter?"

Malcolm's upper lip disappears. He swallows. "Illinois law is crystal clear on this. A custodial parent can't move a child in their care to another state without the explicit approval of the other parent."

"You know the law, you motherfucker, but you don't know shit about Kinsey."

Malcolm flinches. When he speaks, a tiny bit of some-thing soft sifts into his voice. "I just want to be part of her life," he says. "That'll be difficult if she lives in another city."

"Difficult!?" Elena shouts. "You found it difficult to be part of her life when you lived in the same goddamn house!"

"Elena, listen—"

"No, Malcolm! *You* listen!" Elena is standing now, leaning across the island, fists on granite. "You're a selfish prick. You barely noticed her back when she still called you Daddy!"

"Elena—"

"No, Malcolm. Fuck you!"

Malcolm blinks. He opens his mouth and closes it twice, but she can see him decide that he's done. He stands, buttons his coat, and straightens his tie. His face hardens back into his legal mask, and he looks through Elena more than at her.

"Thank you for the coffee," he says quietly, formally, and then he turns and walks out of the kitchen.

"Where you going, Malcolm?" Elena shouts after him. "No next steps? No action items?"

His footsteps echo through the rooms as he makes his way to the foyer. Elena sags on her stool. She rubs her palms across her face. Her shoulders tremble with rage. And when he leaves, she hears the front door click softly shut—the bas-tard doesn't even have the common decency to slam the door after an argument. Elena grabs her half-full mug and throws it as hard as she can against the steel door of the fridge, shattering it into hundreds of tiny shards that clatter almost musically onto the artisanal stone floor.

CHAPTER

11

Undetectable

ALICE WAITS IN the doctor's office. The paper on top of the exam table rustles every time she shifts, so she tries not to move. Instead, she stares at her reflection in the mirror above the sink, trying to fathom how she finds herself in a doctor's office at the age of forty-nine, waiting for the results of an HIV test. Who the hell gets HIV these days anyway? She thought only drug addicts and gay men got HIV. She thought AIDS was mainly an Africa problem now.

Alice never buys the internet when she flies. She usually enjoys the disconnection. It gives her a few uninterrupted hours in the world of a novel, which helps her adjust to landing in a completely different place. Last night, though, she paid the twelve dollars and ninety-nine cents and spent the flight bent over her phone, learning as much as she could, becoming angrier by the minute. Less than one chance in a thousand for Henry each time that he had sex with Lyla. He said that they slept together only a handful of times. He was vague when he talked about it, and the number seemed to change. Six? Eight? Eight out of a thousand. He was either the unluckiest man in the world or a bigger liar than she thought. The odds rise sharply if they had anal sex, but Alice really doesn't want to think about that.

Alice found that she had a one in two thousand chance every time she slept with Henry. She spent part of the flight trying to calculate the number of times that Henry had rolled to her side of the bed over the last two years. Those first six months after she'd learned about Lyla were thin, but it wasn't never. After she finally decided to stay with him, they'd found their way back to their regular rhythm—at least until last month. A hundred times? A hundred and fifty? Enough. Enough that she badgered her way into this appointment. Enough that she demanded the test when she got here. Enough that she can almost feel the virus swimming through her bloodstream, organizing its attack on her immune system.

It's been a long time since Alice thought so much about sex. After thirty-five years it had become just something that happened between Henry and her—like eating dinner and watching Netflix. She kept quiet when the other female agents complained about the way the years had withered their sex lives. But she also said nothing when they talked about the sexual exploits of their youth. Alice has always felt like she and Henry had something special in the sack, but she really had no way to know for sure. That first time she was just fifteen. And he was her first. Her only. Now this, too, makes her angry.

Alice can't remember the last time that she thought about AIDS before Henry said what he said. Back in the eighties it was all anybody talked about—concerts and fundraisers every time she turned on the TV. But sometime in the nineties, it had fallen off Alice's radar. She never really thought about why until now. Maybe it was because all of her friends got married and started talking about lactation and potty training rather than condoms and sexually transmitted diseases. She was shocked when Google told her that more than a million people were living with AIDS in the United States alone. That was probably why she didn't hear about it anymore. It was no longer a death sentence. People were *living*.

Most of the sites that Google sent her toward eventually talked about *undetectable* status. This holy grail is achieved through healthy living, strict adherence to the treatment regimen, and luck, it seems. It means that the viral load can't be measured, but it doesn't mean that you're cured. The virus still lurks. Alice needs to do more research to find out if there are health benefits from becoming undetectable, but all the sites make it clear that you can safely fuck without a condom again, as if that's all that really matters.

When the door opens and Dr. Simpson comes back in, Alice can tell that she's trying to keep a poker face, and Alice knows what this means. Alice reads faces for a living, and she knows that good news always arrives with a relaxed, open smile, while bad news tries to sneak into the room. Dr. Simpson licks her lips and looks down at her clipboard.

"Your test came back positive," she says.

Alice pushes her chin up and looks Dr. Simpson in the eye. "So what's next?" she asks, trying to sound casual.

Dr. Simpson studies Alice for a moment. "We performed an antibody test today. They sometimes return a false positive. We like to perform a second test to confirm."

"How often?"

Dr. Simpson looks confused. "We always suggest a con-firmation test."

"No. I mean how often do you get false positives?"

Dr. Simpson hesitates. "Not often," she admits.

"What happens after the test is confirmed?" Alice asks, because she refuses to be sucked under by hope.

Dr. Simpson talks for several minutes about PrEP and antiretrovirals and inhibitors and antagonists. She talks about regimens and cocktails and side effects. She says *undetectable* at least three times before Alice stops counting. After a while she goes quiet, probably because she can tell that Alice has stopped listening. "All that can wait, though," she says. "It'll take about three days to get the second test back."

Alice nods. She shifts on the table. The paper rustles. She wants to leave.

"Before I send the nurse in, we should talk about con-tact tracing. Was there a reason that you requested the test today?"

This is why she wanted to leave. "My husband tested positive."

Dr. Simpson pauses again. "I see. I know this is uncom-fortable, but have you had other sexual partners?"

"No."

"Intravenous drug use?"

Alice snorts a laugh. "No."

"Does he know how he became infected?"

"He fucked his personal trainer," Alice says, her voice steady, as if she's sharing her birthday or her mother's maiden name. The most humiliating part of her life has become a clinical detail, a data point in her chart. She doesn't want Dr. Simpson to look up from her clipboard. She doesn't want Dr. Simpson to say anything. She doesn't want to discuss next steps. She doesn't want the nurse to come in and take her blood, and she doesn't want to schedule a follow-up appointment with the receptionist. She feels small and wants to make herself smaller until Dr. Simpson can't even see her. She wants to become undetectable herself.

12

Linden Glen

TOMMY ARRIVES AT Linden Glen early. He sits in his car, listening to Dire Straits, and tries to ignore the building. It strikes him as something caught between a hospital and an office park. The double doors under the awning slide open automatically, just like an emergency room. But it's only one story, and a long row of identical windows peer out over the parking lot. Tommy didn't sleep well. Anger kept him awake, and it still simmers. He doesn't quite recognize it as anger, but his breathing comes fast, his lips press against his teeth, and the muscles in his shoulders tighten every time his thoughts drift near Tyler Greavy.

* * *

Malcolm shows up one minute before ten. He gets out of his car immediately and walks to the entrance. He stands under the awning, but far enough from the automatic doors that they don't slide open. Malcolm thinks about the post-close capitalization table for the McGregor deal and how to present it to the target company's CEO in a way that won't infuriate him. As he drove north, past Winnetka, he thought about the cap table to distract himself from what had happened with Elena yesterday. But once he crossed the Wisconsin border, he reorganized that cap table yet again, to keep himself from calling Yuri and to distract himself from where he was headed.

Tommy lumbers toward Malcolm from the parking lot, wearing jeans and a gray shirt with his name stitched over the pocket. Malcolm checks his watch. Straight up ten o'clock. He finally settles on the idea that removing the share classes from the presentation might unruffle things.

"Hey," Tommy says when he reaches Malcolm. He looks tired, and his face is all closed up. His hands are shoved deep into his pockets. "Any sign of Henry?"

"No," Malcolm says, "but he'll be here."

"Did he tell you that?"

"No," Malcolm says. "But Henry could never stand to be left out of anything."

* * *

Henry is exhausted when he pulls up in front of Linden Glen. It's like sand is lodged under his eyelids, and his throat feels like he gargled with bleach. He checked for thrush in the hotel bathroom mirror—just like he's done every morning for the last month—but he found nothing. He managed only a few hours of something resembling sleep, and those few hours were tangled with half-awake dreams about Alice. When he woke, he was startled yet again to find her gone. It took him a long moment of looking around the hotel room to remember that he was in Milwaukee. And then he remembered the argument before she left for the airport, and like the two mornings before, he felt like he might puke. She won't return his calls or his texts. He wonders if she's already moved out. He probably should have flown back to Denver yesterday or the day before, but he doesn't seem capable of that kind of decision. He didn't really decide to stay in Milwaukee, and he certainly didn't decide to come to Linden Glen. He's been letting the decisions make themselves.

As he walks from the car toward Tommy and Malcolm, he can't help but think about what he'll find inside of that building. Malcolm told them about the brain damage and the loss of gross motor skills. Since Alice left for the airport, the disintegration of his marriage has consumed him, distracted him from what he's about to see. But now that he's walking toward the entrance, he can't ignore it any longer, and his mind scrambles for a way to keep himself together, to protect himself from what he's being forced to look at.

"You look like shit," Tommy says when Henry reaches them.

"Thanks for that," Henry says, almost smiling. "Long night."

"Yeah," Tommy says. "Me too."

Malcolm looks at his watch, and his eyes dart from Tommy to Henry. Malcolm looks ironed, crisp, alert. Henry wants Malcolm to say something about his guy so that they don't have to go into that building after all. "It's time," Malcolm says instead. And without another word, he walks toward the doors, and they slide open with a whisper.

* * *

The three men sit uncomfortably close in uncomfortable chairs and say nothing while they wait. Tommy watches the single fish in the enormous tank and wonders if it ate all the others. Malcolm checks his watch. Henry leans his head back against the wall, his eyes closed.

The door clicks loudly open, revealing a woman with a short haircut and a long skirt. She introduces herself as Janet, but she doesn't make them sign anything, which makes Henry wonder about HIPPA regulations, and it makes him wonder just how much Malcolm pays to Linden Glen. They follow her down a long corridor, her heels clacking loud against the tile. There are no windows. The doors are all closed. Successories posters hang on the walls between each door, with words like *Confidence* and *Believe* and *Succeed* in a thirty-point font under pictures of too-perfect landscapes and climbers summitting mountains. Henry wonders whether those posters are meant to motivate the staff or the patients.

"When's the last time you saw Tyler?" Janet asks over her shoulder.

For several strides, the only sound is her heels pounding the tile. All three men try not to think about the last time that they saw Tyler. Tommy wonders what story Malcolm told her when he set this up. All of them know that it's Malcolm's question to answer.

"It's been a long time," Malcolm says.

At the end of the hall, Janet waves a keycard at a sensor to get them through the door, and they follow her into what must be the ward. Most of the doors are open, and sunlight streams through them into the hallway. Men and women in scrubs move from room to room. A lemony disinfectant struggles against the metallic aroma of urine. Janet turns to them.

"Tyler probably won't say anything. He's not verbal."

Malcolm already knows this. It relieves Tommy even as it pisses him off—Greavy couldn't keep his goddamn mouth shut in that Burger King parking lot. Henry eyes the woman's keycard and wonders if he needs one to escape.

"You probably shouldn't stay too long."

Malcolm thinks about his one o'clock back in Chicago. Tommy wonders how long is long enough. Henry knows that they've already been there too long.

"And you shouldn't expect Tyler to recognize you. Given his condition."

She says this with soft eyes, full of empathy, and then turns to walk down the hallway. The three men stand frozen for a moment before they follow, digesting the disconnect between the intention of Janet's words and their implications.

* * *

When they file into the room, for some reason, Malcolm doesn't expect Greavy to be lying in bed at ten in the morning, and he doesn't expect his body to be so thin and still beneath the sheet. Greavy's face is turned to the window, and Malcolm uses that moment of stillness to clutch at details of the McGregor deal, but the numbers and the names and the regulatory filings scatter out of reach. He's left with nothing but that roiling mess of emotions that he'd kept locked away for decades, and the chains clatter.

"Tyler," Janet says. Greavy doesn't move, so she says his name more loudly. "Tyler. Some friends are here to see you."

Greavy turns from the window. His face is skeletal. His head is shaved to a stubble. His blue eyes stare from the caverns of his eye sockets, but they don't seem to land on anything in particular. For a moment Malcom thinks that Greavy is smiling, but it's just the corner of his mouth twitching again and again. Malcolm wants to deny that it's the boy from the parking lot, but then he registers the misshapen nose, and he can't manage it. For a moment all he can feel is the unexpected give of that boy's skull—like a cantaloupe. But that passes quickly, and he's left with the debilitating shame that wrapped him so tightly those first few years. The shame feels warm and familiar, like a favorite sweatshirt that's been lost for so long that it was almost forgotten.

* * *

Henry studies the body under the sheet and pretends it's a cadaver. With the head turned away and the form so still, it's possible to tell himself that. He imagines the paperwork. *Male. Caucasian. Fifty-one years old. 130 pounds. Brain damage. Torso intact.* But then that woman—Henry's forgotten her name already—says Greavy's first name, says it again, and the body under the sheet stirs. Henry looks out the window before the head atop the torso turns toward him. He fixes his eyes on a tall evergreen tree on the other side of a retention pond. He focuses on counting his breath, like Alice taught him back when Alice used to teach him things. Henry stares at the tree and tries to ignore the rustling of the sheets, Tommy's deep breathing, and Malcolm's stillness. He forces himself to wait for the woman with the short hair and the long skirt to say that it's time to go. He prays that nobody will say anything before she utters those magic words, and he wills her not to repeat the man's name, because then he'll be reminded again that the man on the bed was the boy on the asphalt. When Henry again tries to focus on his breath, he realizes that he's stopped breathing altogether.

* * *

Tommy feels his size as he walks into the room where the skinny man lies under the sheet. He felt his size that night in the parking lot too, just like he felt it anytime conflict flared back then. It started in middle school, the year his feet grew four sizes. The big man is never given a choice. He's always elbowed to the front and surrounded from behind when hostilities threaten. When that skinny man under the sheet turns his head toward them, Tommy recognizes his nose immediately, and he hates him. He hates him because he didn't leave that parking lot when Tommy gave him the chance. And Tommy suddenly blames Greavy for all of it—the shattered friendships, the sleepless nights, the guilt that Tommy's been carrying like a sack of rocks for the last thirty years. And Tommy blames him for the lies, for everything he's never told Maggie. The lies feel like termites eating at the beams that support his marriage. He struggles to stretch toward compassion for the man lying on the bed, confused and senseless. But his mind keeps lurching back to Tyler Greavy, the boy, and to Maggie. Tommy blames that boy for the sag in the floor of his life, and he hates him for it.

* * *

Tyler's eyelids flutter and he struggles to focus. But then his eyes lock on Tommy, and they go wide. They flicker to Henry and Malcolm before settling back on Tommy. His breathing becomes labored, and his mouth starts to work, but nothing comes out. He strains to lift his head from the pillow, but the effort is too much, and he falls back. His hands shake with tremors, and his mouth keeps opening and closing.

"He recognizes you after all," Janet says.

Henry looks at Janet to avoid looking at the cadaver on the bed. She's smiling widely, looking from one of them to the other encouragingly. Henry still has no idea what Malcolm told her, but it's clear that she expects excitement, relief, connection. He wants to tell her that she's mistaken about the recognition, that she's deluding herself. He wants to tell her that there are too many years that separate them, too much distance, that connection is too much to ask for, but he knows how all that will sound, so he says nothing.

"He recognizes you after all." These words chill Malcolm to his core, annihilating the warmth of his shame. He can see for himself the recognition in Greavy's gaze, and his mind scrambles across depositions and sworn statements and testimony. But none of that will happen, of course. Malcolm's scanned enough of the reports over the years to know that Tyler won't speak. But those reports didn't warn him about the perception that he finds in Greavy's eyes. The awareness. The humanity.

"Tyler recognizes you," Janet says again, an edge to her voice this time.

Malcolm's eyes are locked on Tyler, but he feels the heat of Janet's gaze. He knows that words are expected of *him*, but he can't speak any better than Tyler can.

"He recognizes you after all." The words catch Tommy off guard, and his anger shatters as they land. Tyler's eyes lend truth to those words. They show Tommy that he's still in there, that he's trapped. Their desperation reminds Tommy that Tyler's been trapped in beds like this, in rooms like this, in his broken body, for the last thirty years. *Tyler*

recognizes you. Tommy realizes with a certainty that bewilders him that Tyler doesn't just recognize the faces of the men who used to be the boys that did this to him, but that he can also sense their shame.

"I think that it's time that you leave," Janet says.

Every bit of warmth has left her voice. Whatever Malcolm told her, it's clear that she now sees the lie of it. Henry bolts for the hallway immediately. Malcolm hesitates, but he soon follows. Tommy urges himself to move, but his legs don't work. He stares at Tyler, and Tyler stares unblinkingly back. Janet shifts, and Tommy knows he has only seconds before she speaks again. Without thinking, without deciding, he reaches out and places his hand over Tyler's. It's dry and bony—more like a claw than a hand. It quivers like a frightened bird. Tommy stops trying to map this man back to the boy in that parking lot, because he can't, and he suddenly realizes that he shouldn't.

"I'm so sorry, Tyler," Tommy whispers. He knows that it's not enough, but he also knows that there's nothing else. Tyler blinks, and his hand goes still. Tommy squeezes it, and then he turns to leave.

13

Strunk and White

AFTER THE THREE men are swallowed by the doors of Linden Glen, Naomi takes the file folder from the passenger seat and opens it. She knows everything in that folder only too well, but she has to occupy herself with something while she waits. Her editor has given her no new stories since Kevin died. He's giving her time, out of concern, out of respect. But time is the last thing she needs right now, so she clings to the folder. The weight of its contents serves as the ballast that keeps her from capsizing.

Naomi takes the sheaf of paper about Tyler Greavy and Linden Glen and shuffles it to the bottom of the pile. A picture of Maggie Rizzo—printed from the district attorney's website—now stares at her. She's almost fifty, but the picture shows a younger woman. It was probably taken a decade ago, when she joined the prosecutor's office. Her eyes are hazel, almost green, and her brown hair brushes her shoulders. She wears the conservative gray suit of a lawyer, red-framed glasses, and the calm smile of someone who has the facts, the truth on her side. Naomi used to smile like that.

Whenever Kevin dragged chaos into their lives, work was always her anchor. Words. Usually just five hundred to a thousand words at a time. She arranges them carefully. Those words are based on facts, and those facts are verified and corroborated, checked and checked yet again. Those facts give the words the weight that hold them to the page. And Naomi arranges those words according to the immutable rules of grammar, the dictates of the Associated Press Stylebook, and the gentle suggestions of Strunk and White. When she has her facts right, she feels settled by the work. She isn't forced to make decisions. The form of the story becomes almost inevitable, and it seems less like writing and more like helping the truth emerge.

Inevitable. Naomi kept overhearing that word at the funeral, and it took all of her self-control to keep from screaming at the people who said it. Susan, Kevin's sister, must have said it a dozen times. Kevin's friends said it. Kevin's coworkers said it. The dirtbag who Naomi suspects was Kevin's dealer even said it. As if everything Kevin suffered, everything that he put her through was preordained. It might be easy for someone who had the luxury of watching from a distance to use that word, but she had been married to Kevin for the better part of a decade. She lived it all up close. She couldn't accept the inevitability of any of it—that was all too simple. The truth of it: Kevin hit the side of that truck at sixty miles per hour because of all the choices he'd made and because of the choices of those three men visiting Tyler Greavy. It might kill her to believe anything else.

The doors of Linden Glen slide open, and the three men emerge. They don't say anything to each other. Henry has

his hands thrust deep into his pockets, and his shoulders
slouch as he walks, head down, to his car. Tommy blinks
into the sun. He seems disoriented, and he changes directions twice before he finds his way to his truck. Malcolm
checks his watch, adjusts his tie, and walks briskly toward
his Mercedes. Tommy and Henry probably think that this
is over. Malcolm doesn't know what will happen next, but
he surely knows that their debt is far from paid.

Naomi doesn't move until after they all drive off. She
looks again at Maggie Rizzo's picture, and she knows that
Maggie doesn't deserve what's about to happen to her.
Naomi knows only too well about the blissful ignorance
before the truth washes ashore. Only one thing seems inevitable: the wives always suffer the most.

14

Marie's Riptide Lounge

MALCOLM DOESN'T REMEMBER leaving Linden Glen. He doesn't remember what he said to Tommy and Henry when they left, and he doesn't remember what they said to him. It's like he's surfaced from dark water, driving down the Edens, and it takes him a moment to realize where he is and how he got there. It's like he woke from a blackout drunk, but he's stone cold sober and driving, and the buildings looming from the Loop are substantial and real. He squeezes his eyes shut, but all he sees is the way that Greavy's mouth hung open and the glistening thread of drool that stretched from his lip to the pillow, so he opens them again.

He checks the clock on the dash, and it says twelve fifteen. He can still make his one o'clock meeting, but he can't remember who it's with or what it's about. He knows it has something to do with the McGregor deal, but his phone's not in his pocket, and he's left to hope that it's in his bag, in the trunk. He's stuck in traffic leading into the junction, and he tries to calculate how long he's been on the road, but his mind isn't up to math, so he abandons that too. It's been a long time since he blacked out, but he knows the feeling well. When he fled to Chicago for college, too many nights were lost to darkness.

A kid on his dorm floor made fake IDs from Nebraska, and at the end of the second week Malcolm paid thirty-five dollars for one with his picture on it. At first, he drank where all the other DePaul students drank—McNulty's, Irish Eyes, The Local Option—but the other students asked too many questions. They asked him where he was from and which high school he went to. And then they'd throw names at him, trying to make a connection. But he didn't want to think about Milwaukee. He didn't want to remember. He wanted to sever all connections rather than reinforce them. So, when he found Marie's Riptide Lounge just west of the expressway, he started taking the number seventy-three bus to the corner of Armitage and Hermitage to get drunk. The Polish regulars downing Pabst and shots of Malört never asked him where he was from. Marie and Shirley never asked him who he knew. They didn't even know his name. They just served him pickled eggs, kept a Maker's and Coke in front of him on the Formica-topped bar, and let him drink in peace.

He tried to stumble home by midnight on Wednesday and Thursday, so that he could will himself through his Thursday and Friday classes. He studied enough Sunday through Tuesday to manage Cs and the occasional B. On Friday and Saturday, though, he'd often stay at Marie's until it closed at four in the morning. Sometimes he remembered how he got home. Other times his memory was jumbled and tilted. But occasionally he'd wake up the next morning with absolutely no memory of going out, the only proof his throbbing headache, the vomit-tinted drool on his pillow, and an empty wallet. But forgetting was what Marie's was all about, really. After the first few drinks, he could forget about the people that used to be his friends. After a few more, he could forget about what happened in that parking lot. Eventually, he could forget about that terrifying surge of anger and those three seconds of stillness.

Malcolm was never an angry drunk. That night in the parking lot, he had been driving, so he had only drunk three beers. And at Marie's Riptide Lounge, the bourbon calmed him as it helped him to forget. The more he drank, the less he spoke, the less he thought. Over time, and usually after he'd been drinking for a while, he thought of the drinking as a project, a responsibility almost. The alcohol sedated him, but it also made the monster inside of him sleepy. And he might have continued that way, sober enough to squeak through college, but drunk enough to forget, if he hadn't woken up that Sunday morning with bloody knuckles.

Traffic eases after the junction, and Malcolm tries again to remember what the one o'clock meeting is about, but all he can recall is the terrible emptiness of Tyler's gaze. He tries to remember what time Marie's opens on weekdays. He once went straight to the bar after a final, but he can't remember if the exam was held in the morning or the afternoon. He's suddenly thirsty, and when he sees the sign for the Armitage exit, he pulls into the right lane. He needs the bite of Maker's on his tongue and the stale stillness of Marie's in the afternoon to settle himself. Somehow, he needs to regain control.

The morning that he woke with the bloody knuckles, he suffered from the usual headache, but his face hurt, too.

When he finally dragged himself from his dorm room bed to look at himself in the mirror, he found his face painted with bruises and one of his eyes swollen almost shut. When his roommate asked him what the hell happened to him, he made up a lie about getting mugged on the way home, because he had no other story to tell. He could no longer tell himself that drinking was a responsibility, the fiction that Maker's Mark kept the monster sleepy, because he didn't know whose blood crusted his knuckles. So he stopped taking the number 73 bus to Marie's Riptide Lounge, and he stopped drinking altogether. No meetings. No twelve steps. He just stopped.

Actually, Malcolm created his own steps, his own system. Self-control became his higher power. He set his alarm for seven every day. He took meticulous notes in class. He read all of the assigned reading twice, and he studied late. And in law school, he took two jobs, because the frenzy of activity allowed him to cage it all in. He scheduled his days—he disciplined himself. He structured his life, and the resulting sense of control replaced the Maker's Mark and became the cage that confined his rage. For a long time, it worked.

He had that dark part of himself restrained and subdued by the time he met Elena, which might be what gave him the courage to ask her out that first time. He was the graduate assistant for an undergraduate course in rhetoric, and she was that sophomore that he couldn't manage to ignore. He waited until the semester ended, because there were rules about that. Her quiet elegance captured his attention, but it was her sense of humor that held it. It didn't hurt that she made no sudden movements, placed no unreasonable demands. She didn't disrupt his system, his ad-hoc twelve steps.

When Kinsey was born, before she could talk, he found fatherhood easier than expected. He managed not to think too much about his own dad, his own childhood. But she did learn to talk, and after that horrible day when the applesauce landed in his hair, thoughts of his father floated to the surface whenever he talked to Kinsey. Malcolm wondered what his dad had been like before Malcolm came along. He wondered if he was different when he first met Malcolm's mom, before they got married, or if he was just better at chaining his own monster back then.

Malcolm's earliest memory of his father centered on yelling. He didn't yell often. He went months without yelling, and during those months, he could be kind and funny and charming even. But that first memory was of the screaming. It might have been because Malcolm wet the bed or because he spilled a drink on the couch or because he failed to pick up his Legos when he was done with them. His father screamed at him for all of those things, but Malcolm can't remember which was the first. His mom usually left the room when his dad started, and Malcolm was glad, because the screaming terrified him, and he didn't want her to be as scared as he was. And he didn't want his mom to hear the horrible things his dad said about him when he finally lowered his voice and leaned into Malcolm's face, nose to nose. He told him that he was a worthless piece of shit. He told him that he would never amount to anything. He told him that he was ashamed to have fathered a son so fucking pathetic.

Every time that Malcolm became pathetic, his mom got clumsy. She slipped in the garage. She fell down the stairs. She ran into too many doors to count. Malcolm never saw his mom's accidents, but for a long time, he thought those accidents were his fault. By the time he found himself in that Burger King parking lot, he had sorted correlation from causality, and he knew that they weren't accidents. But even now, after all these years, he can't think about what he did without feeling his father's hot breath in his face.

When he takes the Armitage exit, he can already feel the heat of the bourbon and the tickle of the Coke bubbles that will carry the taste of it up into his sinuses. He'll have just one, maybe two, he tells himself, even though he's never managed just one or two. But after Linden Glen, there seems no other way to cage any of it. When he pulls up at the corner of Armitage and Hermitage, he finds a parking lot where that old brick building once stood. Expensive cars are penned in by one of those black wrought-iron fences that the last Mayor Daley planted throughout the city. The white dome of a Catholic church peers at him from a few blocks off. He pulls into the stop for the number 73 bus, and he sits there for a long time, well past the start of that one o'clock meeting that doesn't seem to matter anymore. He waits until the taste of the Maker's Mark fades, and the truth settles around his memory of Tyler Greavy's face. He can't cage or chain or sedate the problem. He catches sight of his eyes in the rearview mirror, and they look as weary as he feels. He's worked so hard to convince himself otherwise for the last thirty years, but he can no longer escape the truth: he is the monster.

15

Ridgeline Drive

HENRY STANDS IN his driveway for a long time after the taxi drops him off. He stares at the garage door, at the closed-up front of the house. He's spent the last few days, the entire flight, and the drive from the airport parsing what Alice screamed at him, interrogating her refusal to return his calls, trying to plumb the depths of her anger.

He was going to tell her. He's been searching for the right time to tell her for the last month—ever since the contact tracer called and told him to get tested—but mostly he's been finding excuses instead. He was determined to tell her on Wednesday, but then Tommy called about Kevin. When she decided to come to Milwaukee with him, he couldn't tell her then. There was never a good time to tell her, but Saturday night was most likely the absolute worst.

He thought about getting her a dozen roses or a card or a snow globe of the Milwaukee skyline to make her laugh. But he knows that she'd throw the roses in the garbage, that she's not going to laugh, and Hallmark never tried to capture a sentiment for this particular situation. And now that he's standing in front of their house, he wonders whether she's even inside, whether she's already gone for good. He imagines their house empty and his chest tightens, a lot like it did this morning in Tyler Greavy's room. But when he tries to think about what he'll say to her if she *is* home, no words come to him, and he can't imagine how any of this is going to be okay.

He shouldn't have told her on Saturday, but when he realized that Alice thought he was cheating on her again, the words just fell out. For six months after she found out about Lyla, they went to therapy every week. And every week, they peeled the scab off and poked the wound, watching it bleed again and again. For the six months that he waited for her verdict on their marriage, it felt like he carried a croquet ball in his gut. So when she accused him of cheating on her again, he felt that same weight in his belly, and he couldn't stop himself.

Finally, he musters the courage to roll his bag up the driveway. The door is locked, but she sometimes locks the door when she showers or naps. His key turns. She didn't change the locks. There's that, at least. He closes the front door behind himself and nudges his bag into the corner of the foyer. He stands up straight and listens but hears nothing. The air is still and stale. No windows open. No AC. No heat. Just a silence that screams of Alice's absence. He makes his way into the great room. He peers toward the bedroom. The door is ajar, but he's not ready to go in there yet. Instead, he takes inventory, studies the house for clues. He tries to think like Alice, tries to intuit what she'd take with her.

The picture of her parents still leans on the mantle, but she hasn't talked to her mom since the argument about her mom's turtles. The red clay vase that they bought in Sedona still sits at the center of the coffee table. The watercolors they found in Peru hang next to the windows. The prayer wheel they brought back from Kathmandu after that long, painful trek to the Everest base camp rests on the bookcase. For a moment, the fact that Alice's favorite things remain settles Henry. But then he realizes that he was there for the purchase of all those favorite things. They might be the last things she'd take.

Henry glances at the bedroom, but he's afraid of what he'll find there, so he sits down on the fireplace hearth. He knows that when he talks to her—if she'll let him—she'll want to know why he didn't tell her sooner. And that's the problem. He has no idea why. Just like when he cheated on her—he couldn't verbalize a reason then either. And that day after the Burger King parking lot, when he told Alice everything, the only question she asked was *"Why?"* But all he could do was shake his head and whisper *"I don't know."* The three worst things that he's ever done, and he can explain none of them to her. Henry fears this third unanswered *why* might be the last.

Alice feels to Henry like a dragonfly, ready to flit from their house, from their marriage, with no warning. Her job is portable. She's good at it, and she can be a real estate agent anywhere. And it's made her unsentimental about homes. He tries to think of the weight that might keep her in place. Henry always wanted children and yearns for them now more than ever. Kids—even grown kids—might provide some ballast.

When Henry first raised the topic of children, they still lived down in the city, in South Park Hill, surrounded by houses filled with kids. They were heating up leftovers after the block party when Henry first said something. He forgets the words he used, probably something clumsy, but he remembers her stillness, her silence, when she turned to look at him. He thought that her hesitation presaged a *yes*, that they were about to accidentally drop a birth control pill down the drain of the bathroom sink, but then Alice turned back to the stove and murmured that she wasn't ready yet. Over the following years, *"I'm not ready"* became *"I'm not sure that it's right for us,"* until she finally settled on *"I don't think that we should."*

In the beginning she never said why. Henry thought it was just a matter of time, and he kept asking. Then he blamed it on Alice's work and on Alice's niece and nephew, who were real brats, and even on Alice's mother, who he had always found pathologically distant. It wasn't until they were in their early thirties, just a year before they moved up into the hills, that she came clean. He said something while cooking breakfast on a Saturday morning. She sat at the table behind him, reading *The Post*. He was past asking outright, but he mentioned something that glanced against the question of children.

"I don't want to raise children by myself," she said quietly.

"I was kinda thinking we'd raise them together," Henry said, turning the bacon strips.

"But if you're gone—" She searched for the right words. "I don't want to do that by myself."

"I'm not going anywhere."

"You don't know that."

Henry checked the underside of the eggs. He thought that he knew what she was talking about. "My dad smoked three packs a day," he said. "He was bound to go early."

"That's not what I'm talking about."

Henry turned to look at her, spatula in his hand. "We can't live our lives afraid of what *might* happen in the future."

"I'm not talking about the future," Alice said without looking up from the paper. "I'm talking about the past."

And there it was. She worried about incarceration, not carcinoma. After that, Henry never brought up children again.

Henry finally pushes himself up from the hearth and walks toward the bedroom door. He nudges it open, and he stops breathing again. Alice's clothes are strewn across the bed, the dresser, the floor. He peers at the piles. Are these the castoffs that she left behind or the items about to be shoved into a box or a suitcase? Black spots dot his vision, and he reaches out to the dresser to steady himself, but then Marley rubs against his leg, and relief crashes across him like an orgasm. He hates the cat, but although Alice might leave the prayer wheel or the watercolors or Henry, she'd never leave Marley. Henry bends down and pets the cat. Marley presses his head insistently against Henry's palm. Alice is just out somewhere. She'll be back. He starts to pick at the real problem. What the hell can he possibly say to convince her to put all those clothes back into the drawers and the closet?

* * *

Alice drives up through the foothills from Safeway with a trunk full of confusion. Her grocery bags contain travel-size deodorant, shampoo, and conditioner. And she bought quart-sized Ziploc bags for TSA. But she also bought pork tenderloin and frozen salmon filets. She bought enough greens and vegetables to keep her in salads for a week and enough chicken stock to make a month's worth of chicken noodle soup.

She checks her watch as she pulls onto Ridgeline Drive. Henry texted his flight information, and if his plane arrived on time, he's home by now. She pulls into the driveway, but she doesn't hit the garage door opener, because Henry would hear that. She shifts the car into park and turns off the engine, but she doesn't open the door. She isn't ready to go inside just yet. She isn't ready to face him, because she doesn't know what she'll say or what she'll do. Worse, she still doesn't know what she wants.

She's been deciding what she wants for the last three days, and she keeps deciding differently. She thinks of those weeks that he didn't tell her, and in a rage, she starts packing her clothes. But then while she's packing, a little voice that she doesn't want to hear asks her what's really changed. What has he done that she hasn't already forgiven? Then she walks out to the deck to look at the city below, and while she's standing there, she can almost feel that virus swimming through her veins. But she doesn't know for sure yet. She won't get the results from yesterday's test until tomorrow or the day after, and for a moment her mind stops scrambling for a decision, until she remembers that she's almost certainly positive and that the results of the test don't really change anything between her and Henry.

Alice climbs out of the car and hoists her plastic bags full of confusion from the trunk. She pauses at the front door and almost turns back to the car. She could drive up into the mountains, where the air is thinner, where she can think. She doesn't want to go through that door until she's made a decision that will stick, because she's not used to feeling like this, and she hates it. But the idea that she can't even decide whether to go into her own house pisses her off, so she pushes her way inside.

As soon as she closes the door behind her, she can feel him. She can't see him, and she hears nothing, but she knows. Maybe he's turned on the AC, or maybe it's his smell or his body heat that she feels, but she knows, and that pisses her off too. She makes her way to the kitchen. She sets the bags onto the island and starts to unpack her confusion and put it where it belongs. She's placing the pork tenderloin in the fridge when she feels Henry on the other side of the kitchen island. He's moving quietly, like the cat. She rearranges condiments that don't need rearranging, because she's not ready to look at him.

"Hey," he says, his voice tentative.

"Hey."

She moves the eggs to the shelf with the yogurt and moves the yogurt down to where the eggs were. She hears him pull out a stool and sit. Finally, she closes the fridge and turns to him. He hasn't shaved, even though he always shaves, and his stubble prickles gray. Pouches hang like spoiled fruit under his eyes, and the hair on the side of his head is matted, as if he slept on a board. His shirt, the same shirt he wore on Saturday, is as wrinkled as his face.

"You look like shit," she says.

A smile flickers. "People keep telling me that."

She stares at him, waiting. It's his move, but he doesn't seem to realize it. She bends down to get the colander out of the cabinet and drops it into the sink. She dumps the bag of kale into it and starts to rinse it off.

"We went and saw Tyler Greavy this morning," he says.

Alice wads the kale into a tight ball and squeezes. She switches the faucet to spray mode so that she doesn't have to hear what he says next, but it isn't loud enough.

"He was just lying there when we—"

"Is that really what you think I want to talk about?" Alice's voice sounds shrill, even to her.

"I just thought . . ." His voice trails off.

She shuts the water off and turns on him. She places her hands on the edge of the island, and leans into it, her elbows locked. Her face feels as hard as the countertop. "You just thought what?" she demands. He looks down at his hands and spins his wedding band. "You thought I'd rather talk about what you did to Tyler Greavy than what you did to me?" she shouts. "Is that what you thought?"

"I've thought about nothing but what I've done to you," he says. "I guess I just don't know how to bring it up. How to talk about it."

"Yeah. I guess that you've made that pretty clear over the last month."

Henry closes his eyes and takes a deep breath. "I am so sorry," he says.

He waits for her to respond, but she's got nothing to say to that.

"Have you gone to see your doctor?"

"Yes."

Again he waits. Finally, "What did she say?"

"She told me that my husband should wear a condom the next time he fucks his personal trainer."

Henry's face crumples a bit more, but she can tell that he wants to know more. He made her wait. He can wait too.

"When you first told me," she says, trying to keep her voice steady, "I was so pissed that you went that whole month without saying anything. But when I woke up the next morning, I thought about condoms, and I asked myself what kind of idiot doesn't wear one when he's cheating on his wife? And then I wondered if you were stupid or just selfish. But of course, *then* I started asking myself what kind of fool doesn't ask her cheating husband whether he wore a condom. So I'll ask you this now: What the hell were you thinking?"

Henry's eyes go shiny. He rubs his face with his hands and then peers at her through his eyelashes. "I don't know," is all he manages.

"*I don't know*," Alice spits at him. "You *never* seem to know when it matters."

"I'm so sorry," he says.

"You said that already."

"My doctor said the odds are—"

"Don't tell me about my odds," Alice growls. She turns back to the sink and turns the water back on. She peels clumps from the ball of kale, rinses it, and dumps it into a bowl to dry.

"I was so relieved to see Marley when I got here," Henry says quietly to her back. "When I first came in the house, I was terrified that you were already gone."

Alice scrubs her hands even though they're already clean. "What makes you think that I'll be the one to move out?"

Another long silence while she dries her hands.

"Do you want me to leave?" he asks in a whisper.

Alice hangs up the towel, turns, and crosses her arms across her chest. She locks eyes with him. "Do you really want me to answer that question right now?"

Henry's whole body sags, and his eyes plead. She almost feels sorry for him, but not quite. "No," he finally says. "No. I really don't."

16

Disentanglement

ELENA CLIMBS THE stairs to the office above the shoe store. She was dubious the first time she came to see Luther, because of the worn carpet, the cheap furniture, and the grimy windows. The receptionist is in her sixties and wears cat's-eye reading glasses that dangle from a chain around her neck. She squints at Elena as if she's never seen her before. Elena gives her name to the woman, who calls back to let Luther know that she's there. Elena sits down in the empty waiting room, and she knows that she'll have to wait. Every time she's been to see Luther, he makes her wait. Elena's convinced that he does it on purpose, to remind her how important he is, that she's lucky to have retained a lawyer as busy as he is. Today she doesn't mind waiting, though, because it will give her time to find the right words to tell Luther what she wants.

It's clear what Kinsey wants. Last night, Elena was curled into a chair in the sunroom, reading a Gillian Flynn novel to distract herself from everything that Malcolm had said that morning, so it took her a while to realize that she hadn't seen Kinsey—or heard the mandolin—for hours. Kinsey usually doesn't say much after dinner—just a sentence here, a question there—but she's a lurker. Even though the house is so big—maybe because the house is so big—Kinsey usually appears every hour or so in the room in which Elena has settled. She's like a cat. She'll pad in, maybe stretch, look around, and then pad quietly back out. Elena can tell that it soothes Kinsey to know where Elena is, but she does it more often since Malcolm left, as if she's checking to make sure that Elena's alright. Last night though, the cat didn't stalk through the sunroom, so Elena went to check on her.

Elena watched from the doorway of Kinsey's room for several minutes, pressure building behind her eyes. Bins lined the wall under the windows, and Kinsey walked around her enormous bedroom, collecting things. Children's books. Stuffed animals. Kira's Outback Wildlife Rescue Clinic, complete with cages and exam table and a computer that randomly shouts tips about how to care for koalas. All of it was going into the bins. She seemed ambivalent about the American Girl dolls, because she had those lined up on her bed, but everything else dropped into the bins with a finality that made Elena cringe.

"Whatcha doin'?" Elena said, trying her best to sound casual.

"Giving stuff away," Kinsey said.

"Why?"

"You'll pick our house in Milwaukee. Not Dad," she said. "That means my room will be smaller."

Elena blinked and scrambled for the words to tell her about that morning. "I haven't picked anything yet."

Kinsey looked up, and her lips drifted toward a rare smile. "I know. But you will."

That was the moment to tell her. That was the time to sit down on the bed, ask Kinsey to sit down next to her, and talk it through. Elena told Kinsey *maybe*, and then Malcolm made that *maybe* hard to imagine with any clarity. It was the time to disappoint her, to help her work through that disappointment. It was the time to say she was sorry and deal with the anger and hug Kinsey in the unlikely event that Kinsey would let her. But the moment didn't last, and Kinsey started to move around the room again, a half smile lingering, her eyes glittering like they had north of the Cheese Castle. So Elena didn't say anything. She missed that moment, and now it's gone. Elena was trying to decide what she wants, but that's become irrelevant. Now, she's left to find a way to align what Malcolm wants with what Kinsey wants.

Luther finally emerges from his office. He's short and squat, tucked into a wool suit that looks as expensive as the waiting room looks shabby. His florid face is creased into a grin, revealing his crooked, coffee-stained teeth. He always seems cheerful, as if he loves nothing better than to dismantle families. He shakes Elena's hand with both of his, like a politician. She follows him into his office. His enormous desk sits on a thick green carpet. Golf balls surround the putter leaning in the corner. She sits in the lone overstuffed wingback in front of his desk. Luther leans back in his padded leather chair.

"So," he says. "Tell me about Milwaukee."

"It's a medium-sized city about an hour and a half north. Cheese curds. Summerfest. Bratwurst."

Luther sighs and looks down at his desk. Elena studies his hair. Pure brown on top. Graying around the edges. It's gotta be a rug.

"I know where Milwaukee is."

"I'm going to move there." She decided while climbing the stairs not to use the word *maybe* with Luther.

"With Kinsey," he says.

It isn't a question, but Elena answers anyway. "Of course, with Kinsey."

"You know that your husband has to sign off on that."

"I know."

"And you know that he's not going to do that." Elena doesn't say anything. Luther doesn't stop smiling, but Elena can see that he has to put some effort into it. "Can I ask why?"

"It's where I'm from."

"I mean why does it have to be now?"

"Kinsey starts high school in the fall," Elena says. Her voice remains steady, even as her stomach churns. "I want to move before then."

He scratches the gray behind his ear. He's definitely wearing a toupee. "I usually recommend disentanglement in situations like this."

"Meaning?"

"Meaning that when you negotiate, it's best to deal with one thing at a time. The most important thing first. Don't add another emotional issue to a situation that's already fraught." He pauses, looks down at a fountain pen he's fiddling with. "You should put this move off until after the divorce. Maybe let it sit for a year or two."

Elena wonders why Luther would wear a toupee in the first place. Why not just go bald? And if he insisted on wearing one, why not dye the sides or upgrade every few years to a model with a bit more gray in it? "No," she says.

Luther's smile remains but droops a bit. "What do you mean, *no*?"

"I mean that I'm going to move to Milwaukee this summer. You come highly recommended. Holly Levine swears by you. I'd hate for her to swear *about* you."

Another long stare from Luther, as if he's waiting for her to change her mind. His lips drift toward a straight line. "I can probably make it happen," he says. "But it's gonna cost you. A lot."

"I can pay," Elena says.

Luther's hand twitches as if he's brushing crumbs off his desk. "I'm not talking about my fees. I'm talking about your settlement."

She smiles, because she knew that's what he was talking about, and she can pay that price too. "You were right about what you said," she says.

"Right about what?"

"Deal with the most important thing first."

17

Pizza

TOMMY PUTS THE pizza box on the center of the table and then sets five plates in front of the five chairs. When Emma moved into the dorms down at Marquette, it felt nice to have that extra plate on the table, a reminder to everyone that Emma was still a part of the family, that when she came home, she had a place. Since she and Kyle disappeared, Tommy still sets five places, but that extra plate is heavy in his hands, and that chair feels conspicuously empty.

Jeremy's the first to wander into the kitchen and sit down. His red hair is rumpled, and his first battle with acne is starting to flare. Steam a vegetable, and you have to herd him to the table with a cattle prod, but the boy can smell pizza from the next zip code.

"Is Mom home?" he asks.

"Yeah," Tommy says. "She's washing up."

This tells Jeremy that he has to wait, that he can't just dig in like Tommy lets him when Maggie works late.

"I thought she had a trial."

"Plea deal."

"Damn."

"Watch your mouth."

Sophie can probably smell the pizza too, but she'll need some prodding. "Dinner!" Tommy shouts.

Sophie follows Maggie down the stairs, and Tommy can't help but notice that they're both wearing identical masks of dissatisfaction. Sophie does everything that she can to look different from her mother, but she fails. She wears her thick brown hair halfway down her back, while Maggie's barely brushes her shoulders. Sophie wears contacts so that they don't both wear glasses. But their upturned noses and hazel eyes are identical, and tonight, they both have the same creased forehead and the same slope to their lips. Maybe they got into it upstairs, but Maggie came through the door in a strange mood, so she might have brought that face home from work. And for all Tommy knows, Sophie might be fighting, yet again, with her boyfriend.

"Did you order salad?" Sophie demands as she sits.

"No," Tommy says. "Just pizza."

"There's lettuce in the fridge," Jeremy says.

"Shut up, turd."

"And some vegetables."

"I said. Shut. Up."

Jeremy turns to Tommy, aggrieved. "I try to help, and this is what I get?"

Tommy ignores them both. He bows his head and says grace, murmuring the same perfunctory paragraph that his own father murmured. When he's done, he can see that Maggie's still in her mood, so instead of trying to coax conversation from her, he grabs a corner piece and devours half of it with one bite. He's ravenous because yesterday, after Linden Glen, his stomach felt too slippery for much of anything. This morning, it gurgled when he walked out to the driveway to get the paper, but it settled when he found nothing written by Naomi. The greasy, salty mouthful of sausage and cheese goes down so clean that he almost groans with pleasure.

"Did you do your homework?" Maggie asks Jeremy.

Jeremy looks down at his pizza when he answers. "Yep."

Tommy smiles at this. "What about the math project?"

When Emma disappeared, Tommy and Maggie could think of nothing but that, and both lost track of Jeremy's schoolwork. It took them a couple of months to realize that Jeremy had too—all of his grades had plummeted toward low Cs and high Ds. Tommy now checks PowerSchool every day on his way home from work, but Jeremy hasn't quite gotten used to the renewed scrutiny. He's been bobbing and weaving, hoping it's temporary, a passing storm.

"Some of it," Jeremy says. "It's not hard."

"Then why isn't it done?"

"I like to spread it out," Jeremy says, his lips squirming. "I don't want to have all the fun at once."

Even Tommy has to laugh at this. "PowerSchool says you only have one more day to savor it. And tomorrow you have soccer practice. Of course, you could skip practice to indulge your passion for algebra."

Jeremy's eyes flicker toward Tommy and then land on Sophie. Sophie's staring at her plate, nibbling on the crust of her pizza. Tommy can tell that Jeremy's about to start something with her to change the subject. "What about history?" Tommy asks, before Jeremy can speak.

"I don't have history homework."

"You have a test tomorrow."

"Exactly. So there's no homework."

"You have a C in history."

"That's because Mr. Evans doesn't like me."

"Mr. Evans doesn't like you because you don't study."

Jeremy's eyes flicker about. He takes another bite of his pizza. "It's more of a quiz," he mumbles, his mouth full.

"PowerSchool says test," Tommy says. He starts in on his second piece of pizza and eyes Jeremy, who looks everywhere but back at Tommy. "And your answers on *this* quiz have earned you an evening studying with your father."

Jeremy's eyes harden, Maggie swallows her first smile of the evening, and Sophie keeps nibbling on her crust like a squirrel. Tommy's on his third slice of pizza when Sophie mumbles a question.

"What was that?" Tommy asks.

"I asked if you talked to Emma lately."

Tommy stops mid-chew and looks at Maggie, who has also stopped chewing and is looking right back at him. Every other time that Emma called, Tommy told the kids, to let them know that she was okay. Neither Sophie or Jeremy said anything those other times she called. They just shook their heads when Tommy asked if they had any questions. Tommy would have told them that she called on Saturday if he wasn't so distracted with Kevin and Tyler. He meant to tell them. He should have told them. He nods. "I did. Last weekend."

"How is she?" Sophie asks, more of a challenge than a question.

Tommy looks down at his plate. He feels three sets of eyes on him, but he has no idea how to answer. He glances at Maggie, but her face holds only questions. He looks at

Sophie, who's staring at him with an intensity he hasn't seen from her in years. He doesn't want to worry the kids needlessly, but he doesn't want to lie to them either. And he doesn't want to say anything that he didn't already share with Maggie. He struggles for the words that might describe that sound in Emma's voice, like a stripped gear or a loose belt. "I really don't know," he finally says.

The silence that follows is heavy and lasts a long time. It's broken by Jeremy of all people.

"Why did she go away?" he says, his mouth half full.

Tommy studies him. "We already talked about that," he says.

Jeremy swallows and grabs two more pieces of pizza. "But you never really said anything."

Jeremy's right, because when they talked about it, he and Maggie said a bunch of words that boiled down to *"We don't know why she left."*

"What aren't you telling us?" Sophie demands in that same accusatory tone.

Tommy searches for an answer to that, but Sophie's staring at Maggie now. All at once, it occurs to Tommy that Emma's been calling Sophie. Of course she's calling Sophie. Jeremy is looking at Maggie too. Even Jeremy knows that this is Maggie's question to answer. Maggie avoids all their stares and blinks at the empty chair, the unused plate. Her voice is small and uncertain when she speaks. "It's my fault, Jeremy. She left because of me."

* * *

Tommy's loading the dishwasher, trying to take his mind off dinner, trying to summon the energy to go fight with his son about exponents and colonialism. He feels more than hears Maggie come into the kitchen, but he keeps loading the dishes with his back to her. He knows why she's here. She wants a long hug. She wants him to whisper into her ear that she's being too hard on herself. She wants him to tell her that it's not her fault. But he doesn't turn from the dishwasher because Maggie was right about what she said at dinner. It *was* her fault.

Tommy's pulling the detergent packet from a box beneath the sink when Maggie clears her throat. "Do you know a Kevin McNamara?"

Tommy goes cold, and he finds it hard to move as he struggles to understand why Maggie's asking about Kevin, but that question has no answers, so he pushes it aside because he has to answer the question that Maggie just asked him, and he forces himself to move, and while he puts the detergent in the compartment and snaps it shut, he considers denial, but as he closes the dishwasher and stands, he thinks of all the ways that Maggie can find out that he knew Kevin, if she doesn't know it already, because lawyers are always asking questions they know the answer to, and when he turns, she's leaning against the counter with her arms crossed, and she's staring at him with her eyes narrowed, and he doesn't know what he's about to say even as he opens his mouth.

"Yeah," he admits. "Why do you ask?"

"A reporter from the paper called this afternoon. I'm not sure why she called me, but she suggested that I look into this McNamara about a cold case. A murder." Maggie peers at him with an unsettling intensity. "She said he might have had something to do with it. He's forty-nine and he went to Pius. I thought you might know him."

Tommy's mind spins and his fingers tingle, and he wants to reach out to the counter to steady himself, but it's too far away, and he's not sure that he can move his feet, because he suddenly realizes that he has no idea what Naomi's after or where this will end, so he tries to maintain eye contact with Maggie, and he knows that the longer he says nothing, the more she'll ask, and she'll start asking in her lawyer voice, and the fact that he's even in this situation makes him hate Tyler Greavy on a whole new level, and he doesn't know if he's been standing there a second or a minute, but he knows that he has to say something, and again the truth seems safest. "Did she tell you that he's dead?"

Maggie's eyes bunch, and her mouth squirms with confusion. During the moment that she processes that unexpected bit of information, Tommy searches for something to say to forestall another question. "It was Kevin's funeral that I went to. Last Friday."

Maggie opens her mouth, so Tommy says the first words that come to him. "Motorcycle accident. Hit the side of a truck."

Tommy scrambles toward something else, something true, but Maggie finally manages to blurt a question. "Were you friends with him?"

And there it is. Tommy recognizes it immediately. The question that demands a lie. The way that Maggie squints at him makes him wonder if she realizes the same.

"No," Tommy says. "He was just a guy that I knew."

18

Tommy's Basement

THE FOUR BOYS were watching the Brewers play the Orioles that last time they were all together in Tommy's basement. They always hung out in Tommy's basement, except in the fall when Tommy's life was consumed by football practices. It was unfinished, as were all their basements. Most of it was devoted to Mr. Rizzo's workshop. He built furniture as a side gig, so a lathe, a table saw, and a drill press were lined up next to the workbench. A half-finished kitchen table stood in front of the workbench, and concentric circles of debris—sawdust, discarded fragments of cherry, oak, and pine—surrounded it. Old bicycles, Tommy's brother's hockey equipment, and an ancient wooden playpen lay abandoned in a corner. Canned goods that Tommy's mom had bought on sale lined shelves, next to boxes with words like *Winter Clothes* and *Children's Books* and *Quilt Scraps* printed neatly in marker on the sides.

The boys had claimed one corner for themselves. They found two old couches on curbs that they wedged down the stairs and arranged at an angle to square off their domain. Henry found one of those couches after a rainstorm, so even though they let it sit out in the sun for three or four days, its stink, like a wet dog, mingled with the smell of WD-40 and sawdust and Jumpin' Jack Monterey Doritos, a bag of which had been abandoned and forgotten, leaning against the far end of one of the sofas. Alice brought an old area rug that her mom was going to throw out because the cat puked on it, and she spread it across the concrete between the couches and the television. The boys rested their feet (and their beer cans when Tommy's parents were out on bowling night) on milk crates that lay scattered atop the rug. They had to buy the TV that sat in the corner on another milk crate, but they got a deal from one of Kevin's mom's boyfriends, so it only cost them fifteen dollars each. Mr. Rizzo helped them splice it into the cable box for free.

It had been almost two weeks since the night in the parking lot. Baltimore was up three to one in the fourth, but none of the boys cared much about the game, because the Brewers and the Orioles both seemed to be battling their way to the bottom of the division. They mainly had the game on to distract themselves, to keep themselves from talking about that night yet again.

They'd talked about that night relentlessly the previous two weeks. They tried to use words to make sense of what had happened, but they could find no sense in it. They had agreed to tell absolutely nobody, although by the time they agreed to that, Henry had already told Alice, so she was grandfathered in. They shared the shreds of information that they gathered from the newspaper and from listening carefully to rumors and conjecture, and they tried to arrange those fragments into something that resembled an explanation of what had happened after they left the parking lot. They talked about what they would do if a cop showed up at one of their doors, and they agreed that they should remain silent and ask for a lawyer, because they had all watched enough cop shows to know that's what you're supposed to do. They concocted elaborate lies that might serve as an alibi. Henry joked about running to Mexico, and they actually spent a couple of hours discussing it. But none of them owned a car, and they barely had enough money between the four of them for the gas, much less food and shelter. Besides, none of them spoke a lick of Spanish.

Certain things they did not discuss. They did not talk about the details of the night—just the aftermath—because they were all reliving those details in their minds, and it seemed like too much to hear them aloud. And they certainly didn't talk about how they felt—the guilt, the shame, the constant hum of anxiety—because teenage boys don't have many words for that. All of them were thinking about that night, even as they watched the game and complained about the middle of the infield and the middle of the batting order. They were always thinking about it. They thought about it at school as they went through the final motions of their final year, and they thought about it when they were in the shower and while their parents filled the silence at the dinner table with questions that they responded to with grunts or single-word answers. Even when they were taking tests or playing basketball or masturbating, it was there. It was always with them, like a shadow on a sunny afternoon. It was a heavy pressure leaning against everything. Like a tumor.

Over the last few days, the conversations about that night had thinned, even though it was still all they could think about. Henry, Malcolm, and Tommy all wanted to stop talking about it, hoping that the whole thing would fade over time, like a bruise or like that puddle of blood on the asphalt.

"Has anybody heard anything?" Kevin asked.

Tommy shifted his weight. Malcolm closed his eyes, leaned his mullet back against the couch, and breathed heavily through his nose. Henry narrowed his eyes and stared at Kevin, a faint smile smudging his lips. "Yeah. I heard that the Brewers might trade Bosio to the Cardinals for two minor leaguers and some spare bats."

Tommy snorted a mirthless laugh. Malcolm didn't stir. Kevin kept his eyes on the TV. "You know what I mean," he said quietly.

Henry leaned forward, his elbows on his knees. "And I heard your mom is having a spring sale. Blow jobs for fifteen bucks. Hand jobs for a bratwurst."

Usually when Henry made jokes about Kevin's mom, it would set Kevin off, but that day he remained still, expressionless, blinking at the TV. "I'm thinking about calling the hospital," he said.

Malcolm's eyes snapped open. "No. You won't do that."

The words came from Malcolm louder than the other three boys expected, with a clear, cold finality. They had agreed to lay low, and now Kevin was suggesting otherwise, but Malcolm's voice dripped with a malevolence, a hatred even, that was entirely new and unexpected. They all tried to get a read on him, but his eyes remained locked on the television, so eventually their gaze drifted back to the game too.

The silence hardened around the soothing voices of the play-by-play announcer and the color guy. Kevin seethed. Tommy hoped that the silence would hold. Malcolm thought about what he would say when Kevin spoke again, because he knew that Kevin would say more. Kevin always said more. Bosio walked another batter. Henry always found it difficult to sit with the silence. "These goddamn Brewers could trade for Babe Ruth, Ty Cobb, and Jackie Robinson, and they'd still suck a dick."

Tommy heard this as Henry trying to change the subject, and he was grateful. Kevin heard this as the feeblest of apologies, but he was still pissed off because you just don't have to say something like that about anyone's mother. Malcolm didn't really hear him because the space between his ears was abuzz. They watched Bosio load the bases before Trebelhorn finally tapped his arm for a reliever.

"Aren't any of you curious?" Kevin asked.

"I'm curious about when you're gonna let it go," Malcolm growled.

"I mean, we don't even know if he's still alive," Kevin insisted.

"My mom said that he's alive," Tommy said. Tommy's mom was a nurse at Waukesha Hospital, where Tyler Greavy had been sent. She said it over dinner, like she was telling Tommy's dad what time the fish fry started, or like she was telling Tommy's aunt about the latest plot twist on *Knots Landing*. She said it so casually because she knew that it didn't have anything to do with them. "That second boy looks like he's gonna make it," she said. "The one from the Burger King." Tommy managed to swallow the mouthful he was chewing. He kept his eyes on his plate and carefully cut another piece of Salisbury steak.

"That was more than a week ago," Kevin said.

"You call the hospital, Kevin, and you're just gonna stir up shit," Malcolm said. "We've been through all this."

"And what if he recovers?" Kevin insisted. "What if he remembers everything and gives the cops a description, and we get hauled in?" Kevin was talking fast, like he did when he got worked up.

"Ask for a lawyer," Malcolm said. He grabbed the remote and turned up the sound. The hum of the crowd in Baltimore filled the basement. "And keep your goddamn mouth shut."

Kevin looked down at his hands. "None of it would have happened if I had kept my mouth shut that night."

They all knew this was true. If he had just kept his mouth shut—something that Kevin always had trouble with—none of it would have happened. They had turned this idea over and over in their heads while they were staring at the ceilings of their bedrooms, waiting too many hours for sleep to come, but there was no point in saying anything.

"I'm thinking about talking to somebody," Kevin said.

Malcolm hit the mute button, and the basement went very quiet. "A therapist? A school counselor? Your mommy? What the hell are we talking about here?"

"I was thinking about talking to the cops," he said quietly.

They all sat there, stunned, Kevin as astonished by what he'd said as the others. "What the fuck are you talking about?" Henry finally demanded.

"I think about their families." Kevin stared through his knees at the milk crate in front of him. "They don't know anything. They don't know why."

"You have got to be kidding me," Malcolm said, his voice a mixture of disbelief and disgust.

"It just seems like the right thing to do."

"The right thing to do," Malcolm said flatly. "What makes you think you get to decide what's right for the rest of us, you motherfucker?"

"I wouldn't bring you guys into it, I'd just—"

"Bullshit," Malcolm said. "Everyone saw us together at Josh's party. It wouldn't take Cagney and Lacey to figure out we were with you."

Henry leaned forward again. "Kevin. I think what Malcolm's trying to say is that you might have started it, but he finished it. He's got more at stake here."

Malcolm turned on Henry, his eyes flashing. "What the hell are *you* talking about? You weren't exactly innocent."

"Not exactly guilty either," Henry said.

"*Fuck. You.* We both have just as much to lose."

"Bullshit, Malcolm. We all saw what happened. This would have all just been another funny story if you hadn't lost your shit."

"We were all there," Tommy said quietly. "We were all part of it."

"We're all gonna regret this," Kevin said. "In the end the truth's gonna come out."

"Just shut! The fuck! Up!" Malcolm shouted. He pushed himself up from the couch and stood over Kevin, his fists clenching and unclenching. "I'm so sick of your self-righteous bullshit. You started the whole goddamn thing, but then you turned pussy. You kept your hands clean that night, and now you want to drag the rest of us through the mud so you can sleep at night."

Kevin closed his eyes, bent his head forward, and held his hands clasped between his knees. He wished that he hadn't said anything.

Tommy glared at Malcolm. "Do you really think that what you did that night was so courageous?"

Malcolm's body became very still. His face twisted in a way that made it difficult to tell if he was going to cry or spit or yell. "What does that mean?" he asked, a hitch in his voice.

"You just called Kevin a pussy—for what he didn't do. You think what you did that night makes you tough? Some sorta goddamn hero?"

Malcolm stared for a long time at Tommy. His shoulders gradually sagged and his fists unclenched. Kevin wasn't sure what he'd wanted when he started talking, and he had become less sure as they argued. Henry wanted to take back what he'd said to Malcolm. But Tommy meant exactly what he'd said, and he was glad that he'd said it. Without another word Malcolm stalked to the stairs and climbed them for what none of them knew would be the last time ever.

The TV was still muted, so all they heard were Malcolm's footsteps above them and the front door slamming. For a long time, they said nothing. They didn't look at each other. Ripkin found a fat one, high and away, and sent a grand slam over the center field wall, but none of the boys were watching. Henry stared at the milk crate in front of him. Tommy stared at the weeds in the window well. Kevin stared at Tommy's father's lathe. It was Kevin who finally broke the silence.

"I was just trying to—"

"Kevin," Tommy said loudly, to shut Kevin up, "just get the hell out of my house."

CHAPTER

19

The Attic

MAGGIE CALLED IN sick. Her throat *does* hurt, but she knows it's probably just acid reflux. After Tommy leaves with the kids, she climbs out of bed, makes herself coffee, and sits quietly with her suspicion. A twitch in her stomach, that bitterness at the back of her throat, that tiny pressure at the base of her skull convinced her that Tommy was lying when he told her that Kevin was just a guy that he knew. If she hadn't been a litigator for the last twenty years, she could probably ignore her body, but the fact is, her body has proven right too many times.

A few months after they'd first started dating, they began introducing each other to their friends. There were Tommy's work friends—mostly men his father's age, with grease under their fingernails. And there were his softball friends—he played on three different teams back then. She met his poker friends only when Tommy hosted after they moved in together. Tommy has always had a lot of friends. People are drawn to his gentle nature and his dry sense of humor, and his size means that once someone meets Tommy, they tend not to forget him. He never went to college, so there are no college friends, but the absence of high school friends and friends from his childhood always puzzled her. They live just a few miles from the house where he grew up, a few miles more from his high school, yet she's never met anyone but family who knew Tommy as a child. When she asked him about it, his answers were uncharacteristically vague, and she learned not to press him, because after a certain number of questions, he would shut down completely.

But ever since Maggie asked him about Kevin McNamara, she can't stop thinking about those blank pages in Tommy's life and all those long-ago evasions. Her body tells her that they aren't unrelated to last night in the kitchen. She knows that her body is fallible, that it sometimes gets things wrong. But she also knows that it's persistent, that it will keep nagging her until she finds out one way or the other. And that's why she can't stop thinking about that box.

When Tommy's mom moved in with them for good, when they sold her house, they gave away what they could and sold the rest at an estate sale. Besides his mom's clothes, her jewelry, and the photo albums, Tommy only brought three items: the Sacred Heart statue that had belonged to his grandmother, the ugly yellow cookie jar that sat on his childhood kitchen counter, and the cardboard box with his name written in marker across the top and sides. The Sacred Heart statue now perches on a shelf in the family room, although they only sometimes go to church. The cookie jar clutters up the counter next to the toaster oven, although they still keep the cookies in the pantry. Tommy took the cardboard box straight to the attic. When she asked him what was in it, he mumbled something vague about *"stuff from when I was a kid."* She didn't think too much about it until her stomach started twitching last night. Now, she can't stop.

Maggie tries to enjoy her coffee. She's so seldom in her house alone, and she tries to take pleasure in the silence. She thinks about the platter that she left cooling on top of her kiln a few nights ago—a gift for an old friend entering her second marriage. She considers the design that she'll paint on it, the colors she'll use, the glaze that she'll bake onto it after she paints it. But none of this distracts her from the tug of that box. She gets up and pours her coffee down the sink. She tells herself to go down the stairs to check on the platter, because if it warped while it cooled, she'll need to start over, and she needs to ship it by Wednesday if she wants to get it there in time for the wedding. But it probably didn't warp, and it's a second marriage, so if the gift isn't perfect or turns up a little bit late, it doesn't really matter.

So she grabs the flashlight from where Tommy keeps it on top of the fridge and climbs up the stairs rather than down. At the end of the second-floor hallway, she uses the hook to tug open the trapdoor to the attic, and pulls down the ladder. She climbs into the heat and the musty mess of the attic. She can stand up straight along the center line of the house, but the roof slopes to meet the floor at the edges. She plays the light across old furniture and Jeremy's hobby horse and the boxes of clothes she should have taken to Goodwill years ago. She has a sudden urge to sort and restack and purge, but she pushes that aside and starts scanning the boxes for Tommy's name.

She walks the length of the attic and back again. Twice. She peers behind old furniture, moves Tommy's golf clubs, shines her flashlight across box after box. She's starting to wonder whether Tommy really did bring that box up to the attic, when, behind an old dresser and at the bottom of a stack of boxes, she finds Tommy's name scrawled on the cardboard. She sets the flashlight on the dresser and moves the two boxes on top of it. One of them contains Jeremy's wooden Thomas the Train set. The other is full of maternity clothes that she packed away a decade ago. There's no reason—at least no reason that she's ready to contemplate—why Tommy's box would sit beneath the other two. She drags it to the rocking chair that they moved from the nursery when Jeremy got his big-boy bed, and she sits.

Maggie tucks the flashlight under her armpit, unfolds the flaps, and starts to pull items out. Baby shoes and his lacy christening outfit. A large P and a smaller P—his varsity and junior varsity letters. Snow globes of the Sears Tower, the St. Louis Arch, and the Golden Gate Bridge. She sets aside a stack of report cards wrapped in a rubber band. First grade is on top, and she knows without looking that Tommy's mother arranged them all in order. She sets aside a bundle of birthday cards and the stacks of photos. She finds the yearbooks at the bottom. They also are precisely ordered. She ignores the thin, soft-covered volumes from St. Francis Elementary on the top. She finds his senior-year Pius yearbook at the bottom of the stack.

Maggie pages to the M's and immediately finds Kevin McNamara. He's got his hair parted down the middle and feathered like Leif Garrett—like half the boys on the page. But Kevin McNamara refuses to blend in. His big ears poke through his hair. His lopsided smirk doesn't reveal any teeth. And unlike the other boys, he's got his top button undone and his tie loosened, as if he'd just arrived home after a hard day at work.

Maggie shines the light on that face for a long moment before shifting her attention to the inside covers. They're scrawled with messages and signatures. She means to scan for a note from Kevin, but she finds herself reading every inscription, trying to peer into Tommy's past. Many reference his ability to swill copious quantities of beer. Some are vague and formulaic, from people he probably knew only glancingly. But some are specific: *"I'll always remember Springsteen at Summerfest." "That week at my uncle's cabin will live in infamy." "We'll have to go to Chicago again when we're legal!"* She finds more of the same on the back cover, tiny windows into Tommy's life. Way at the bottom corner, in careful print, she finds a note from someone named Kevin. There's no way to know if it's from Kevin McNamara, of course, but the visceral directness of the message makes Maggie's mouth fall open. *"Tommy, I love you like a brother, and I always will. Kevin."*

Maggie sets the yearbook aside and starts on the photographs. There are three bundles, each held snug by a rubber band. The first stack features Tommy as a baby and as a toddler—at the pool, at Christmas, at Easter. The second rubber band holds elementary school. She sees Tommy with his mat and lunch box in front of the school bus on the first day of kindergarten. He's carving his Pinewood Derby car. She finds him playing soccer and football and baseball. She sees him in a canoe with his father. Mixed in with all of it are pictures of Tommy with three other boys. They're building a snow fort and sledding and skating on a pond. They're jumping off a diving board and fishing and peering down from a treehouse.

The third bundle features the same four boys growing awkwardly into high school bodies. She finds Tommy in his uniform, with his helmet under his arm. A grainy shot of a football game taken from the stands. Again and again, those same four boys drape their arms over each other's shoulders, grinning toward the camera at parties and at dances, and looking uncomfortable in white and powder-blue tuxedos at the prom. There's the short one, the tall one with blond hair, and next to Tommy—always next to Tommy—stands that boy with his hair parted down the middle, his too-big ears, and that closed-mouth, lopsided smirk.

20

Applesauce

MALCOLM HANGS UP the phone and turns to his monitor. The call with McGregor's executive team did not go well. Emotions always run hot as the close approaches, and Malcolm had to force the CEO to face some very large and uncomfortable realities. Malcolm logs in to his computer so that he can start responding to the venom inevitably pouring in from the McGregor team. This brush fire will take a while to extinguish. He considers telling his assistant to send Tommy back to Milwaukee, but decides to let him wait in the lobby. It annoys him that Tommy came to his office unannounced, but he's also curious about what brought him.

As he opens his email, his desk phone rings. He hits the speaker button. "Yeah?"

"Peter's on line one."

Malcolm frowns. Peter is Malcolm's divorce attorney. They've known each other since law school, and Peter knows better than to call Malcolm during the workday, especially during a deal. Yet another distraction that he doesn't need. Malcolm punches the button. "What's up?" he snaps.

"Sorry to bug you," Peter says, but he sounds giddy, not sorry at all. "I just got off the phone with Luther. Elena wants to cut a deal."

Already the emails are streaming in. Lots of exclamation points, capital letters, and bold-faced words. "Seems like this can wait until later," Malcolm says.

Peter laughs. "No. Deals this good have a shelf life of hours. She's bound to change her mind."

Malcolm clicks on the first email, from the CFO. He scans it, hits "Reply," and starts typing. Peter takes his silence as permission to continue.

"Lump sum of two hundred thousand. Five thousand a month for maintenance for five years. Another five grand for child support until Kinsey's eighteen."

Malcolm's hands slip from the keyboard, and he blinks. He's certain that he's misheard. Elena knows their net worth. She knows what he makes. Peter's good, but he's not *that* good. "Two hundred thousand and ten grand a month?"

"Right? I need the green light on this fast. She's going to change her mind. Oh, and you get to keep the house."

Malcolm stands, plants his palms on the desk, and leans over the phone. He asks the next question even though he already knows the answer. "What else does she want?"

"She wants the kid. Sole custody. Visitation one night every month." Peter stops talking, but Malcolm doesn't say anything because he knows what's coming. "And she wants to move to Milwaukee."

Malcolm walks over to the window and watches a gull circle. The updraft must be weak, because it's gliding lower fast.

"You still there?"

"I'm here."

"So, this is a go, right?"

"No," Malcolm says. "Not yet."

"What?" Peter demands. "Are you kidding me, Malcolm? This is as good as it gets. Better than it gets."

"I need to think about it," Malcolm says to the window, to the bird as it drifts down, almost out of sight.

This leaves Peter speechless. When he finally gathers himself, Malcolm can tell that he's struggling to stay calm. "You need to tell me what you want, Malcolm. If you don't tell me what you want, then I can't do my job."

At this, Malcolm smiles because, of course, Peter's right. It's a straightforward deal: he trades control for the money. He evaluates and makes more complex decisions a dozen times every day. And he knows that he can't control Elena and Kinsey, no matter where they live, so he's really giving up nothing that he didn't surrender years ago. A dozen years, to be precise.

Elena was out. Kinsey was two. She had been talking for a while, but she was just beginning to grasp her ability to manipulate the world with words. She was strapped into her booster chair, the yellow plastic one with frogs on the side. Saturday lunch like so many others. Malcolm gave her applesauce for dessert, but she wanted ice cream. He should have just given her the ice cream, but he was tired and distracted by the work for the Cellutec deal that he was neglecting. She said, "Ice cream." He said, "Eat your applesauce." She screamed, "Ice cream!" He said, more firmly, "Eat your applesauce." He doesn't remember exactly how many times she screamed for ice cream, but he vividly remembers the applesauce hitting him in the face. More than that, he remembers the terrible things that he shouted next, words that a man should never shout at his daughter. And he remembers how much the low, guttural rasp of his voice sounded like his father's.

By the time Malcolm changed his shirt and rinsed the applesauce from his hair, he had reminded himself that he had a plan, that he had a system, and that he had allowed himself to drift away from it. By the time that Elena arrived home, Kinsey seemed to have forgotten about the shouting, but Malcolm never did. By late afternoon, he was back at work, and in the following weeks he let the Cellutec deal swallow him whole. Since then, he's contented himself with those quiet, safe moments watching Kinsey sleep, and he's watched her grow to resent his absence as much as Malcolm had resented his own father's presence. That's the problem, he now realizes—there are so many ways to hurt the people that you love.

But Peter is waiting for an answer, and as the bird drifts out of sight around the corner of a building, the real question shifts into focus: is Malcolm going to try to fix things, or is he ready to give up? When he turns from the window, he has to work hard to keep his voice steady as he says words that he hasn't said aloud for years, maybe decades.

"I need to decide what I want."

* * *

Tommy's been waiting for two hours when he hears the clack of heels on marble approach his chair. When he looks up, he finds a short, middle-aged woman wearing a gray pantsuit with her hands clasped behind her back. "Mr. O'Donnell will see you now," she says.

She turns without another word, so he gets up and follows her. She leads him through a maze of carpeted hallways,

and they all look the same. So do the offices and the desks,
and the men and women behind those desks. The sameness
is broken by the occasional wooden bookcase lined with
leather-bound tomes that don't look like they've ever been
cracked open, but after they pass a few of those, he realizes
that they're all the same, too. Before he knows it, before he
wants it, really, the woman has ushered him into an enormous corner office where Malcolm sits behind a sleek black
desk that's completely different from the others. The sun
slants in through the wall of windows, and Malcolm squints
at his monitor as if he's reading about a cancer cure or a plan
to deliver peace to the Middle East.

The woman closes the door, but Malcolm doesn't look
away from the screen. Tommy stands in front of the desk for
a moment, looks out the window. Finally, he sinks into one
of the low-slung chairs.

"Hey," Tommy says.

"Claire said it was important," Malcolm says, but he
still hasn't looked away from that goddamn monitor.

Tommy gets to the point. "Naomi called Maggie."

Malcolm's eyes finally dart to Tommy. He leans back in
his chair, digests the information.

"Maggie's your wife," he says, but of course he knows
that. Tommy told him at the funeral, and Malcolm has
always vacuumed facts, sorted them, and filed them away
until they're needed.

"And she's an assistant DA," Tommy says. He didn't tell
Malcolm this, and he can tell by the way Malcolm goes still,
doesn't even blink as he sorts through the implications, that
he didn't know that Maggie was a lawyer.

"Which jurisdiction?" Malcolm asks.

"Waukesha County," Tommy says.

He watches *those* implications settle across Malcolm's features. Malcolm doesn't respond, as if waiting for Tommy to say more, but after sitting in that lobby for two hours, Tommy decides to let Malcolm wait.

"What did she tell her?" Malcolm finally asks.

"She said she's doing a story on a cold murder case. And she told Maggie that she should look into Kevin McNamara as a suspect."

Malcolm's mouth falls open for a moment, the first authentic reaction that Tommy's seen from him since high school. But just as quickly, Malcolm forces his face into that tight-lipped lawyer's mask. "Did she tell Maggie that Kevin's dead?"

"No," Tommy says. "But I did."

"Why would you—"

"She told Maggie that Kevin graduated from Pius in '90," Tommy says, cutting Malcolm off. "Maggie asked if I knew him. It was only a matter of time before she found out it was Kevin's funeral last Friday."

"Did Naomi tell her that she was married to Kevin?"

"Not that I know of."

"What else did you tell Maggie?"

"Nothing," Tommy says. The list of things he's kept from Maggie seems so much longer than what he's told her. "Not yet."

"What does that mean?" Malcolm says quietly, leaning forward now, his elbows on his desk.

It means that Maggie isn't stupid, that recognizing lies and discovering unsaid things is what she does. It means that with every day that goes by, his silence adds yet another lie to the stack that he's been building for decades. It means that when Maggie finds all those lies—and Naomi seems determined to show her exactly where to look—she'll never forgive him. "She's my wife, Malcolm. My marriage is at stake, for Christ's sake."

"There's nothing to tie us to that night," Malcolm says. "Kevin's dead."

"But Naomi's not."

The two men stare at one another, and then Malcolm blinks, glances at the monitor. "I'll take care of Naomi," Malcolm finally says.

"What does that mean?"

"I'll talk to her. Figure out what she wants."

Tommy already knows what she wants—she wants to destroy all three of them. "All she has to do is call my wife one more time," Tommy says.

"I understand that you're scared," Malcolm says softly. "But if Maggie finds out—from you or from Naomi—I go to jail for murder."

"We all go to jail," Tommy says.

"Maybe," Malcolm says. "Henry would probably testify against us. You might get a few months for obstructing justice." Malcolm looks out the window and then back at Tommy. "But I'll go away for years—even if I plead it down to manslaughter."

The office goes silent, and Tommy licks the sweat from his upper lip. It would have been so much better to tell her back when she was a public defender. No, he should have told Maggie right when they started dating, while she was still in law school. He meant to tell her, even tried to tell her, although he never actually said any words. Every few months for the last twenty-two years, he has spent days and weeks working up the nerve to tell her, but the urge always faltered—he never had the balls to tell her who he really was.

LIKE IT NEVER HAPPENED

"What about self-defense?" Tommy asks.

"You sound like Kevin. I'll call my guy again. Make sure he's prioritizing this appropriately."

Disgust climbs Tommy's throat—the same bitterness he tasted when Malcolm first started talking about *his guy*. He's disgusted with Malcolm, but he's disgusted with himself even more, because he knows as soon as Malcolm speaks that getting Malcolm to call his guy is exactly why he drove down to Chicago and sat in that waiting room for two hours. "What if he doesn't find anything?"

"There's always something," Malcolm says. "Just keep your mouth shut until he finds it, and this too will pass."

"Keep your mouth shut." Tommy has become only too good at keeping his mouth shut. He looks down at his hands, and he feels Malcolm wait for his response. He knows that he should just get up and walk out. He should drive back to Milwaukee and tell Maggie everything, but he knows that he won't. He doesn't look up when he speaks. "This guy of yours," he says. "You think he could help me find someone?"

21

Your Brother

H ENRY SITS AT his desk in his home office and reviews the details of the MedScope event in Hilton Head. He's sourced all but four of the cadavers. He sends a flurry of emails to his regular sources and a few that he's been cultivating. They've got almost eighty of the top orthopedic surgeons flying in from around the country for three days of steak, bourbon, golf, and training. MedScope recently introduced a new scope that they claim significantly improves the outcomes on most back surgeries. Henry knows that's probably bullshit, but the new scope sells for thirty thousand more than the one it replaces, so the facts are irrelevant. And all the medical-device companies learned long ago that if you invite surgeons to a suburban training center in New Jersey, none will show. But to sell their devices, they must train the surgeons. So they need steak, bourbon, golf courses, and torsos. Forty torsos wouldn't usually be a problem for Henry, but with the new attorney general in Maryland and the bad press in Texas, he has to work harder for them than usual.

His email pings, and he goes still when he sees the name of the sender: Tommy Rizzo. His mouse hovers over the message for a long moment before he clicks it open.

Hey,

Just checking to see how you are. I'm worried about you.

Your brother,
Tommy

Henry reads the message twice, testing it for sarcasm, for aggression, but it's just Tommy. It's a simple message, but those words set him off balance: *Your brother.* Those words send him tumbling back decades, to before that night, to when their friendship was unquestioned, to when they *had* considered themselves brothers. Milwaukee was such a shit show last weekend that, although he was tugged into the past, he mostly managed not to allow his mind to drift back to all those years before that night in the Burger King parking lot. He blinks at those words, and their tenderness, the vulnerability that it took to write them, after everything, makes him click the reply button. His fingers rest on the keyboard, and he tries to think of what he might write.

In the early years, right after he and Alice left Milwaukee for Denver, he thought often about calling Tommy, to try to repair what had been broken. He knew that if he was going to patch things back together, he would have to start with Tommy, but he never managed to pick up the phone. Last Friday at the bar after the wake, he thought that they might be starting down that path, but then Kevin did what he did, and they found themselves in Tyler Greavy's room. And just like that, Henry's back in that room at Linden Glen, and he sees Greavy's thin, still body lying under that sheet. He feels that same vertigo, that same overwhelming disgust and shame that forced him to stare out the window at that evergreen tree. He remembers why he never called Tommy and why he never will. He clicks the "Reply" window closed and deletes Tommy's email. He kneads his face hard with the palms of his hands and forces his mind back to the familiar task of searching for cadavers.

He follows up with the sources that have committed. He's always very particular about the logistics—the packing, the refrigeration, the transportation—and he double-checks that all the torsos will move like they're supposed to. He reviews and submits the Virginia paperwork because he knows that Virginia actually pays attention to the paperwork. He checks in with his onsite supervisor, to make sure that everything will be ready when the cadavers arrive.

Henry hangs up the phone, stands, and stretches. He looks out the window and down the hill at the city. Marley rubs against his shin, and he gives the cat a not-so-gentle kick. This time of day is usually his favorite, the late afternoon light lending a warm glow to everything. But Tommy's email makes him feel gritty, and a haze drapes the skyline, making the whole city look dirty. Besides all that, Alice is due soon.

Before, when she arrived home from work, she'd wander into his office, rest her hand on the back of his neck, and

stare out the window while she told him about her showings. They played a little game where he would guess the
prospective home buyers' occupations based on how she
described them. The goal wasn't to guess accurately, but to
make her laugh, because he finds the trickle of her laughter
irresistible. Since he got back from Milwaukee, though, he's
learned to dread the sound of her car in the driveway. Now
her arrival means that the house will fill with a deafening
silence, punctuated by muffled noises from the bedroom as
she packs or unpacks her things, depending on her mood.

Henry's email pings again. He hesitates before sitting
back down at his desk. He's relieved to find that the email
is from Everglades Crematorium, a new source just south
of Atlanta. He's been courting them for a few months, but
they haven't yet supplied anything. It's one of those places
that offers free cremation. You have to read the fine print
to learn that they only burn your corpse after your torso is
packed in dry ice, shipped to a resort town, and cut open
by hungover surgeons in a hotel ballroom. In the beginning, the size of that print niggled a bit, but it certainly
doesn't bother him now, because the email says they have
inventory—they can deliver three of the last four torsos in
time for the event.

Henry hears Alice's car in the driveway. The front door
opens and then slams shut. Her footsteps fade down the
hallway, and another door slams. He stares out the window
at the haze for a long time before he stands. He walks to the
door of his office. He can see down the hallway to their bedroom door. Marley stands outside it, mewling loudly. Henry
tries to piece together the words he could say to Alice, words
that might slice through her unbearable silence, but none
come. Something heavy falls to the floor in the bedroom.

Marley jumps and then meows again. The bedroom door opens just a crack, the cat slips in, and the door closes. Henry stands there for a long time before he turns and walks back to his desk, grateful that there is one more cadaver to find, one more corpse to distract him from the silence.

22

Payment

NAOMI SITS AT her secondhand kitchen table, stacks of paper spread around her, the keys of her laptop under her fingers. She finds that when she's digging through the documents, when her hands are moving, when she's piecing together the story, the need to cry doesn't feel quite so urgent.

Those first couple of days after Kevin died, all she did was cry. Their house seemed so empty without him, no matter how many people stopped by to put casserole dishes in the fridge and hug her and ask her how she was holding up. Their home is empty, but it's full of him too. His Packers jersey, where he left it draped across the arm of the couch, and his books on the bookcase and his couscous in the kitchen cabinet all demand that she think of nothing but Kevin. After nine years together, she had stopped thinking of his things as his, but now that he's gone, every item makes it hard to breathe. It doesn't help that she knows it was no accident. It certainly doesn't help that she issued yet another ultimatum just before he slammed the door behind himself, his helmet under his arm.

She started writing the story three days after Kevin died, before dawn on the morning of the wake, but really she's been writing the story in her head for the last nine years. Nobody came by that morning because they all knew that they'd see her at the wake, so she was left by herself with all of his things. It was too early to pack them away, of course, but she couldn't look at them either. So she started writing the story to keep her eyes off his Carhartt work pants hanging on the hook near the door and his fishing pole leaning in the corner and his Brewer's cap on the coffee table. And she wrote the story to try to make sense of it all, even though she knew that no sense would come of it. Kevin had spent thirty years trying to make sense of it, and just look at how that turned out for him.

She knew nothing about the story in the beginning, but it wasn't just that story that he was hiding from her then. She fell in love with the clean Kevin, and it wasn't until they'd been together for almost two years, after they'd married, after they'd bought the house, that he began to tell her the story. He started to come home with glazed eyes and his shoes untied, but at that point she just thought he was stopping at the bar after work. He shared the story in tiny bits—just dribs and drabs. He finally told her about what happened in the parking lot just a week before that first overdose—the first overdose that Naomi was forced to deal with anyway.

When Kevin was clean—and she'd learned, just like every junkie's wife, to recognize when he was clean and when he wasn't—he was funny and kind, and he bristled with energy, but he was stingy with the story. When he came home late with that glazed look, though, the story would spill from him. She learned not to ask questions when he was telling it—even though her nature and her training inclined her toward questions—because when she asked questions, Kevin's face would close up and he'd stop talking. He'd push himself up from the couch and drift into the bedroom, where she would find him curled into the fetal position on top of the bedspread, fast asleep. When she just listened, though, when she offered up silence, he filled it with scraps that she collected and curated, sewing those fragments into a patchwork quilt of a story. But until the day of Kevin's wake, she never wrote any of it down.

It didn't take a psychology degree to draw a line from that night to the needle, but Naomi wanted to know every last detail of the *why*. Back when she thought that she could change him, the *why* seemed so important. She thought she might be able to help him weave some of those threads into something resembling context, insight even. By the time he got on his motorcycle for the last time, she knew that it was far too late for that, but the *why* of it still matters to her. Every time he talked about that night, his own shame glittered, and its edges seemed to scrape against his nerve endings. She was unsettled by the blame that he pinned on Tyler Greavy, but stranger still, he never fell out of love with Tommy or Henry or Malcolm. He called them brothers. He missed them more than he blamed them. When she pressed him, he could never explain it, and she could never understand it. The story speaks for itself, and she's still angry that he never blamed them. He wasn't the only one pricked by that needle. He wasn't the only one living in their tidy little bungalow who had paid an enormous price for that night.

Naomi pushes back from the table and walks to the stove, where she pours herself another cup of tea from the pot. She sips the Earl Grey and stares out the window at their tiny square of yard, shaggy with uncut spring growth. When they bought the house, she thought that backyard might someday contain a swing set. She clung to the idea of that swing set for the first half of their marriage. But her dreams of motherhood were governed not by the rhythm of the moon, but by the cycles of Kevin's addiction. He would stack up clean months, years even, and the first three times through the cycle, she thought that they might have beaten it. But every time, just before she built the resolve to say something, he'd come home with his eyes glazed and his shoes untied. That empty patch of grass where the swing set should stand amounts to just another price that they paid for that night in the Burger King parking lot, but she doesn't write that part of the story.

There's a lot that she doesn't write about. Like the stiff breeze on that day they first met. She was walking through the Firefly Art Fair when she saw the bugs that he made—sculptures welded from rebar and scrap metal—some big enough to sit upon, others small enough to fit in the palm of your hand. He made her laugh that day with a joke that she can't remember. He ignored his other customers for more than an hour while they talked, and he sent her home with his phone number and a tiny metal grasshopper, no charge. She won't write about the way he would sneak up behind her and lick her ear when she was trying to work or watch TV or read. She won't write about how he could make a harmonica sound like it was weeping or how he pulled half dollars from her nephew's ear or the spicy sweetness of the jambalaya he made every year for her brother's Superbowl party.

The morning of the funeral, she started writing the story as a way to keep her fingers and her mind moving, so that her thoughts wouldn't settle on the emptiness and the fullness of their house. Not long after dawn she had a draft, so she started to research because that's what she always did after she wrote a draft. You need details and facts to transform a draft into a story. Kevin had told her so much about Henry and Tommy and Malcolm as children and teenagers, but he never told her anything about them past that last argument in Tommy's basement. She never learned where they went, what they did, how they turned out. Until she started her research, they were all just boys, frozen in amber.

But then Facebook and Google and a variety of public records databases freed them, and she learned about children and homes and careers, about lives that stretched far beyond that basement. None of them had paid the terrible price that Kevin had paid, that she had paid. As she took notes and printed source materials, a black rage began to mix with her grief. By the time she showered and dressed for the wake, the general shape of a plan had begun to form. By the time she parked at the funeral home, it had become tangible yet flexible, ready to wrap itself around different reactions and circumstances. She clings to that plan. It helped her to hold back the tears when she saw Kevin's body in the coffin. It holds them back now as she studies that patch of grass where the swing set should be.

Naomi sits back down at the table and continues to revise the story. It's not just a story anymore—it's an invoice. It's grown to almost three thousand words. She knows that her editor will never print it. He'd demand evidence, corroboration, and secondary sources that she could never provide. But she knows that there are so many other ways to unleash this story into the world, into the lives of Malcolm and Henry and Tommy. She has a backup plan—and a backup plan for her backup plan. She's not yet sure how this will all play out, but she's certain of one thing: she will make them pay.

23

Miss Katie's

TOMMY IS EARLY and Emma is late. Emma is always late. It was her idea to meet at Miss Katie's, but it feels perfect to Tommy. When the kids were young, Tommy would take the three of them to the little diner down on 19th Street whenever Maggie was fighting through a tough trial. It gave her a few hours to sleep or catch up on work without the kids underfoot. Miss Katie's, with its speckled linoleum, sticky vinyl booths, and aproned waitresses, became their place. They usually perched on the metal stools along the yellow and red breakfast counter, but today demands a degree of privacy that the counter won't offer. Emma's tardiness gives Tommy more time to think through what he'll say to her, time to craft the gentle questions that might help him learn what's going on without scaring her off. It gives him time to make sure that he doesn't act like Maggie did the last time they shared a meal with Emma.

Before Emma disappeared, the three of them had gone to dinner at the Olive Garden near Marquette on the first

Monday of every month. Tommy met Emma for lunch often, so mostly the dinners were for Maggie. Tommy was there to translate for them and to smother the flames when the brushfires started.

"How's Kyle?" Maggie asked over salad, after the usual interrogation about classes and roommates and basketball games.

Tommy glanced sharply at Maggie because of the way her voice landed hard on Kyle's name.

"He's fine," Emma said, picking the onions out of her salad.

She answered in the same bored monotone that she answered all of Maggie's questions, because she didn't hear what Tommy heard. Of course, Tommy was tuned to it, because he and Maggie had argued about Kyle just the week before. He knew about the file Maggie had brought home from work. He thought that they'd ended that argument on the same page, but suddenly he wasn't so sure.

"You have plans for spring break?" Tommy asked quickly, trying to steer the conversation back to safer ground. He worked to catch Maggie's eye, but she was sorting the onions from her own salad.

Maggie spoke again before Emma could answer his question. "Is he staying out of trouble?"

Emma looked up, fastened her eyes on her mother. "Why would you ask me that?"

"Maggie—"

"Let her answer, Dad." Emma's lips settled into a thin straight line, just like Maggie's did when she was angry.

Maggie continued to pick out the onions. "It just seems important that he keeps his nose clean," she said. "After what happened in high school."

Confusion edged in alongside Emma's anger. "What are you talking about?"

"Maggie—" Tommy said.

"I thought that you knew." Maggie finally looked up from her plate. "I just assumed that he told you about his arrest."

Emma went very still.

"Goddamn it, Maggie," Tommy said.

"What?" Maggie said, trying and failing to sound sincere. "I thought that she knew."

"What are you talking about?" Emma asked again, her voice softer, crackling with uncertainty.

Maggie turned back to Emma. "I'm talking about the two pounds of marijuana that the police found in his trunk when he was sixteen."

Emma's face hardened. She leaned back in her chair and crossed her arms across her chest.

"He didn't tell you," Maggie said.

Tommy could see Emma take it all in, try to digest it. She stared at her mother for a long time before she spoke. "And how did *you* learn about this?"

"That's not relevant," Maggie said. "What's matters is—"

"Was it even legal?" Emma interrupted. "The way you found out?"

The same question that Tommy had asked. "Selling drugs isn't legal," Maggie said, a sharp edge leaking into her voice. "They say he was supplying his entire high school."

Emma picked her napkin up from her lap and placed it carefully on top of her salad. "Are we done?"

"Yes," Tommy said too loudly.

"No," Maggie said even more loudly. "We're not done. I want to know if you're going to keep seeing this boy who breaks laws and then keeps it from you."

Tommy shifted uncomfortably in his chair. "Maggie."

Emma stood, and her chair scraped across the tile behind her. She glared at her mother. "It's none of your fucking business who I see."

Maggie leaned forward, glared right back. "As long as we're supporting you, it *is* our business."

Tommy searched for words that might make Emma sit back down, words that might shove them both away from the argument, back toward a conversation. But before he could say anything, before he could do anything, Emma turned and threaded her way through the tables to the front door. And then she was gone.

*   *   *

He almost doesn't recognize Emma when she comes through the door of Ms. Katie's. She's wearing makeup and dressed in a blouse and a skirt instead of her usual sweatpants and sweatshirt—as if she's meeting him for an interview. Her brown hair is pulled so tightly into a ponytail that it hurts to look at. She seems to have lost a few pounds, weight that she couldn't really spare to begin with. Tommy climbs out of the booth and wraps her in a hug. She feels fragile. Her hair smells like leaves and smoke. She pulls from his embrace before he's ready to let her go, and she slides into the booth.

"I've missed you," Tommy says quietly as he sits.

"Me too," she says.

He can hear from the tone of her voice that she, too, is being careful with her words. "You look good," he says, even though he doesn't care for the makeup and the fancy clothes. She seems older, but more spent than mature.

"How're Jeremy and Sophie?" she asks.

Tommy notices that she doesn't ask after her mother. "Jeremy is Jeremy," he says. "He thinks he's funny, and sometimes he is. Sophie's dieting again, and she's been fighting with her boyfriend. But I think that you probably already knew that."

Emma looks down at the menu and says nothing. She and Sophie *have* been talking. The waitress comes, and Tommy orders the corned beef hash skillet and a stack of buttermilk pancakes for himself, a Belgian waffle with strawberries for Emma. They always order exactly the same thing at Miss Katie's.

"How are you?" he asks when the waitress leaves.

She hesitates before answering, which tells Tommy more than the words that follow. "I'm good."

"How's Kyle?" he asks, not because he cares, but because Kyle is another tiny window into Emma's new life.

A longer pause this time, and her eyes slip toward the window. "He's good," she says quietly.

The way she says it, as if it's something that she wishes were true, tells Tommy everything. Her eyes dart around the restaurant, out toward the street, and then back again, like she's ready to scramble into the weeds. Those eyes tell Tommy that he's got to be careful.

"I've been worried about you," he says. "All of us have been worried about you."

Emma unwraps her silverware. She folds the paper napkin in half and then in half again. "I'm an adult now, Dad."

Tommy wants to argue. He wants to tell her how little she really knows. He wants to tell her about the responsibilities that come with the freedoms, the weight of adult consequences, but he knows she won't be able to hear it, so instead he says, "I know."

"Then why don't you treat me like one?" she demands without looking up from the napkin.

Why don't you start acting like one, he wants to snap, but he knows that will send her into the brush. "I'm learning to," he says instead. "I know that you'll make your own decisions, and I've come to grips with the fact that there's nothing that your mother or I can do about that."

"And what about Mom? Has she arrived at any epiphanies?"

This is the hard part for Tommy. He and Maggie are so different, but they've never talked badly about one another in front of the kids. Until now. "Your mom has control issues."

This pries a bitter laugh from Emma. "*That's* an understatement."

He knows he has to go further, that he has to throw Maggie fully under the bus in order to earn a sliver of Emma's trust. "What she said—at Olive Garden that night—that was way out of line."

Emma cocks her head, surprised by his candor.

"Prying into Kyle's past like that. Telling you what to do. None of it was right," he says. "But she did it because she cares about you. Whenever she sees one of you kids make a mistake—or doing something that she thinks is a mistake—she can't help herself."

"Good intentions," Emma says. "Mom always says that good intentions aren't enough."

"I'm just telling you the reasons," Tommy says. "I'm not making excuses."

"Kyle and I love each other."

Tommy stifles a smile and concentrates on what he'll say next. One wrong word and he knows that he'll have two meals to eat. "Sometimes that's enough," he says. "And sometimes it isn't."

Emma swallows, looks Tommy directly in the eyes. "Is it enough for you and Mom?"

The question stuns Tommy. Not just its audacity or the insistence with which she asks—its accuracy sends him reeling. It lands on that soft spot that he's been pressing for months. "Tell me what's wrong," he says instead of answering. "I can tell that something's wrong, and I want to help."

The waitress arrives with the food just then. The settling of plates gives Emma an excuse not to answer right away. She pours syrup over her waffle and cuts it into tiny squares. She eats a strawberry and then a bite of the waffle. Finally, she looks up. "If I tell you, you can't tell Mom."

It's Tommy's turn to look down at his plate, to push food around. He tries to imagine how he would feel, what he would do if he found out Maggie was having lunch with Emma without telling him. "We don't usually keep things from each other," he says. He shovels a forkful of corned beef into his mouth because the word *usually* tastes wrong.

Emma looks out the window, down at her plate, toward the door. Tommy can feel her dissatisfaction with his answer.

"You know how she'll act," Emma says. "She'll decide what she wants to happen, and she'll call her cop friends, and she won't do things *for* us. She'll do things *to* us." She pauses, let's her words sink in. "That's not the kind of help we need."

Tommy thinks of all the other things that he hasn't told Maggie, and he can't decide if one more straw fits on the camel's back. But then he parses Emma's words. *"Cop friends. The kind of help we need."* He considers everything that lurks beneath those words. He tries to convince himself that Maggie wouldn't want anything to get in the way of him doing the right thing for their daughter. "Okay," he finally says. "I won't tell her."

"You have to promise," Emma says immediately.

He feels her eyes on him as he arranges the bacon strips into perfect rows. He thinks of the implicit promise he made to Maggie when they married, and he thinks about how he broke that promise even before he made it. He doesn't want to make another promise that he may not be able to keep. He wants to bob and weave, say some words that might pacify her while falling short of a promise. But when he looks up, he sees the desperation written across Emma's too-lean face, and he can't help himself.

"I promise."

CHAPTER

24

What's-His-Name

ELENA MIXES FLOUR and eggs and butter with her mom's old wooden spoon. Kinsey sits next to her at the island, her hair hanging around her face as she stares down at Elena's phone, swiping through the photos that Elena took in Wauwatosa yesterday afternoon. Elena watches for a reaction, but of course Kinsey betrays none, so Elena pays attention to which photos Kinsey lingers over.

"That one's your bedroom," Elena says. Kinsey swipes. "And that's the family room."

It's a little three-bedroom ranch built in the seventies. The whole thing measures less than two thousand square feet, but that should be plenty for the two of them. It hangs back from the street, and it's got a nice front yard, even if the hedges need a good trim. The backyard has a fish-pond and not too much grass to cut. The school district is the right one—Kinsey's cousin Mia will be a sophomore at the high school next fall. The kitchen was remodeled a few years back, but it wasn't overdone. The appliances are

Whirlpool and GE and Frigidaire, but they're all black, and they all work. Best of all, the kitchen is small. Cozy. Two steps from everything.

"What do you think?" Elena asks when she can wait no longer.

Kinsey swipes through a few more pictures, swipes back to look at the bedroom. Elena worries that she finds the house too small or too old-fashioned.

"We'll probably replace the carpet," Elena says. "And the wallpaper in the bathroom."

"How far is it from Uncle Dom's house?" Kinsey asks.

Elena licks her lips to keep from smiling. She was hoping that would be the only thing that really matters. "Six blocks. You can ride your bike there."

Kinsey clicks the lock button on the phone and sets it on the counter. "When do we move?"

"I haven't even made an offer yet," Elena says. "Can you get me the Crisco?"

Kinsey climbs off the stool and drifts to the pantry. She moves bottles and boxes until she finds the blue can in the very back. Elena uses Crisco only for chocolate chip cookies, because they just don't taste like her mom's without it. Kinsey sets the can on the counter and sits back down, studying Elena.

"But that's the one?" Kinsey asks.

"Yeah," Elena says. "That's the one." The price is right. The kitchen is right. The location is right. It feels surreal to say it, to slip away from their life in Winnetka so easily, but it also feels so, so right. "We'll probably move in a month or two."

"In time for school?"

"Definitely in time for school."

"Did you tell Uncle Dom yet?"

"Yeah," Elena says. "He's excited. Oh. I almost forgot—he's coming to your concert on the seventeenth."

Kinsey doesn't quite smile, but her lips wriggle. "Did you tell Grandpa that we're moving?"

"Not yet," Elena says as she spoons the shortening into the bowl. She hasn't even told her dad about the divorce yet. She should have stopped by yesterday on the way out of town, but she didn't. Instead, she took the coward's way out and told Dom. She's hoping that her brother will tell him, so that Dom can answer the inevitable questions before Elena talks to her dad again.

He'll be ecstatic to have her back in Milwaukee, and he certainly won't miss Malcolm. He could never remember Malcolm's name when they first started dating—more likely, he refused to remember it—and by the time he learned it, he decided that he didn't like Malcolm, so he still calls him *what's his name* when Kinsey's not around. But she sat at the kitchen table as a girl too many times, listening to her father ask the same two questions whenever Elena's mom told him that somebody from the parish was getting divorced. *Did he hit her? Did he cheat on her?* Those were the only two questions he asked because, for him, those were the only two reasons to divorce. Those questions always pissed off Elena's mom, and some of her parents' most memorable fights were about other people's divorces. She wishes, for the thousandth time, that her mom were still alive, this time to help her dad reconcile Elena's reality with the Pope's. But her mom is dead, and her dad is old and Catholic, so it's probably best if Dom talks to him first.

"What are you going to do about Dad?" Kinsey asks. This is the closest that Kinsey has come to acknowledging what she told Malcolm at dinner.

Elena turns the oven on, so that her back is to Kinsey, so that Kinsey can't see her face. She called Luther on the way home from school today, but he still didn't have an answer. He said that Malcolm's attorney seemed as bewildered as anyone. "We'll work it out," she says, even though she has no idea how or when or who *we* even includes.

Elena's phone rings and Kinsey looks down at it. "Milwaukee number," she says.

Elena thinks it might be the real estate agent, so she answers. "This is Elena."

"Hi, Elena." Not the agent. A stranger's voice. Low and even. A woman.

"Who is this?"

Elena feels Kinsey's eyes on her.

"I used to be married to a high school friend of your husband's."

Elena tries to think of a single high school friend of Malcolm's and fails. "How can I help you?"

"You can't," the woman says. "But maybe I can help you."

"Who is this?" Elena demands again.

"I understand that you're going through a divorce."

Elena's mind churns quickly through the tiny list of people that she's told. She turns to the fridge and opens it, even though she doesn't need anything from the fridge.

"If things get complicated—and they usually do—you'll need leverage. Ask Malcolm about Burger King." A pause. "That might make him a bit more flexible."

"Who are you?" Elena asks. She closes the fridge without taking anything from it.

"My name is Naomi," the woman says. "Malcolm will know who I am."

The woman hangs up. Elena sets the phone uncertainly on the counter and picks up the spoon. She churns the greasy wad of Crisco into the mix. She doesn't look up, because she's trying to sort out what just happened, but she can feel Kinsey's eyes pry at her.

"Who was that?" Kinsey asks.

Elena keeps her eyes on the bowl. "Nobody," she lies, trying to keep her voice casual. "Telemarketer."

Kinsey goes more still than usual, but Elena won't look at her. She stirs and stirs until the Crisco has disappeared, until everything is smooth and even, and then she stirs some more. Finally, Kinsey gets up without a word and leaves the kitchen.

25

Redstone

A LICE SITS DOWN at the bar at Redstone and orders a gin and tonic. Hendrick's. The good stuff. If she's going to pay fourteen dollars for a gin and tonic, then she might as well enjoy it. It's only half past six on Thursday, but a man in a bow tie is already playing the piano in the corner, and the bar is filling with women who look hungry.

Alice just finished showing a condo around the corner. It's priced a bit high, but the seller seems flexible. Her client is a divorced woman. She didn't say that she's divorced, but Alice can always tell. There's just something about the way that divorced people hold themselves that helps Alice sort them from the never married. Her client was almost sixty, and she seemed settled, content. Alice knows the type. Alice has been categorizing clients for decades. All realtors do it, and the best are good at it. And it's especially important to categorize the divorced women, because they all want something so different.

Alice has probably shown thousands of homes to hundreds of divorced women, so she knows the types well. The grieving, the busy, the numb, the hungry, the resigned, the fierce, the empowered, the happy. Today, she can't stop wondering what makes the difference. Is it the circumstances of the divorce? Is it the personality or the character of each woman? Or do they all follow a progression over time—the types just depressingly predictable phases that every divorced woman fights her way through on the way to peace?

Her client likes the condo. When someone starts mentally arranging their furniture in the rooms, Alice knows that they're leaning toward an offer.

"We could put the couch against that wall," the woman said quietly. "The loveseat against that one." She looked at a third wall. "The TV there."

We. The plural caught Alice off guard, and for a split second it seemed as if that *we* might include *her*. She almost answered, but the way the woman whispered told Alice that *we* referenced someone else altogether. She appraised the woman again, tried to imagine whom she'd found. Alice wondered how long it took her and what she'd had to sacrifice to find her way back to *we*. But then the woman told Alice that her daughter and her granddaughter would be living with her. That explained the *we*, and to hear it made Alice's chest ache, because there was no hope in that *we*, at least not for Alice.

Maybe Alice stopped into Redstone because it was so close and because she'd already paid for parking. Maybe she chose the bar because she wants to eat somewhere crowded and noisy instead of that house on Ridgeline Drive, so heavy with angry silence. Probably she's sitting at the bar at Redstone because Wyatt from the office, who's ten years younger, told her that Redstone is where he goes cougar hunting.

Cougar. She's always been mildly disgusted by the term. For some reason, she's always associated desperation with the word, but she's unable to remember why. A cougar is sleek and strong and merciless. As she gains distance from that trip to Milwaukee, as the betrayal and humiliation melt toward rage, she feels all of that.

Alice looks more closely at the people gathered so far around the glossy mahogany bar, and she finds that Wyatt wasn't wrong. There's one couple, grabbing a quick bite to eat, and there are a pair of old men at the back nursing whiskeys, neat. The balance of the crowd are women who seem clustered around Alice's age. Some together, others alone, but each with at least one empty barstool next to her. One drinks a martini, the rest drink wine, mostly red. All but the Black woman are unseasonably tan, and most are taut for their age, from Pilates and yoga or eating too little. All of them look around the bar, taking the measure of each other. It suddenly occurs to Alice that these women could become her rivals, her friends, or both.

As Alice sips her gin, men filter in, all of them alone. They don't seem to evaluate their options before they choose a stool, or they decide so quickly and so discreetly that Alice doesn't see them do it. Each of the men introduces himself to the woman next to him, just after the bartender delivers a drink. And then the woman sizes him up, much as Alice sized up the competition a few moments ago. Alice feels like Marlin Perkins, but she can't tell who is hunting and who is prey.

The first Hendrick's goes down smooth, and it's an easy decision to order another. If only she could decide so easily what to do about Henry. She wakes up every morning and spends the first few hours trying to decide whether she wants to keep the house or move to Spain. A few hours later, she's

trying to decide whether to sell the china or pack it away in
storage for some hard-to-imagine dinner party in the distant future. Should she keep those watercolors that she and
Henry bought in Cusco? She loves them, but she knows
they'll always remind her of Henry. But then she finds herself making excuses for his month of not telling—it would
be so hard to tell someone that you infected them with HIV.
And that's when it hits her all over again—he infected her
with HIV—and she goes back to deciding whether to keep
the house or move to Spain.

She's wrapped so tightly around this axle. She needs to
gain some objectivity, some perspective. Maybe *that's* why
she's at Redstone. You would think that living with Henry
would have taught her to put some distance between herself
and the ugly. God knows that he's good at it.

She can't help but think of that trip up Highway 1 a
couple of years after they married. They were driving the
coast from Los Angeles to San Francisco when Henry took
a work call. The ocean was pounding the shore below them.
The steep cliffs to her right blurred past. She had almost
drifted off to sleep the first time he said it, so it didn't quite
register. Then he said it again, and she heard him too clearly.

"I didn't know that you called them that," she said after
he hung up.

"What's that?" Henry asked.

"I didn't know that you called the bodies 'meat.'"

"Not bodies," Henry said. "They're cadavers."

"Whatever," she said. "You just told that man to be sure
to keep the 'meat' cold."

Henry stared hard at the road, his hands at ten and two.
For almost five miles he didn't respond, and Alice was starting to think that he wouldn't. "It helps," he finally said, his

voice hoarse. "It's a hard job if you think of them as bodies. If you think of them as people."

They drove in silence a while longer, and Alice's thoughts rubbed raw against Henry's words.

"Does it help with that other thing?" she asked.

"What thing is that?"

"Burger King?"

Henry gripped the steering wheel more tightly and stared out the windshield at the winding coastal highway. By the time they reached Half Moon Bay, she realized he wasn't going to answer, and she didn't ask again. His silence was answer enough.

Alice needs her own answer now, but everything looms so close that it overwhelms her. She'll decide when she can see the whole of it. She doesn't know when she'll decide, but she knows how. Like a cougar, she'll decide what's best for herself, and if that's not what's best for Henry, then he can go fuck himself.

A man sits down next to Alice. She keeps her eyes fixed on the TV above the bar, but she can tell it's a man by the way he smells and the amount of space that he takes up. She doesn't look at him because she doesn't want to seem eager or desperate, and she still isn't sure why she came to Redstone. She doesn't know what she wants, and turning to him seems like a decision that she's not quite ready for.

When the bartender comes to take his order, he asks for the small-batch bourbon menu, and Alice begins to dislike him. Finally, he orders, and Alice keeps her eyes on the television. The Avalanche are up by one in the first period, but the Blackhawks have a man advantage. She decides to leave when the power play is over, when the Avalanche stop scrambling to cover too much ice.

"I don't think I've ever seen you here before," the man says.

Alice turns, hoping to find a troll or a boy half her age, someone who will make the right decision easy. But he's lean, with a strong jaw and broad shoulders, and enough gray in his full head of dark hair to convince her that he's past forty.

"That's probably because I've never been here."

"Can I buy you a drink?"

"I don't drink bourbon," she says, to buy herself time, to see how he reacts, and because it's true—she hates bourbon.

He smiles wryly, swirls the enormous single ice cube in the brown liquor. "Neither do I, actually," he says. "I prefer gin, but when I got divorced, my brother told me that real men are supposed to drink bourbon."

Despite herself, Alice smiles at this. "Do you always do what you're supposed to do?"

He studies the glass in his hand and shakes his head. He looks up at her. "Not often enough, I guess."

She meets his gaze, and his eyes are a dark brown, nothing like Henry's. They look at each other for an uncomfortably long moment.

"You never answered my question," he says. "Can I buy you a drink?"

Alice considers what she wants, her whole body tense. It takes all of her effort to keep her smile relaxed. She doesn't really decide, she just pounces. "No," she says. "But I'll buy you one." She raises a hand and the bartender wanders over. "Two Hendrick's and tonics."

* * *

They eat dinner sitting at the bar. Alice has a cheeseburger, and Mark—his name is Mark—has the Cobb salad. Alice

knows that she should have ordered a salad, that a cheeseburger breaks an unwritten rule of the bar at Redstone, but
after three drinks, she's past caring. And she knows she
needs some bread in her stomach to soak up the fourth.

Mark sells polymers, whatever the hell those are. He
explains it to her, but she doesn't really care, so she doesn't
really listen. He hikes, and he's got an eleven-year-old son
and fresh wounds from a divorce that did not go well. Alice
tells him that she's recently divorced too, and the lie rolls
off her tongue so easily that it frightens her. Maybe it's the
gin. Maybe Henry's rubbing off on her. Maybe it's close
enough to the truth. Maybe it's becoming more true with
each moment that passes.

If she's just learning to lie, she hasn't forgotten how to
flirt. The last time she flirted, the Berlin Wall still stood
and Reagan was president, but she realizes as they talk
that flirting isn't so much different from showing a house.
You take the measure of the client before you enter. You
ask them questions, learn what's important to them and
what will turn them off. Then you reveal the property to
them in a way that will build excitement. It's all about
order and emphasis. You have to show the flaws along
with the features, but at the end of the most effective
showings, that amazing view or that outdoor entertaining
space or that beautifully appointed master suite will make
them forget all about the crawl space that may or may not
contain mold.

So Alice talks about every hike that she's ever taken.
She tells him about the campsites and that bear and the
waterfalls and the sunsets. She doesn't tell him that it's been
more than a decade since she's hiked. And she edits Henry
from the narrative, because Henry is not the place to start.

Decades as a realtor have also taught her to read body language. When a couple is looking at a house, they draw closer to each other and touch each other if it's a good fit. They whisper. The wrong house sends them wandering into separate rooms, and they shout about what they find there.

Mark's body tells Alice all that she needs to know. He never glances at the other women at the bar. In fact, his eyes only leave her to look down at his salad or to search for the bartender to order another drink. He touches her forearm when making a point. He laughs at everything she says, even though most of what she says isn't all that funny. He leans toward her when he speaks, and he listens to her in a way that Alice isn't used to. Alice can feel the chemistry, the static between them, and it moves both ways.

Mark is telling a story about a ski trip to Aspen in February, but Alice only half listens. She feels herself sliding downhill toward something inevitable, and it feels like she's gaining speed. She wonders how fast things move at the Redstone bar. She doesn't know the rules, but there must be rules. And although she wants to think that she and Mark are meandering down the mountain on a green named Sunnyside or The Long Way Home, she suspects that they're racing headlong down an icy black diamond. Her body and the gin coursing through it urge her forward, but that virus swimming in her bloodstream with the alcohol is telling her to slow down. She's trying to remember the numbers that she read on the internet, the odds—Mark's odds—when she realizes that Mark is no longer talking. He's looking at her expectantly, as if he's asked her a question.

"What was that?" she asks, embarrassed.

"I said that I've got a special bottle of California red back at my place. Do you want to help me drink it?"

And there it is, the answer to the question about how quickly things move at Redstone. She realizes, all at once, the number-one rule of dating when you're fifty—that all of the showings start in the bedroom. You need to go through the bedroom before you're allowed to browse the bookshelves or see what's in the kitchen cabinets, and this makes her angry all over again. Angry with Henry and angry at herself for staying with him these last two years. That virus swimming with the gin makes everything complicated when it should be simple, but when she opens her mouth, it's the cougar that speaks.

"That would be lovely," she says. "But you must let me pay for dinner."

*   *   *

Alice was wrong—she gets a good look at Mark's bookshelf while he's in the kitchen gathering the bottle, the corkscrew, and the wineglasses. The living room is spartan—just a large television on one wall and a floor-to-ceiling bookcase on another. The coffee table is glass, and the couch is black leather, of course. She sees it all the time—it's as if divorce courts issue black leather couches to every man when his marriage is dissolved.

Alice finds Morrison and Groff and Zusak and Saunders and Foster Wallace on the bookshelf, and she wonders if they're like the bourbon—props selected by his brother. Mark sits down on the couch, sets the glasses on the table. He struggles with the cork. Alice runs her fingertips over the spines. They all look untouched. Either he's a very careful reader, or the bookshelf has been staged. When Alice turns, she's startled again by Mark's beauty—and her own nerves. She sits down in the center of the couch. Close enough to smell him, but far enough away to keep things ambiguous. Mark hands her a glass. She takes a sip and lets it sit on her tongue before swallowing. Mark was right about the wine—it's balanced, with just a hint of something like coffee at the bottom of it. It finishes long and strong.

"How is it?" Mark asks.

"Excellent."

"I have a confession to make," he says, smiling. "I know less about wine than I know about bourbon, so I'll have to take your word for it."

Alice smiles, swirls the wine in her glass. She thought he was going to tell her that he, too, was still married. "Your brother again?"

He nods. "My brother."

"What's your favorite?" Alice asks, nodding toward the bookcase. And after she asks, she decides that if he can't answer that question, if his brother picked out his books too, then she'll leave after one glass of wine.

"Favorite book?" he asks, squinting at the shelves. "That's an impossible question."

Alice swallows her disappointment with another sip, because his answer tells her that she's sitting, half drunk, on a generic black leather couch with a generic divorced man. She starts to formulate her excuse.

"If I had to pick a top ten, I'd have to include *The Road*," Mark says. "Partly because I have a son. Mostly because that prose is the most pristine I've ever read. Not an extra word in the whole book. McCarthy has a way of stripping things down to the essential."

Alice glances back up at the hundreds of books on the shelf. *Okay, he's read one.*

"McEwan's my guilty pleasure. I've probably read every book he's written."

"*The Cement Garden?*" Alice asks, raising her eyebrows.

"Okay. That was a bit much. He was young, though. *Lincoln in the Bardo* makes the cut, because it's like nothing else. If you're only gonna write one novel, that's probably the one. Toni Morrison's probably my favorite, though."

Toni Morrison. "Why?" Alice asks.

Mark thinks about it, takes a sip of wine while he thinks. "So many of her books are love stories disguised as something else. And all of them allow me—force me, really—into a subjectivity so far beyond my experience." He takes another sip, looks at Alice. "I guess, in the end, that's why I read."

Alice has grown warm, and it isn't just the wine. She looks back up at the shelf, sees the fat one, and she can't help but ask. "Foster Wallace?"

Mark looks at the shelf and laughs. "Nope. My brother gave me that for Christmas a few years ago. I tried. But I couldn't fight my way through the first chapter."

Alice smiles into her glass as she takes another sip. "Me neither."

* * *

Alice washes her hands in the bathroom. She avoids looking at herself in the mirror. The more she and Mark talk, the more three-dimensional he becomes, and it becomes difficult to think of him as prey. But then she thinks of the virus, which makes her think of Henry, and that angers the cougar. So, when she sits back down on the couch, she sits right next to Mark, and she rests her hand on his thigh. And when he leans hesitantly toward her, she kisses him, and he kisses back hungrily.

They don't stop kissing as they tug and unbutton and unclasp. Mark is down to his boxers, Alice to her panties, and she's straddling him on the couch. The cougar bites his earlobe and purrs in his ear and arches her back when the sandpaper of his chin scrapes her nipple.

"The bedroom," he says, his voice husky.

They touch and grope as they stumble down the dimly lit hallway. Halfway to the bedroom, Mark presses her urgently against the wall. He kisses her breasts and then her belly and starts to tug at the elastic of her panties with his teeth, Alice can't help but notice the photographs on the opposite wall, and her eyes lock on a picture of Mark and a boy that must be his son. It's a selfie in the woods, on a hike no doubt, and even in the low light she can see that both of their smiles are enormous. And then her drunken mind scrambles for the data, trying to remember the odds—Mark's chances—but the numbers blur together, and she can't remember if they relate to sex with a condom or unprotected sex or anal sex, but it doesn't matter anyway, because with that eleven-year-old boy staring at her, the generic divorced man comes into focus as a very specific father.

"I can't," she says.

Mark stops moving. His teeth release her panties. He looks up at her. He laughs a humorless, almost angry laugh. "What do you mean you can't?"

For a moment, Alice considers telling him, but it's too late, or it's too early—as if there's a right time to bring up *that*.

"I shouldn't."

Mark takes his hands off her thighs, settles back on his haunches. Alice still won't look down at him.

"You shouldn't," he says flatly. He climbs to his feet. He leans against the wall of pictures, runs his hand through his hair, and looks toward the bedroom door. "You tell me this now?"

Alice bites her upper lip to keep from responding, to keep from crying. She walks back out to the living room, sorts through the jumble of clothes. She finally finds her bra under the coffee table, and she realizes just how drunk she is when she tries to clasp it. He stands in the doorway and watches her dress. It feels like a clumsy striptease in reverse. She steals a look at him as she struggles. He leans against the wall in his boxers, his face a stew of confusion and disdain. She pulls on her jeans. "I'm sorry," she says as she buttons them.

At this, he finally looks away. He brushes wordlessly past her to gather the wine bottle and the glasses. As far as he's concerned she's already gone. He disappears into the kitchen, and she hears him rinsing the wineglasses as she slips quietly out the door.

26

Going Dutch

ON THE DRIVE north, Malcolm distracts himself from the meeting that waits for him by sorting through what he knows about ElekTek. Breck Sneddon, the managing partner, stopped by Malcolm's office this morning to congratulate him on the McGregor close. He also told Malcolm that he'd met the CEO of ElekTek, playing squash, and that he'd wrangled a dinner for the seventeenth. Malcolm checked his calendar, and Kinsey's concert made him pause for a long moment before answering. But he knew that there was only one answer, because if he said no, Sneddon would take someone else, and the ElekTek deal would slip from his grasp.

After he crosses the border into Wisconsin, he can ignore where he's headed no longer, so he calls Yuri. He's used Yuri a half dozen times, and he usually finds something in a day or two. One time it took a week. Only once—for that Dutch guy—did he come up with nothing. Yuri would have called if he found something, but it's been four days, and Malcolm desperately wants leverage for the conversation that he's driving toward, so he calls him.

"Hello," Yuri answers quietly in his thick accent.

Malcolm doesn't say his name because Yuri doesn't like to use names on the phone. "Did you find anything?"

"There is nothing."

Yuri says it with certainty, but Malcolm presses. "What about her family?"

"I check her mother and father and brother. I check her cousins and aunt and uncle. Nothing."

Malcolm passes the Mars Cheese Castle and considers the line he's about to cross. He has no choice, though. Naomi has given him no choice. "I need you to go Dutch."

The connection goes silent. When Yuri came up with nothing on that recalcitrant Dutch executive, he manufactured a sexual assault. The man was removed from the board in days, and the deal closed without issue. The divorce didn't come until six months later.

"That will cost more," Yuri finally says.

"I know," Malcolm says. He thinks through what will prove most effective, what will provide the most leverage. "Go after her father," he says.

More silence. "One day," Yuri says, "maybe two." And then he hangs up.

Malcolm drives for another ten miles, his eyes fixed on the road. Finally, he calls HR about an associate that needs firing, to take his mind off what he's just done.

*　*　*

Naomi carries her tea to a table where she can see the door and where she can keep her back to the wall. She shrugs off her sweater and hangs it, along with her purse, across the back of the chair. She hates Starbucks with its long lines and loud talkers and pretentious Italian names for small, medium, and large, but she refuses to let Malcolm O'Donnell sully her regular place with his presence. She sits, settles the tea in front of her, runs her fingers through her hair, and smooths the wrinkles from her blouse. She works to steady herself because she refuses to let Malcolm O'Donnell see what a mess she is.

Her editor finally gave her a story yesterday. Just a filler piece about the city council deciding not to make decisions about zoning, but she hasn't written a word of it. She hasn't worked on Kevin's story—Malcolm's story—either. Since yesterday afternoon, she's been curled up on the couch, smelling her own stink and staring glassy-eyed at the television that she didn't have the energy to turn on. It wasn't Malcolm's call that sent her into a tailspin. She's been expecting that call, prodding him toward it. Talking to his wife forced Naomi into the fetal position. That call went just like she'd planned, but discussing the O'Donnells' divorce made Naomi think about her own divorce—the divorce that she never quite managed.

Every time that Kevin started using, Naomi felt betrayed all over again, and every time she thought again about ending their marriage. She fantasized about the relief she would feel when she set down the burden of keeping him alive. She imagined a fresh start in a new house with someone she could trust. She dreamed of a swing set in a different yard. Twice she called a lawyer to start the process. Once she even paid the retainer, but every time she let those fantasies slip away. She knew that if she left him, Kevin would be dead within a year.

The door opens and Malcolm walks in like he owns the place. He's wearing another version of the expensive suit he wore to the funeral. He scans the shop until he sees her. He glances at the line, and Naomi can see him decide that the caffeine isn't worth the wait. He pulls out the other chair and sits. The bags under his eyes tell her that he hasn't slept much, and this at least gives Naomi pleasure. She wonders if her call to Maggie Rizzo or her call to his wife dragged him north to Milwaukee.

"Thank you for agreeing to see me," he says. His voice comes soft, almost deferential.

Naomi just nods.

"You called Tommy's wife."

So, Elena hasn't gone after him yet. Naomi works hard to hold her gaze steady. "I did. To be honest, I thought that I'd hear from you sooner."

"You told her to investigate Kevin."

Naomi forces her lips toward a smile. "I didn't think he'd mind."

He waits for her to say more, but Naomi refuses. This is his meeting.

"I guess that you're trying to send someone a message."

"Or Kevin is."

"What do you want?" he asks.

Naomi takes a long sip from her tea. What does she want? She wants him and Henry and Tommy to experience every ounce of the pain that night heaped upon Kevin, upon her. She knows that she can't have that, though, so she'll have to settle for what Kevin asked of them in that basement so many years ago. She'll demand what they refused to give him then. "I want you to tell the truth."

Malcolm sighs heavily. He glances at the two women at the table next to them who are arguing about window treatments. Finally, he looks back at Naomi. "And what exactly does that mean?"

Naomi reaches into her purse and pulls out the slip of paper with the Hoyers' name and address. She sets it in the center of the table and watches him. For a long time, his hands don't move. Hot milk hisses from behind the counter. Finally, he reaches for it, unfolds it, and reads it. He looks up at her.

"You want us to go to Florida?"

Naomi nods.

"And what purpose would that serve?"

"He was their only son," she says. "They still don't know why he died."

"*I* don't know why he died," Malcolm says.

Naomi studies his face, but it gives away nothing. She can't tell if he's claiming innocence or speaking to the senselessness of that night. Kevin never could make sense of it. The only sense he could make of it was that it was his fault, because he'd started it. He'd thought they would win. There were four of them, and one of those four was Tommy. It wasn't until it was over that he realized that they would all lose that night. Naomi feels her resolve weaken. Against her nature and against her better judgment, she feels herself giving Malcolm the benefit of the doubt. Maybe he, too, is still trying to make sense of that night.

"Then you can at least tell them how," she says.

Malcolm stares at her for a long time without blinking. "That's simply not going to happen," he finally says. He puts the scrap of paper back on the table and shoves it toward her.

Naomi takes a sip of tea and swallows it along with her disgust. Stupid to think that this man was capable of self-reflection, of compassion. She sets her teacup carefully on the saucer. She pulls her sweater from the back of the chair and shrugs into it. "I need to get back to the office, then. I need to present what I have to my editor, see if there are any holes that need filling before I file the story."

Malcolm leans forward, but his expression doesn't change. "That's libel. I'll sue you. And the paper. And your editor."

Naomi shrugs. "I'll tell him that you said that. If he decides not to print it, I'll box it all up and deliver it to Maggie Rizzo." She sips from her tea and then places the cup carefully on the table. "Although I might send it to Elena's attorney first. I haven't decided."

Malcolm's body goes still, but his eyes start blinking. His lashes are long, like Kevin's, but darker. "If we go visit them, you bury it," he says.

The closest to an admission she'll ever get from this asshole. Naomi stands, puts her purse on her shoulder. "Maybe. Maybe not. But if you don't go to Gainesville, there is no *maybe*."

"*Maybe*'s not good enough," he says.

Naomi forces herself still, even as her gut quivers. "Who the fuck do you think you are? Kevin already decided that you'll go to Florida. After that, *I'll* decide what *I'm* going to do. You made your decision thirty years ago. You don't get to decide anymore."

27

Weight

Tommy and Roy climb the steel stairs to the crawl space under the roof of the science building. Roy is skinny and bald, with the wire-rimmed glasses of a professor, but the flannel shirt and worn jeans of a plumber. Tommy swings open the short steel door at the top of the stairs. They turn on their flashlights and bend through. They don't have to crawl, but Roy must stoop, and Tommy bends almost double to avoid hitting his head.

"Where do they want to put it?" Roy asks.

Roy is the structural engineer that the university uses whenever they're considering anything big and heavy. Tommy leads him through the maze of pillars and beams and wiring harnesses until they are stooped just to the west of the ductwork snaking from the existing HVAC system. They hear and feel its rumble and clatter. Tommy shines the beam of his flashlight across the ceiling. "Right about here," he says over the din.

Roy plays his own light across the beams and the nearby pillars. Tommy knows he's looking for the path that three tons might follow down to the foundation. "Dumbasses," he mutters as he takes out his notebook, his pencil, and his tape measure.

While Roy measures and considers, Tommy checks his phone again to see if Malcolm has called or texted or emailed. Nothing. To keep his mind from slipping toward Maggie, he thinks again about his lunch with Emma. He's deeply unsettled by what she told him about Kyle. The details themselves, although not terribly surprising, are disturbing enough, but the fact that Emma shared them with Tommy tells him just how terrified she is. He knows Emma well enough to realize that she didn't tell him everything, that she withheld the worst bits. That's what scares him most.

Tommy doesn't like Kyle any more than Maggie does. He's a good-looking kid. He's tall. He works out a lot. His face is too long, but his shoulder-length hair distracts from that. The first time he came to pick up Emma, he just honked, and that set Tommy immediately on edge. The second time, after Tommy had a very direct conversation with Emma, Kyle came to the door and introduced himself. He was well spoken and nice enough, but nice in the polished and too-smooth manner of a knife salesmen or an undertaker. The night that Emma borrowed Maggie's car and came home with Kyle's puke all over the floor mats told them everything that they needed to know, but by then it was too late.

Tommy listens to the rumble of the HVAC system, to the clatter that's gotten progressively worse. It's seventeen years old, and they should have replaced it last summer. It's gone down four times since September. Tommy agrees with Roy—most HVAC salesmen are stupid, lazy, or both.

Gary, the guy who designed the new system for the science building, proves no exception. He convinced the purchasing manager to install it right next to the old system. That way, they wouldn't have to shut the building down, he said. They could redirect the ductwork and switch to the new system over a weekend, so they wouldn't have to wait until the summer. More to the point, Gary could get his commission check before the end of the second quarter.

But Tommy sees what Roy sees. The weight. When Tommy first started with the university, his dad taught him about heaviness. He taught him to look closely at a building and separate the flesh from the weight-bearing bones. He taught him to see how weight rests on those bones, how it distributes itself, traverses from joist to beam to pillar, and how that weight finds its way down to the earth. Back then, before the board of trustees became cluttered with lawyers, a building engineer like Tommy's father was allowed to evaluate the bones of his building and decide where to put the weight all by himself. But now Tommy must pay Roy to prove with careful measurements and calculations and schematics what Tommy already knows to be true.

Emma says she's in love with Kyle. Tommy tries to remember what he thought love was shaped like when he was that age. Boys are different from girls, of course, but he's learned that in so many ways they're frighteningly the same. At that age love is built around bodies, smiles, and compliments. Long, mysterious silences are weighted with too much meaning. He remembers how parental disapproval can harden lust into something brittle that can seem like love.

At fifty, he knows that love is delineated by sharp angles, plumbed with upset stomachs, and measured by the willingness to push past the loud angry arguments to a place of compromise. At fifty, love is more about what you've endured together than what you expect to happen next. The transition from teenage love to fifty-year-old love isn't marked by a particular experience or threshold or transformation. The meaning of love is warped over time under the weight of shared sacrifice, divided responsibilities, and unspoken commitments. But even though it happens gradually, those two loves are as starkly different as night and day. Emma, of course, knows none of this. And she doesn't yet know that if the weight comes too quickly, drops all of a sudden, love can crack and splinter and shatter, hurting everyone badly.

"You're right," Roy says, studying his clipboard. "I don't need to crunch the numbers on this one. Those beams don't bear weight. The distribution vectors are uneven at best. You put three tons up on that roof, it won't stay there long. Looks like you might have to rip and replace."

Tommy nods. "There might be another option," he says. "Follow me."

Tommy shuffles to the center of the building, where the Otis machines rumble, sending stacks of steel plates down the shafts as they pull cars full of students up. His dad always called the elevator shaft the spine of a building. He said that the strength and stability of any building radiates from that spine. Tommy shines his flashlight beam on the steel pillars surrounding the elevator.

"These go straight to the foundation," he says.

"The Otis mechanicals use the roof, though?" Roy asks.

Tommy shifts the light to the ceiling south of the elevator, toward the existing HVAC. "Wouldn't take much to cantilever support beams out this way," he says.

Roy nods as he studies the ceiling.

"It's a straight shot from here to the existing ductwork," Tommy says. "It'll cost a little bit more, but it'll keep the downtime to a minimum."

Tommy watches as Roy imagines the leverage of the cantilever, the flow of the weight down the spine toward the bedrock. Roy likes elegant solutions as much as Tommy, and Tommy sees a smile creep across Roy's lips.

While Roy measures again and scribbles the notes that will help him prove that Tommy's idea will work, Tommy sits next to one of the thin little windows that line the walls of the crawl space. The glass is grimed over, so he can't see much, just a slice of sky and the outline of the student union across the street. He can see even less of the future, what might happen to him, to Maggie, to Emma.

Tommy was surprised when Maggie came home with Kyle's file. Her ethical lapse stunned him, even if the truth in the file didn't. Kyle never seemed like the type to sell knives door to door, so the pot seemed almost inevitable. In Madison, evidently, he's learning to diversify.

Emma told Tommy that Kyle decided to sell heroin because of Maggie. She didn't say it like that, of course. She said that when they moved to Madison, they needed money, but Kyle didn't want them to get regular jobs with taxes and W-2s, because then Maggie would be able to find them. So, he was forced back into selling weed. He didn't *plan* on selling heroin, but with pot going legal in Illinois, he had to expand his offering. Maggie and market forces, Emma didn't quite say. The people that come to their place to buy heroin are different from the ones that come for weed. Emma looked out the window of the diner, and her face hardened when she said this, so she didn't have to tell Tommy how much they scared her.

Emma's a smart girl. She's flooded with hormones and saddled with a too-narrow understanding of love, nurtured by the Disney Channel and John Hughes movies, but she's got good judgment. That's the part that Maggie always forgets. Given time, Tommy knows that one of two things will happen: Kyle will mature into the man that Emma believes that he'll become, or she'll recognize him for the boy that he'll always be. The weight is heavy in Madison, though, and Tommy's not sure that she and Kyle have the time for all that to sort itself out. He's afraid that the emotions that they call love are no match for everything that's about to crash down upon them.

Tommy's phone vibrates in his pocket. He pulls it out, and he sees that it's Malcolm. Tommy looks over at Roy, back down at the phone, and then answers.

"What's up."

"I talked to Naomi," Malcolm says.

"What did she say?"

"We're going to Gainesville, Florida. Tomorrow."

28

Iron Mountain

MAGGIE SITS IN her office with the door closed and her earbuds in. She's playing Coltrane loud, to help her concentrate. She's filing a motion to dismiss a murder case, and it's important that she get this one right. The victim's wife is certain that the suspect in custody is the man that killed her husband, and the press can't get enough of the story. The murder made the ten o'clock news many times in multiple months because pictures of the blood-splattered wall leaked out, which always makes for good ratings.

Usually when Maggie writes a motion to dismiss, she does it reluctantly, dismissing a charge when she knows the suspect is guilty. Usually, she's describing a lack of evidence or a witness that has disappeared or a mistake by the police that springs the defendant on a technicality. Or she's explaining why the guilty will escape justice because it can't be proven beyond a reasonable doubt in a court of law. Usually, she's not making the case that the suspect is really innocent.

Maggie's doubts surfaced with the inconclusive ballistics report, and they deepened when she re-interviewed the alibi witness. Unfortunately, she knows the detective who obtained the confession. He's old school, and his file is cluttered with complaints of abuse and coercion that would find their way into the courtroom. When she studied the forensics reports closely, she was able to read some ambiguities underneath all the technical jargon that didn't match the narrative that the police put forth. Footprints that shouldn't be at the crime scene, DNA samples that were never processed. She started to see the possibility of an alternative narrative that seemed more likely with every piece of evidence she examined.

All of her instincts tell her that he's innocent, and her gut is seldom wrong. She let it sit for a couple of weeks, mentally prodding her revised narrative for holes, but she can't find any. Leonard isn't going to like this motion one bit, but the defense attorney that Maggie will always remain at her core just won't allow her to press forward with a case as flawed as this. Nobody's going to like what she's writing— the cops, the media, the wife. So she plays Coltrane loud and considers every paragraph, every sentence, every word with great care. The intense focus will help her get it right. And it allows her to avoid thinking about Tommy.

When she first started dating Tommy, she paid such careful attention to everything he said, testing it for strength. Maggie became certain that he never lied to her, and it became the rock-solid foundation upon which she built the sense of her husband. And that foundation was buttressed by Maggie's belief in her own ability to sort truth from lie. But what he said in the kitchen after dinner just couldn't square with what she found in the attic. She cried in the attic for a long time before she climbed down, and since then, she's been questioning everything. Everything that he's said and done and her own ability to sort it all out. She hasn't said anything to Tommy yet, but the cracks in the foundation have become fissures, and the whole damn thing feels like it is crumbling.

Maggie doesn't hear the knock on her door because the music is too loud, but she sees it open out of the corner of her eye. She looks up to find the old guy from the mailroom, but her eyes lock on the Iron Mountain envelope that he's carrying. She pulls the buds from her ears. The man steps into her office waving a clipboard. "I need you to sign for this."

Maggie merely nods and scribbles her signature on the form where the man presses his finger. He sets the envelope on the edge of her desk, between the plant that needs water and the family photograph from five years back. She stares at the envelope. It usually takes four days for off-site records retrieval—she didn't expect it until tomorrow. But there it is, and she can't take her eyes off it. She knows that she won't be able to focus on the motion until she reads what's in that envelope.

When she finally leans across her desk to pick it up, it feels lighter than she expects. She wonders whether she accidently requested the wrong file, and she can't help but hope that she did. She tears open the seal and slides the file folder onto her desk. She opens it and studies the top sheet. It's brittle with age, and she sees immediately that it's an autopsy report for a Michael Hoyer.

The autopsy's detached, clinical prose can't hide the brutality of the murder. The temperature in her office seems to rise with every page she scans. Seven broken ribs.

Collapsed lung. Dislocated shoulder. Subdural hematoma. Shattered skull. They always say *fractured*—she's never seen the word *shattered* in an autopsy report before. She sets the autopsy aside and reads the police report, such as it is. The only witness was the boy's friend, who was mentally incapacitated by the beating he suffered. She takes her sweater off as she reads. No crime scene forensics to speak of. No leads. No meaningful investigation.

But Maggie recognizes the intersection where the Burger King stood. Before Tommy's mom moved in with them, they used to drive past that corner every time they went to visit. It's a Starbucks now, and it sits less than four blocks from Tommy's mom's house, his childhood home. Maggie lays the police report on top of the autopsy and straightens the stack as best she can. She closes the folder, her fingers clammy with sweat. The coldest of cold cases. Until now.

CHAPTER

29

I Don't Know

H ENRY SITS IN the dark. The only light comes from
the full moon rising over the city and the blue wash
of the computer monitor. He's clicking through pictures of
mountains and waterfalls and the Milford Sound with that
phallic peak thrusting from the water. Ever since Alice told
him the verdict from Dr. Simpson, the house has grown
too quiet. She leaves early in the morning and sometimes
doesn't come back until late. If there's going to be conversation, no matter how thin, it falls to him to start it. He asks
her what she wants for dinner and about work and about
whether to invite the Wesolowskis or the Kopecs to dinner
in the city, but an alarming number of her answers consti-
tute just three words: *"I don't know."* And the tone of her
voice—or maybe it's the cadence of those three words—
doesn't sound like indecision. Maybe he's just imagining it,
or maybe all the silence that surrounds those three words
lends them too much weight, but they sound like an echo of

his own nonanswers, a none-too-subtle reflection of his own inability to explain what he's done.

When Alice is home at night, she spends most of her time in the bedroom, moving her clothes around, building boxes, packing and then unpacking suitcases. He can't tell whether she's messing with him or if she truly can't decide what to do, but he knows from last time that he has to wait. Last time, the waiting was broken into manageable slices by the therapy sessions. Every single one of those sessions felt like Alice and the therapist were squeezing his balls in a vise, but at least he was *doing* something then. Two days ago, he asked her if she'd go back to the therapist with him, but all she said was "I don't know" in that infuriating tone that falls just short of a taunt, and then she retreated back into the bedroom to sort her things. Henry's learned to avoid the bedroom until he's ready to sleep, but he makes himself go in there every night. To retreat to the guest bedroom seems like a capitulation that he's not ready for yet, so every night, he clings to his edge of the bed and tries to ignore the silence as he waits too long for sleep.

The noises coming from the bedroom—the screech of packaging tape, the thud of suitcases when she moves them from the bed, the slam of the closet door—tell him that he has to do something. He thought about buying jewelry, a big-ass diamond necklace or some outrageously expensive earrings. But in the unlikely event that Alice wore whatever he bought her, every time she looked in the mirror it would remind her of what he's done. So, instead, he's considering a trip from the very top of Alice's bucket list.

Henry's phone vibrates on the desk, and he sees that it's Malcolm again. He doesn't answer, but he watches it until the screen goes dark, and then tries to ignore the ping of another voicemail. He deletes the message just like the rest of them because he doesn't want to hear what Malcolm has to say. He continues to scroll through pictures of the Milford Track. They call it "The Finest Walk in the World," but it looks miserable. Seventeen hours in two planes to get to Christchurch, an eight-hour drive to Te Anau, and then four days and thirty-three miles of humping up and down mountains in the rain. All to arrive at the Milford Sound so that they can stare at the reflection of that giant pecker. But Alice has been talking about it for a decade. Every year or so, she brings it up. She leaves articles about it torn from Condé Nast on the counter.

Of all their vacations, Alice best loved their hike on the Inca Trail and their trek to the Everest Base Camp. Henry hated every minute of both. In Peru he got altitude sickness at fifteen thousand feet. He sprained his knee on the second day. He still can't quite wash the taste of roasted guinea pig from his mouth. Before their trip to Nepal, he failed to break his boots in properly, and by the third day his blisters felt like a hacksaw across his heels. Halfway through, he contracted dysentery, and every few miles he dug a hole in the scree and deposited what little was left in his bowels. On both trips, though, Alice seemed more alive than he had ever seen her. The exertion, the thin air, and the enormous mountains made her almost giddy.

It takes him a half hour to line up the permits for the hike and the reservations in the backcountry huts. The flights cost a fortune because they're only a week out, but he books it all and pays in full. She's not going to like the short notice, but the trekking season ends May first, so he can't book it any later. He prints the itinerary along with a picture of the Milford Sound and staples the packet. He'll tell her tonight and show her the details tomorrow. She'll know what he's trying to do, but she'll be tempted. Most importantly, he knows that it will make her decide. It will force her to say something soon—something besides *"I don't know."*

His phone vibrates again, and he picks it up. He's not surprised to find Malcolm's name on the screen, and he's about to press the red button again, but his thumb hovers. Malcolm's not going to stop calling, and Henry wants this over too, so he presses the green instead.

"This is Henry."

"Did you get my voicemails?" Malcolm asks without preamble.

"No."

"I talked to Naomi today."

"And why in the hell would you do that?"

"We need to go to Gainesville. Tomorrow."

"Florida?"

"Mike Hoyer's parents live there. She wants us to go see them."

Mike Hoyer. It's a name that's been rattling around Henry's brain since he spoke it aloud at that diner. To hear Malcolm say it in his clipped voice makes it hard to form words, but they come.

"No fucking way," he finally says. "Enjoy your trip."

"She made it clear that unless all of us go, she'll publish an article."

Henry closes the browser and the penis mountain disappears. "I didn't do shit, Malcolm. You're the one who killed him. This is *your* problem."

"I'm guessing that Kevin didn't quibble about who was at fault when he told Naomi about it," Malcolm says. "She said that if her editor won't print the story, she'll send everything she's got to Maggie Rizzo."

Henry's about to say, *"That's Tommy's problem,"* but then he remembers that Tommy's wife is a prosecutor. "She's bluffing," Henry says, trying to sound more confident than he feels. "She won't contact Maggie."

For a long moment, Henry hears only silence.

"See, that's the thing," Malcolm says, his voice thick. "She already did."

* * *

Alice lies in bed, her lamp on, trying to read a book set in Berlin after the war, because she doesn't want to think about now. But the words dance, and she has trouble keeping her place. Maybe there are too many characters with similar names. Maybe she's just tired. Probably it's Mark that keeps dragging her back from Berlin.

She could have slept with him safely if he wore a condom—she knows that now. For a day or two after she fled Mark's apartment, she felt suffocated by the idea that the virus, the deadly debris of Henry's infidelity, might be the very thing that keeps her trapped in this house with him. She was afraid that the virus would make it difficult, if not impossible, for a middle-aged woman to find her way back to *we*. But a more thorough examination of the internet convinced her that condoms drag the risk down to an ethically acceptable level. She should have ignored that damn picture of Mark's son. She should have continued down that hall to his bedroom. She should track him down. It wouldn't be difficult—another visit to Redstone, maybe two. A search of Facebook or Tinder would probably bring him to the surface. Instead, she lets her hand creep under the covers and slip inside her sleep shorts. She holds the book open with the other hand, but the words start to blur. She's tasting that California red on Mark's tongue, and she's feeling him press her against the wall in the hallway. Her eyes are drifting closed, and she's following him into that bedroom when Henry comes through the door and ruins even this.

Alice grabs the book with both hands, and she rereads a paragraph that seems vaguely familiar. She tries again to sort Greta from Gabrielle while Henry strips down to his boxers and T-shirt. She thought he might move into the guestroom that first night he came back from Milwaukee, but he's been climbing silently into bed every night. He's either oblivious or stubborn. She thought about banishing him, but he has the good sense not to creep toward the middle, and he usually doesn't say anything more than goodnight.

"I'm flying to Florida tomorrow," he says.

"For work?" Alice murmurs, although she couldn't care less.

"I'll be back by seven or eight. In and out."

Alice finds her place. She settles back into that abandoned warehouse in the American sector, near the wall, and she remembers that Greta is the young, pretty one.

"I also booked us tickets to New Zealand," he says. "For the fifteenth."

Alice lays the book on her belly and looks at him. He's staring at the ceiling. "And why would you do that?"

"It gets too cold in May for the Milford."

Alice stares at him. *The Milford.* She's been bugging him for years to go walk the Milford Track. He always makes excuses about work and weather, but she knows that he hated Peru and Nepal. The Milford. He thinks he can buy his way out of this. Ten grand and four days of hiking as penance for what he did, for what he didn't tell her, for what he can't explain. She picks her book up and stares at it, but it might as well be written in German.

"I know that you've always wanted to do that hike," he says to the ceiling. "And God knows it would be good for us to get away for a bit. Together."

Together. The word rings hollow between them. Are they together? Will they be together? The thought of a long plane ride with Henry, even walking along a gorgeous trail with him, leaves her cold. The fifteenth. One week away.

"What do you think?" he asks.

His anxiety rounds the edges of his voice. They both know that he's asking about more than just a vacation, a nice walk in the woods, but despite all that, she's grateful for those tickets, for the deadline. It took her six months last time. She can't keep living like this, unable to make up her mind. For a moment she wants to decide right then, but instead she just says, "I don't know."

Henry doesn't say anything more, and Alice forces herself back to that warehouse in Berlin. She's almost fully back into the story when the bomb maker, an American, walks in. He's introduced to Greta, and his name is Mark. Alice almost laughs out loud, but she manages not to. She thinks about turning off the lamp so that she can slip her hand back under the covers. She considers taking her book and a joint out to the sunroom, to clear her head a different way. But that taste of cabernet on her tongue won't let her. She stares at the words for a long time and then pulls back the covers and sits up. She puts her feet on the floor and studies her clothes, folded neatly and stacked in piles along the wall. She puts the book on her bedside table, and before she quite decides to, she tugs her T-shirt over her head and drops it to the floor.

She can feel Henry's eyes on her bare back, and she stretches straight and rolls her neck. Then she stands and thumbs her shorts off her hips and shimmies them, too, to the floor. The cool air licks at her nakedness, and she hears Henry shift on his edge of the bed. She takes a deep breath and then lies down on top of the covers. She closes her eyes, folds her hands across her bare belly, and waits. She doesn't have to wait long—the sheets rustle, and the mattress gives as Henry wriggles to her. He nibbles her ear, of course, and kisses her neck gently. His hand begins to wander, and she lets it, but she keeps her eyes closed. His lips leave her earlobe, and his hand leaves her inner thigh, and she hears him struggle out of his own clothes. Then he's back, on his hands and knees, straddling her. She still doesn't open her eyes. His mouth brushes hers, and she opens her lips. He kisses her hungrily, and she kisses Mark.

She grabs his neck as they kiss, and then she gently pushes his shoulders down with her wrists. He takes the cue and nibbles her neck, then her nipple, and he drags his tongue down her belly. She feels the scape of his chin and his cheeks against her thighs, and then she feels his tongue at the center of her.

She presses her palms hard against the sheets and takes herself to that bedroom that she never quite made it to. She takes herself to a cold stream in the mountains, to a tent in the wilderness. When the tingling starts in her thighs, she runs her fingers through his hair, and that hair feels brown with flecks of gray. Her back arches and her hips lift. She presses herself against his tongue and he keeps pace. The heat rises to her groin and then to her stomach, and she's in a hut on the Milford with Mark. The heat rises to her chest, and her breath comes heavy, uneven, and she squeezes her eyes tight because she has to. Her whole body tingles, and she tumbles back into that bedroom in Washington Park. She grips Mark's sheets in her fists and tries not to make noises because she's in a strange bedroom with a man she's just met. But the wave starts to swell, and she holds his head tightly with her hands, pressing him to her. She wraps her legs around him and digs her heels into his back. The wave builds and builds, and she starts to gasp and groan as her hips buck against him. As the wave finally curls and crashes, she can't help a strangled cry. Her head tilts back, her mouth open, until she finally sinks back to the mattress, gasping for breath.

Her hands fall back to her sides, her legs go slack, and she feels the bed shift as Henry slides back up to her side. She finally opens her eyes, and although she knows what she'll see, she's jolted by Henry's self-satisfied smile. He presses himself against her thigh because he thinks he knows what happens next. But not tonight. She rolls to the side of the bed and drops her feet to the ground again. She feels only stillness behind her as she stands, slides her shorts back on, and slips the T-shirt over her head. She grabs her book from the table and manages not to look at him as she walks from the room. She doesn't want to see the expression on his face, his nakedness, his swollen need, because the last thing she wants to feel right now is pity.

30

War

E LENA LISTENS TO the plunk of the mandolin drifting down to her office from Kinsey's room and reviews her spreadsheet one more time. *Burger King.* Those two words have been rattling around in her brain for the last few days, making more and more noise. They mean nothing to her, and she can't even begin to guess what they mean to Malcolm. *Leverage.* She knows in her gut that those two words will escalate everything. Those two words might be her ticket to Milwaukee, or they might be a declaration of war, and she has no idea how to tell the difference.

Tomorrow she'll apply for her mortgage preapproval, so it's time to finish what she started this morning. She felt sneaky at the bank, opening an account in her own name—and then felt foolish for feeling sneaky. The spreadsheet includes a twenty percent down payment on the house and Elena's best guess at what she and Kinsey will need through the end of the year. She doesn't know what game Malcolm's playing, she doesn't know the rules, but she knows that she needs to get settled in Milwaukee well before school starts, so she's hatched plan B. The divorce should work itself out long before the end of the year, and she expects that she'll have a teaching job in Milwaukee in the fall, but she wants to be safe.

It took her most of yesterday—adding, subtracting, estimating. She wants to make sure that they're covered, but she doesn't want to take more than they'll need either. There's more than eleven million in the Vanguard account. She thought about taking half of it. Just kick the shitcan over and see what spills out. But Malcolm is Kinsey's father, no matter how she and Kinsey feel about it. Moving to Milwaukee won't be the last time that she'll have to deal with him. It won't be the last time that they'll have to cooperate. But she knows it's her pride more than anything else that keeps the number on the spreadsheet low. She's been telling Malcolm for a decade that the money doesn't mean anything to her. It makes her feel dirty to take even this much. She looks forward to living within her means. *Her* means, not Malcolm's.

Elena surveys the numbers one last time and then closes the spreadsheet. She navigates to the Vanguard website and types in her username and password. She must have typed it wrong, because it fails. Annoyed, she types the password again, more carefully. It fails again and her annoyance swells toward something else entirely. She types it a third time, careful with each character, and when it fails yet again, she blinks at the screen and goes rigid. She pays the bills. She moves the money. She's logged onto this site a hundred times without issue. The account is in both their names, a joint account, but suddenly she wonders what that even means. She forces herself to click on the link that taunts her: *Forgot Your Password?* She knows that she hasn't forgotten her password, but she types her username into the box provided anyway. She clicks "Submit."

Username not found.

Elena hugs herself and starts to shiver. That son of a bitch. That goddamn son of a bitch. Just then her phone vibrates on the desk, and she can see, before the screen goes black again, that it's a text from Malcolm. She stares at the phone, wondering if he set up alerts to notify him about her login attempt. Finally, she picks up the phone and reads the text.

> can u tell kinsey i can't make the concert? i've got an impor-
> tant work thing that night

Elena grips the phone tightly and feels everything harden within her at once. She was such a fool to think that Malcolm would cooperate with her, that leverage wouldn't be necessary. She thinks about having Luther call Malcolm to ask about Burger King, but she wants to do it herself. She saved Naomi's number. If Malcolm plays dumb, she'll call the woman back and ask for more details. Malcolm wants a war. A fucking war he will get.

"Hey, Mom."

Elena turns to find Kinsey in the doorway. She wonders how long she's been standing there. She wonders how long the mandolin's been silent. But then Kinsey's features collapse from calm satisfaction to confusion, to distress, and she knows all at once that it's the expression on her own face that causes that unfolding.

"What's wrong?" Kinsey demands.

Elena forces her mouth toward a smile, but she knows that she manages only a baring of her teeth. "Nothing's wrong," she says. "How was the mandolin tonight?"

Kinsey doesn't answer, and Elena can see that Kinsey knows that she's holding back, that she's lying. Kinsey stares right at Elena—through her really—and the worry drains from her face, leaving just cold, clear rage.

31

No Good Reason

MALCOLM AND TOMMY don't say much as they wait at O'Hare for the flight to Jacksonville, and they both wonder whether Henry will show. Henry doesn't board until the last minute, and he doesn't say anything to Malcolm as he passes through business class on the way to coach. They talk only for the first fifteen minutes of the drive from Jacksonville to Gainesville. That's how long it takes for Malcolm to review the plan three times and for Henry to stop complaining. They pass billboards for pawnshops and Disney World and megachurches. Tommy thinks about what he'll say to Emma when he talks to her next, and he thinks about all the things that he should have told Maggie but didn't. Malcolm rehearses what he'll say to the Hoyers and worries about what the other two men might say after that. Henry tries to imagine the future, but he has trouble imagining the end of this car ride, much less next week or next month or next year.

When they exit the expressway in Gainesville, all three shift in their seats a bit, trying to get comfortable. A few signs are the only evidence of the university. The Red Robin and the Walmart and the endless strip malls make Gainesville seem like any other small city, but as they drive north, the familiar quickly falls away. The road narrows, lined by ancient trees, their branches sagging under curtains of moss. Horse farms give way to dense forest, broken only by gravel driveways with signs next to them declaring "Private Property" and informing potential trespassers of second amendment rights. Barbed wire snakes from tree to tree.

When the GPS tells Malcolm that the next driveway belongs to the Hoyers, he slows. Tommy peers through the woods, trying to glimpse the Hoyers' house. Henry is staring, stone-faced, at the back of Tommy's head. Malcolm chooses his words carefully. "We're here. It's important that we stick to the plan."

"We heard you the first dozen times you said that," Henry says impatiently. Henry regrets, yet again, that he came. He knows in his gut, plan or no plan, that this can only end badly.

Tommy stares at the dense underbrush. Now that he's here, he feels strangely settled, as if this visit was inevitable. But he's still not sure about Malcolm's plan. He can't see the holes in it, but he can feel them.

Malcolm turns onto the gravel track. He drives slowly, but the car bounces across the ruts. After the first hundred yards, the forest abruptly gives way to a field of tall, thin pine trees, a carpet of needles beneath them. Malcolm can see the house now, but it's a mobile home, not a house.

He pulls the car up front, and parks it next to an old blue pickup with rust gnawing at the fenders.

Malcolm turns off the engine. Without the hum of the motor and the AC, the car becomes too quiet. Nobody moves. Tommy can hear the other men breathe. The trailer is small, but the outside is tidy. Rusty buckets at the bottom of the stairs spill over with flowers. The truck gleams where the rust hasn't gotten to it, as if it was recently washed and waxed.

"We should have called," Tommy says.

Henry thinks they should flee while they still can, but he says nothing.

Although arriving unannounced is central to Malcolm's plan, Malcolm wonders if Tommy is right. "It's too late now," he says at last. "Let's get this over with."

* * *

Malcolm knocks firmly on the door of the trailer, and they wait. Tommy is on the top step with Malcolm, and he's already sweating from the heat and from the anxiety of what's about to happen. Henry hangs back at the bottom of the stairs. For a long time, they hear nothing but silence, and Malcolm begins to worry that the Hoyers aren't home. But then he hears quiet footsteps, and the door pulls open just a crack. A woman's face, old and weathered, peers at them. Malcolm is about to introduce himself when the door eases shut. "Rodney!" the woman shouts from inside. "There's some men here!"

They wait, and then they hear sharp words and slow, uncertain footsteps. The door swings open wide, and an old man stands in the doorway, scowling at them. He's wearing a red sleeveless T-shirt tucked into jean shorts. His socks are pulled up around his scrawny calves, and his belly strains against his shirt. His wife peers at them over his shoulder. "What's this all about?" he demands.

Malcolm holds his hand out. "Mr. Hoyer, my name's Malcolm."

Mr. Hoyer looks distrustfully at Malcolm's hand and doesn't shake it. Malcolm knows that the next few words are critical, that the way he delivers them can help make this go easy. Henry looks at Malcolm's pocket and wonders whether he left the keys in the car. This whole thing is a bad idea, and he's more certain than ever that he wants no part of it. If the keys are in the car, he could go sit in the air-conditioning and wait for this fiasco to play out without him. Tommy studies Mr. Hoyer, and something about the way his nostrils flare and the way his eyes dart from one of them to the other reminds Tommy of the expression on Mike Hoyer's face just before Tommy punched him.

"We're here to talk to you about your son's death," Malcolm says. "To tell you what happened."

Mr. Hoyer's eyes bulge and his hands curl into fists. Mrs. Hoyer closes her eyes. "What the hell do you know about that?" Mr. Hoyer demands.

"The three of us were there," Malcolm says. "The night he died."

At this Mr. Hoyer grabs the doorframe. Tommy wants to reach out and steady the man, but his instincts tell him not to. Henry glances at the car to see if the windows are all rolled up. He peers at Malcolm's pants pocket again, but he can only make out what looks like a money clip.

"I know this comes out of the blue, but we can shed light on what happened that night," Malcolm says in a voice as gentle as he can manage. "If that's what you'd like."

"Who are you people?" Mr. Hoyer asks, looking confused.

"We were there that night," Malcolm says again. "The night your son died."

Mr. Hoyer blinks, and something else builds in his expression alongside the confusion. When he speaks, his voice comes loud and loaded with gravel. "You come and knock on our door *thirty years* after our son died? *You* want to tell *us* about our son?" His face goes red even as the knuckles of his hand gripping the doorframe drain to white. "Who in the hell do you think you are?"

Henry starts to turn toward the car. Tommy thrusts his hands into his pockets and looks down at the weathered wooden steps. Malcolm says, "My apologies. I'm sorry that we intruded. We'll let you be."

"Let them in," Mrs. Hoyer croaks from behind Mr. Hoyer.

Henry considers pretending not to hear, to continue walking toward the car, but he still doesn't know where those keys are, and he'd feel foolish leaning against the car while Tommy and Malcolm go inside, so he stops and turns. Malcolm looks at Mr. Hoyer, whose eyes remain hard. His mouth closes then opens and then closes again. Tommy looks over Mr. Hoyer's shoulder at Mrs. Hoyer, and even though he's standing in the bright Florida sun and she's shrouded in gloom, Tommy can see that her eyes glisten.

Finally, Mr. Hoyer turns, so that he's only blocking half of the doorway. He glances at his wife, and something passes between then. He looks back at Malcolm and nods curtly. Malcolm takes this as agreement and steps into the trailer. Tommy has to turn sideways to get past, and he still brushes the other man's stomach. By the time Henry comes through the door, Mr. Hoyer has stepped inside and is scowling at Tommy and Malcolm.

It takes a moment for their eyes to adjust from the sun to the gloom, but they smell the trailer immediately. Underneath the cigarettes, Henry smells mothballs. Malcolm smells mildew and rot. Tommy smells Pine Sol, which reminds him of his mother.

"Sit," Mrs. Hoyer commands, pointing at a maroon suede couch against the wall. "Please," she says more gently.

Malcolm sits at one end of the couch. He's driven past mobile homes before, but he's never been inside of one. It's bigger than he expected, but it seems flimsy. When Tommy moves near him, the floor gives a little. All the walls are covered with fake paneling, the kind that covered the basements of his childhood, the kind that begs for a fist to punch a hole through it. The kitchen cabinets are particleboard, and they don't pretend otherwise. The TV, a relic from another time, perches across from the couch on what looks like a dresser.

Tommy sinks into the other end of the couch. His uncle lived in a mobile home for a while, so he's familiar with the layout. It's a double-wide, so there are two bedrooms and a dining room around the corner. He can tell from the sound of the AC unit that's hanging in the window that it's running low on freon.

Henry squeezes into the middle of the couch, but it's closer to a loveseat, so his legs are touching Malcolm's and Tommy's. Tommy's bulk puts a big dent in his end of the couch, so Henry has to lean toward Malcolm to keep from falling into Tommy.

Mr. Hoyer settles into a recliner, but he doesn't recline. Mrs. Hoyer perches on a wicker chair with a flowered cushioned seat. She's withered, like a raisin. She wears a powder-blue housedress with flowers embroidered around the neck and the cuffs of the sleeves. It reminds Tommy of something his grandmother would wear. It reminds Malcolm of Elena's mom just before she died. Henry has never seen anything like it. Although she deferred to her husband when three strangers showed up at the door, she's the one that invited them in. All four men wait for her to get settled. Once she learned that this is about her son, it became her meeting, and all four men seem to know it.

"This is Henry and Tommy," Malcolm says to her. The plan has Malcolm doing most of the talking. "And I'm Malcolm." Their last names are not part of the plan.

Mrs. Hoyer picks lint from her knee. "What happened to Michael?"

Malcolm knows how important it is to start a lie with as much truth as possible. "We never saw your son or Tyler Greavy before that night," he says. "The three of us and another boy named Kevin McNamara were in one car—driving through McDonald's to see if we could find Henry's girlfriend. Tyler didn't like the way one of us looked at him when we drove past. Words were shouted from both cars. Tyler followed us from McDonald's to the Burger King parking lot. That's when things got out of hand."

Malcolm pauses for a moment to let the Hoyers digest what he said. That was the easy part for Malcolm, because he's been through it so many times in his head and because what he's said so far is true. He glances at each of the Hoyers. Mr. Hoyer still wears that scowl, and his gaze remains fixed on Malcolm. Mrs. Hoyer is still plucking lint from her dress.

"Did you know Tyler well?" Malcolm asks.

Mr. Hoyer snorts. "We knew him well enough."

Malcolm tells the Hoyers about how Tyler jumped out of the car screaming and cursing, and that their son never said a word. He tells them about how their son didn't really have any choice, that the real problem was Tyler Greavy. But he doesn't tell them how Tyler and her son ended up on the ground, because that isn't germane, and it isn't part of the plan to tell them about that. And then he pauses. Partly to let the Hoyers digest it all. Partly because the rest will be harder for the Hoyers. Mostly because Malcolm learned long ago that lies require more precise language.

"After your son and Tyler Greavy went to the ground, Kevin McNamara, the fourth boy in our car, kicked them both repeatedly," Malcolm says. "In the head. In the ribs. We tried to pull him off, but we couldn't stop him. It was like something snapped in him."

"This McNamara," Mr. Hoyer says. "Where in the hell is he at?"

"He died," Malcolm says. "Last week. None of us have seen him since shortly after the night that your son was killed."

Mr. Hoyer snorts. "Isn't that convenient."

It *is* convenient. The plan was built around that convenience.

"So you wait thirty years?" Mr. Hoyer asks, incredulous. "You wait thirty goddamn years and then come knocking on my door to tell me that somebody else—a dead man— killed my son?"

"I'm terribly sorry," Malcolm says carefully. He glances at Henry and Tommy but wills both of them to stay silent. "Like I said, none of us have seen each other since 1990. At Kevin's funeral, we decided that it was time to come tell you. I guess that we thought it might bring you some peace to know what happened. I'm sorry if we were wrong about that."

"Get the hell outta my house."

For a moment nobody moves. Malcolm tries to hide his satisfaction that the plan held together. Tommy's knuckles ache as if he punched those boys yesterday. Henry can't take his eyes off Mrs. Hoyer, who is visibly struggling with something. Malcolm is the first to push himself up from the couch.

"Before you go, I want to show you something," Mrs. Hoyer says. She says it quietly, and she's still looking at her lap.

"Aw, Helen," Mr. Hoyer says. He says it with resignation and a low-grade venom that speaks of an argument that's been simmering for decades. "Don't you go there."

Henry watches as whatever was roiling through Mrs. Hoyer consolidates and hardens. She looks up from her lap, and she glares at her husband. "I want them to see it," she says.

"And what good is that gonna do?" Mr. Hoyer demands.

Malcolm checks his watch. Whatever she wants to show them is *not* part of the plan, and his mind scrambles for an excuse to leave.

"They're gonna see it," Mrs. Hoyer says, and she says it with a certainty and a strength that makes it clear to all four men that the argument is over.

When Mrs. Hoyer stands up and walks down the narrow hallway, Mr. Hoyer doesn't get up from his recliner. Instead, he stares stone-faced and still out the front window. Malcolm considers walking out the front door because he can't think of anything good coming from walking down that hallway, and a plan is a plan. When Tommy stands, the phone in his pocket vibrates. He wonders if it's Emma, and he, too, looks at the front door. Henry's pits and the backs of his knees are slick with sweat. His stomach is twisted in a way that he didn't expect, a knotting up that he hasn't felt in a long, long time. And when he stands up from the couch, he finds himself following Mrs. Hoyer down that narrow hallway. Tommy and Malcolm glance at each other, but neither finds anything useful in the other's expression. Malcolm knows that he needs to make sure that Henry doesn't do or say anything stupid, so he follows. There's nothing for Tommy to do but to join them.

Mrs. Hoyer pauses at the first door before turning the knob and pushing it open. She steps aside, and all three men file in. There's barely space for the three of them, because as they take it in, they see that the furniture was bought for a larger room. The curtains are open, and the men's eyes are drawn first to the posters. They all stop breathing for a moment, because the posters tell them all at once what they are being shown. That perfect spectrum of light emerging from that white triangle against a black background—a poster depicting the cover of the album that all three men still believe to be the greatest ever made. And on the adjacent wall, the head tilt, the radiant smile, the red swimsuit that any boy born in the early seventies remembers with a visceral, chapped clarity.

Malcolm tears his eyes away from Farrah and studies the desk set beneath the window. Textbooks are stacked neatly in one corner, their spines visible. Physics, calculus, advanced French, AP government, business law. On the other corner: *The Catcher in the Rye, The Great Gatsby, To Kill a Mockingbird.* A Black Warrior pencil lies on an open notebook—calculus from what Malcolm can see. His throat tightens as he remembers his first taste of differential equations and reading about that green light on Daisy's dock and the trinkets that Scout found in the crook of the tree.

Tommy's eyes drift from Farrah to the particleboard shelf in the corner of the room. Every square inch is filled with models of Camaros and Thunderbirds and Corvettes and fighter jets. There's a battleship and a ship in a bottle. The Millennium Falcon sits on the top shelf, and next to it, C-3PO stoops protectively over R2-D2. Tommy remembers the first few models that he tried, with their incomplete instructions and all the tiny parts that he pinched from the plastic frame. He can feel the sharp kinks in the aluminum tube of glue and its sweet industrial stink. And he remembers his dad helping after that first failure—a '57 Chevy—and how his dad used tweezers and toothpicks and chopsticks because his fingers were way too big.

Henry's gaze slips from Farrah to the shelf above. It's lined with wrestling trophies, arranged by height just like Henry's basketball trophies were arranged in his own room. Silver and gold boys dressed in singlets and crouched, ready for battle. Ribbons wrap the trophies, and medals dangle over the edge of the shelf. A faded photograph leans against the largest trophy. Mike Hoyer, with his too-long hair parted down the middle, looking (except for the smile) exactly like he did that night in the Burger King parking lot. Much younger versions of Mr. and Mrs. Hoyer stand on either side of him, but it's their smiles, rather than their youth, that makes them so difficult to recognize. And then he sees the balsawood bridge on the shelf. Henry built a bridge just like that for physics class, and just like Michael Hoyer's, Henry's bridge buckled under the weight. Henry threw his bridge out, but of course, Michael and his mother saved his, and it sits there on the shelf, crumpled beyond repair.

It takes Tommy, Malcolm, and Henry just seconds to digest what they see, to understand what they've walked into. In those seconds they travel thousands of miles and dozens of years, to their own rooms, to the rooms of their friends, to that parking lot, and back again. They don't think of the woman behind them in those seconds that they are gone, but then they notice the clutter. The unmade bed. The clothes hamper half full. The bottle of Polo cologne with its cap off on the nightstand. The acid-washed jeans and the tube socks crumpled on the floor in front of the closet. Suddenly, and as one, they feel the grief radiating from the woman behind them, the terrifying despair that would make this woman pack up her dead son's room in Wisconsin and recreate it in such painful and painstaking detail in this trailer home just north of Gainesville. What did it cost her to arrange the dirty clothes that her son shucked in front of the closet as he prepared to go out that Friday night in the spring of his senior year with his friend Tyler Greavy? The night that he was killed for no good reason at all.

CHAPTER

32

The Burger King Parking Lot

MALCOLM WAS DRIVING his dad's old maroon Cutlass Supreme. Henry sat on the other end of the vinyl bench seat, Kevin and Tommy in back. A party over in Pewaukee had been busted by the cops, and they still had a few beers left from the case that Tommy bought earlier that night at T.J.'s Liquor and Smokes. It was a little bit before midnight, and Malcolm had to get the car home by twelve thirty. They decided to drive through McDonald's because they might find Alice there, and Kevin was still trying to make traction with one of her friends from the volleyball team. But mostly they were just killing time and those last few beers.

Malcolm didn't like the look of the old Chevelle, even before he saw the driver. It was matte black, like someone had painted it in their garage. The tires were extra wide and glass packs on the exhaust gave off an ominous rumble. Malcolm especially didn't like the look of the driver. He had greasy, shoulder-length hair of an indeterminate color.

One hand gripped the steering wheel, and his other arm hung out the window, bicep bulging. But it was the driver's stare as he scanned the Cutlass for offense, for affront, that made Malcolm look away quickly. Evidently, Kevin looked for too long, because the Chevelle screeched to a stop, and the driver shouted.

"Fuck you lookin' at?"

Malcolm stopped the Cutlass. Not because he wanted to. He was compelled by the unwritten rules that govern the lives of eighteen-year-old boys. And the math made him stop. Only two in the Chevelle compared to four in the Cutlass—and Tommy was one of those four. If he didn't hit the brakes, if he let that insult pass, the others would call Malcolm a pussy, and nothing damages the psyche of an eighteen-year-old boy like being called a pussy by his friends.

"I'm not really sure," Kevin shouted through the back window. "But it looks like a fucking douchebag."

Malcolm watched the driver's face as he took that in. His eyes pinched tight with annoyance, then widened in confusion, and finally bulged with fury. The tendons stood out on his thick neck as he leaned out the window. He opened his mouth to shout something else, but instead ducked back inside and opened the door. That's when Malcolm hit the gas. The unwritten rules and the math were washed away by the certainty of the violence that waited at home if his dad's Cutlass got scratched or dented. As Malcolm sped from the parking lot, Kevin laughed maniacally. Malcolm heard the squeal of tires and the roar of the Chevelle's engine. As he pulled out onto Northview, the Chevelle's headlights swerved into place behind them. Malcolm hit the gas, but those headlights closed fast.

"They're following us," Henry said, peering into the sideview mirror.

"No shit."

The Chevelle's high beams flicked on, filling the Cutlass with glare.

"There's only two of them," Kevin said.

Tommy said nothing.

A light turned red. Malcolm thought about running it, but he knew the Chevelle would follow, and they still had beer in the car, so he stopped. The Chevelle pulled up so close that the inside of the Cutlass went dark. Malcolm watched his own sideview mirror to see if the Chevelle's door would swing open. Instead, he felt a jolt and heard a scrape as the Chevelle bumped the back of the Cutlass.

"Goddamn it," Malcolm muttered. If that left a mark, his dad would beat his ass.

"They fucking hit you," Henry said, outraged.

"No shit," Malcolm said.

"There's only two of them," Kevin said again.

Tommy still said nothing.

The light changed, and Malcolm sped off. The adrenaline surging through his body forced his foot down on the accelerator and made him grip the wheel too tightly. The Chevelle sped behind them, just feet from their bumper.

"Pull into the Burger King," Henry blurted.

Malcolm still sometimes wonders why Henry said that, and he wonders why he listened. It wasn't the math that Kevin kept going on about. It wasn't the scrape on his dad's car or the blood pounding in his ears or the dizzy, almost giddy way the fear made him feel. But he turned into the Burger King parking lot, drove around the back, and pulled up next to the dumpster. The Chevelle squealed to a stop a few feet away.

"There's only two of them," Kevin said yet again, but this time his voice hitched when he said it.

The four of them climbed out of the Cutlass, and Malcolm still remembers the shaky feeling in his legs and the way his hands were curled into fists. He's replayed those moments in his mind a thousand times. He sometimes thinks that there was really no way around what happened, that once Kevin looked too long at the driver of the Chevelle, everything that followed was inevitable. They were all playing their roles, roles filled by countless teenage boys in thousands of parking lots in hundreds of cities and towns every Friday and Saturday night. And Malcolm vividly remembers the look on Tommy's face when he climbed out of the Cutlass, stood to his full height, and slammed the door closed. He seemed resigned to what they were about to do, the role he would play. He seemed weary, even as everyone else in that parking lot vibrated with energy and aggression and fear.

When Tommy climbed out of the Cutlass Supreme, he knew what was expected of him. He saved everyone the trouble of jostling and elbowing. He walked past the stink of the dumpster toward the two boys from the Chevelle and felt the other boys close ranks around him. He sized up the two boys quickly. They were both about the same height, but the passenger looked nervous, shifting his weight from one foot to the other, even as he balled his fists tightly. The driver was the one. His stringy hair, his dirty jeans, and the hard look in his eye told Tommy that he was the reason, the only reason that they were all in that parking lot. He was almost a head shorter than Tommy, but he had the lean, muscled body of a wrestler. His nose bent to the left as if it had been broken, and acne clawed at his forehead. But it was the eyes that Tommy couldn't ignore. Cold, hard, careless eyes. Tommy walked up to the driver—close enough to let the boy feel his size, but far enough to give them all a way out.

"What seems to be the problem?" Tommy said, careful to keep his voice even, gentle almost.

"Fucker called me a douchebag." The boy twitched his head toward Kevin but kept his eyes on Tommy. The smart ones never take their eyes off the big man.

"Yeah," Tommy said. "I heard him. He probably shouldn't have done that."

The boy shifted forward, and Tommy felt the toes of his shoes against his own. He smelled of oranges and unwashed hair. He stared defiantly up at Tommy. "But he did, didn't he? Scrawny little twat."

"Fuck you, man," Kevin said.

"Kevin," Tommy said calmly, "shut the fuck up."

"You hear that, bitch?" the boy said. "Daddy says to shut the fuck up."

And when the boy said *bitch*, a drop of spittle flew from his mouth and landed on Tommy's cheek. He resisted the urge to wipe it away, but he couldn't ignore it. It felt warm and heavy. Tommy spoke slowly and not quite so gently. "Why don't you get back in your car and get the hell out of here," he said. "That might work out better for everyone."

"Tyler—" the other boy said.

"Shut up, Mike. I'm talking to someone," Tyler growled through his teeth. Then he poked Tommy in the chest. "Why don't you make me leave, lard ass."

And that's when Tommy knew for certain that they wouldn't leave that parking lot without someone getting hurt. He had learned through too many repetitions to distinguish the boys that stand and shout, and then shout some more as they get back into their cars, from the boys that have been looking for a fight all night and refuse to go home without one, whatever the cost, because they really have nothing to lose. Malcolm, Kevin, and Henry seemed to sense it too, because the circle tightened. Tyler stared unblinkingly at Tommy for what seemed like a very long time, but it might have been only seconds, and Tommy shifted his attention to Tyler's shoulders, because the cold, careless eyes already told him all that they would. With a kid like this, the shoulders would telegraph the punch, and it wasn't Kevin who would get hit, because they always go after the big man first.

Tyler was quick. An uppercut to the jaw that came just after his shoulder twitched. He was quick, but Tommy's right hand was already moving before the punch landed, and the shock of the pain—always a surprise—made Tommy's hand move faster and harder, and when it connected with that crooked nose, his fist kept moving, and the boy went down, just like they always did. The other boy hesitated for a fraction of a second, and Tommy willed him to take a step backward, but he stepped toward Tommy instead, because he, too, had a role to play. His punch was tentative, and Tommy blocked it easily. Tommy's own punch was half-hearted, but when it landed on the side of the boy's head, he, too, went down.

And that's where it was supposed to end. Exit stage right into the Cutlass, finish the last few beers on the drive home, and put a bag of frozen peas against his jaw to keep the swelling down. But it didn't end, because after those two boys hit the ground, Henry went terribly and irrevocably off script.

Henry knows why he kicked Tyler Greavy that first time. Tommy was watching Hoyer fall while Greavy pushed himself up to his hands and knees. Henry didn't think about kicking him, he just felt the necessity of it, and he kicked him hard. He felt Greavy's ribs crack so easily, like balsawood, and Greavy crumpled to the ground with a groan. Henry's been able to convince himself over the years that the first kick was a responsibility, his role to play. He had to protect Tommy. But he still can't explain away that rush of something like joy that caused him to kick Greavy again, and he's never been able to explain to himself what compelled him to start kicking Hoyer. It happened so quickly, and he was drunk from the violence as much as from the beer, so he doesn't know how many times he kicked them. He could never explain that giddiness to Alice, so he never tried. He remembers the horrible sound of his instep hitting their bodies and Kevin screaming, *"STOP!"* and Tommy screaming, *"STOP!"* It was only after Tommy pulled him away, when he still heard that terrible sound of shoes hitting flesh, that he realized that Malcolm had started.

When Henry first kicked Greavy, Malcolm desperately wanted him to stop. The sound of Henry's shoe striking the boy's body was so muted, like a beanbag falling to the earth, or a pillow fight without all the giggling. When his dad used to hit him, all he heard was a loud buzzing in his ears until it was over, but the time that he heard his dad beat his mom, it sounded just like Henry's shoe striking Greavy. His dad had thrown him against the wall for leaving the milk out. Malcolm knew what was coming next, and lay on the floor, his hands covering his head. *"Leave the boy alone,"* his mom had shouted in a high strangled voice that didn't sound like hers. His dad became still, confused, but when he turned to her, he moved across the room more quickly than Malcolm thought possible and grabbed his mom by the arm. He dragged her down the hall to their bedroom. He didn't bother to close the door before he started to beat her, so Malcolm heard everything, although he doesn't know whether his dad used his feet or his fists, because he only managed the courage to walk halfway down the hall. He stopped and listened to those dull thuds and did nothing, even as a terrible rage built in his gut and expanded into his eight-year-old chest. He felt that same swelling in his chest that night in the parking lot. He can still sometimes convince himself that he meant to grab Henry and stop him, but after that first step with his left foot, his right foot swung toward the boy on the ground. He still tells himself that he meant to kick him in the back, but the boy convulsed after a blow from Henry, and Malcolm's boot met his skull with a crunch that Malcolm felt more than he heard.

When he felt the boy's skull give, the anger collapsed with it and twisted into something righteous and terrible and sublime and shameful, like an orgasm, but black and ugly. He never felt that way before, and he's never felt that way since—he's spent most of the last thirty years trying to suppress the echoes of it, but he can still feel it reverberate when he sits very still. He doesn't know how many times he kicked him, and he didn't even realize that he had started kicking Hoyer until Tommy wrapped him in a bear hug and lifted him off the ground. When he stopped squirming, Tommy set him down. Kevin let go of Henry, and for a few seconds—two, maybe three—all of them stared at those boys on the ground, at what they'd done. It was during those three seconds, watching the blood trickle from that boy's ear onto the asphalt, that the adrenaline ebbed,

making room for disbelief and then horror and the barest
beginnings of the shame that would consume them. It was
during those three seconds, before they turned, wordlessly
as one and ran toward the Cutlass, that they realized the
terrible thing they had done, and they began to know that
the last few minutes had changed everything.

33

Let Him Talk

NONE OF THE men look at Mrs. Hoyer, because they're afraid to see the expression on her face. Tommy thinks of his own mother standing in that hallway, and he knows she would never have survived the grief. He sees that all the surfaces in the room are clean, and he thinks about Emma's room in his own house. He goes in there sometimes when Maggie isn't home. He closes his eyes and smells Emma's perfume and the powdery scent of her makeup and the dust that is starting to lie across everything.

Malcolm also thinks of his mother, but he knows that she wouldn't have built this shrine if she had lost him, if he had died that night instead of Mike Hoyer. He knows with certainty that she would have packed all his things into boxes and put them in the corner of the basement so that she could make a home office out of his bedroom—just like she did the moment that he left for college. He thinks about Kinsey and Elena, and he misses both of them with an ache in his lungs that he forgot so long ago was called sadness.

Henry feels Mrs. Hoyer behind him, and she seems so close—too close. He wants to move away from her, but there's nowhere to go. He thinks of Alice and knows that there was a time that she would have missed him deeply, maybe as viscerally as Mrs. Hoyer misses her son, but he knows that time is long past. He looks at those crumpled clothes by the closet and he knows with certainty that Mrs. Hoyer never washed those clothes. He knows that back when those clothes still held her son's scent, when Mr. Hoyer was out, she would bury her face in those clothes and smell him, and he knows that now she misses even that.

And suddenly he smells all the death that he's been trying so desperately to suppress all these years. So many human beings related to people who loved them and grieved them and smelled their clothes for as long as even a tiny whiff of their bodies remained. When he dies, in a year, in five, in twenty, he's terrified that nobody will clutch his clothes to their face, nobody will hold him in their heart like Mrs. Hoyer holds her son, and his body really will be nothing more than a cadaver.

"She comes in here," Mr. Hoyer says from the doorway. "Every morning at six thirty." His voice is soft now, and none of them turn. "That's what time she used to wake him for school."

Henry's legs begin to quiver, so he sits down on the edge of the bed. He props his elbows on his knees and kneads his face with the palms of his hands. He finally looks up at Mrs. Hoyer, and she squints at him, her mouth hanging open. Every day she gets up at dawn to wake her son who will forever sleep, and there's absolutely no way to gain distance from *that*.

"That night—"

"I think we've given the Hoyers enough to digest," Malcolm says. Something about the way Henry's body sags where he sits, something about the whisper of his words, tells Malcolm that his plan is about to buckle under the weight of everything in that room. "It's time to go."

Tommy's hands curl into fists, and Malcolm's voice grates. It's suddenly like the Hoyers aren't there. It's just the three of them, hashing it out yet again, this time without Kevin. As he opens his mouth, he thinks about what he's about to do to Maggie, but even as the words form in his throat, he knows that they are *for* her.

"Let him talk," Tommy says.

"Tommy—" Malcolm says.

"I said, let him talk."

Henry hasn't taken his eyes off Mrs. Hoyer. He can see the tension in her stillness. She waits, unblinking, and she's waited so long.

"I kicked him," Henry whispers.

"What did you say?" Mrs. Hoyer manages.

"I kicked him," Henry says louder. "Your son. When he was lying on the ground. I don't know why I did it, but I kicked him in the ribs and in the stomach. I might have kicked him in the head, but I just don't know for sure."

Tommy's fists finally unclench. "I punched them," he says before Malcolm can start in again. He looks at Henry, but he can feel the Hoyers' eyes on him. He forms words out of the worries that have haunted him for decades. "I knocked both of them down. I hit them hard, and they went down hard. I'm not sure if they hit their heads when they hit the ground." His shoulders sag. "I've always wondered if they did."

Malcolm wants to argue, he wants to redact and object and retract, but for a moment, the words of the other two men leave him mute. And despite himself, as they say words that he's never heard them say, Malcolm leaves that bedroom in a trailer home just north of Gainesville, and he's standing in a parking lot, breathing heavily, staring down at two boys who have stopped fighting. It's never the fight that comes back to Malcolm when his nightmares come. He never feels angry in those dreams, he never hears the dull, thick sound of his boots striking the boys' heads. Instead, he always dreams of those three seconds of silence before the four of them dashed toward the car. He knows what's expected of him. He knows what he must say, but instead, he forces that box closed.

"I think it's time we go," he says in a whisper. He looks at Mrs. Hoyer because he can't look at Tommy or Henry. "I'm sorry that we disturbed you."

34

The Tipping Point

MAGGIE STARES AT the Hoyer/Greavy file on her desk. It sits by itself between the dying plant and the family portrait. They were all smiling in that photo—even Sophie. Smiles that seem genuine. Emma was starting high school—Jeremy was in just second grade. Everything was so easy back then, so simple.

The file remains thin. Each case has two distinct phases for Maggie. In the first, she looks for truth. She doesn't add anything to the file, just sifts through what's there, asks questions, checks facts. That first phase might take hours or days or weeks. She works to convince herself of the perp's guilt or innocence. She follows her intuition, her heart, rather than her head. She's only trying to convince *herself* in that first phase. Eventually, she always reaches a tipping point, where the evidence and the testimony and the corroboration convince her one way or the other. Until then, the file stays thin.

Maggie's pretty sure that Tommy lied to her again this morning. He told her that he had to work late tonight—maybe as late as midnight. A special job—a dry run for a data center cutover. He was only responsible for the electrical and the cooling, but he had to be onsite for the whole thing, he said, just in case. There seem to be a lot of special jobs lately. Maybe she's looking for lies where they don't exist, but he was wearing jeans and a shirt that he never wears to work. Church jeans. Church shirt. And he was bent over the coffeemaker when he told her about the data center. He didn't kiss her before he left. She's not certain that he's lying about the data center, but he definitely lied about knowing Kevin McNamara. Maggie's time in the attic made that clear. The deeper she dug into that box, the clearer it became that Kevin wasn't just a guy he knew. Kevin McNamara was Tommy's best friend.

Maggie and Tommy have always fought plenty. There's so much that they don't see the same way, but their differences always seemed like small things until Emma disappeared. Tommy blames Maggie for Emma leaving. He's never said so, but Maggie can tell, and she isn't entirely sure that he's wrong. They haven't really fought since Emma left, but it's not because of a special closeness forged during a hard time. It's more like Tommy's steering clear of any arguments because he's afraid of what he'll say. Through all that, Maggie worried plenty about Emma, but she never worried about Tommy.

The tipping point came today. The box in the attic told her about Henry Duncan and Malcolm O'Donnell, but her intuition told her to find out all that she could about Kevin McNamara. She checked all the usual databases, but the results were thin. One speeding ticket. No arrests or warrants or liens. But the marriage license database coughed up a document, and Maggie stared at it for a long time. Her gaze locked on the name of Kevin's wife, and her mind scrambled in a dozen different directions, searching for a reason that Naomi would call Maggie and ask her to investigate her own dead husband for a crime that nobody cares about anymore. But every mental thread she follows leads to the same place. And there's only one reason that Naomi would mention that Kevin was forty-nine and that he went to Pius. Naomi's really trying to get Maggie to investigate Tommy. And with a clarity that the evidence doesn't yet support, a clarity that comes from her intuition, from her heart, she realizes that Tommy isn't just guilty of lying, but that he's guilty of something far, far worse.

Maggie feels unsteady when she stands. She grips the edge of her desk for a moment, until her head clears. She grabs the file and walks down the hall. Jerry's office is only four doors from Maggie's, but they seldom talk. He doesn't share Maggie's passion for the law. She's not sure that he's passionate about anything but his pension. Jerry's desk is littered with stacks of files, but he's cleared a spot at the center of it large enough for his pastrami sandwich. He takes a big bite when she walks in, and he looks at her suspiciously while he chews. He puts the sandwich down and wipes his mustache and fleshy face with a napkin. He swallows. "What's up?"

"I need a favor," Maggie says.

Jerry's eyes narrow as they lock on the file she holds. "What kinda favor?"

"I got a call from a reporter," Maggie says. "She gave me the name of a guy that she thinks is implicated in a cold case. A murder."

Jerry's eyes flick down at his sandwich and then back to the folder. "How cold?"

"1990."

He laughs. "1990."

"Yeah. 1990."

They both know that he owes her, that she's picked up the slack for him too many times to count. She can sense that he wants to argue, but he looks at the sandwich again, and she can see him decide that an argument will delay lunch. Finally, he reaches out a greasy hand, and Maggie hands him the folder. He sets it on the tallest pile, on the corner of his desk farthest from his sandwich. They both know that he'll do nothing with that file. Another file will land on top of it and then another. She knows it will be a long time before Jerry comes across that file again, and she guesses that when he does, he'll send it back to long-term storage.

"I'll give the reporter your number if she calls again," Maggie says. "Her name's Naomi."

Jerry takes another bite of his sandwich and doesn't respond. Maggie turns from his doorway, and she heads farther down the hall toward HR, because she's afraid that if she heads back to her desk now, she'll lose her nerve. She walks into Fran's office, closes the door, and sags into the chair in front of her friend's desk. Fran's got her glasses perched on the end of her nose, and she's biting her lip like she always does when she's writing a particularly sensitive email. Fran hits "Send" and then turns to Maggie. She puts her glasses on the desk and checks her watch. "Lunch?"

"Not today," Maggie says.

Fran leans back in her chair and studies Maggie. "What's wrong?"

"Nothing," she lies, even though Fran can always see through to what Maggie is really feeling. "I wanted to give you a heads-up. I'm going to start looking for another job."

"What? Really?"

"I haven't started looking yet, but I know how long it takes you to find someone. I don't want to leave you in a lurch."

"Why?" Fran asks, her forehead wrinkled. "Leonard?"

After all the lunches that Maggie's spent complaining about her boss, she should have known that's where Fran's mind would go, and she decides to let it. She can't tell Fran about Naomi, about Tommy. She won't tell her about the file she just abandoned to the oblivion of Jerry's desk. She doesn't want to wrap words around her loss of faith in her ability to sort truth from lies, or the impossibility of sitting down at the prosecutor's table ever again, papers stacked neatly in front of her, prepared to send someone else to prison.

"It's just time to do something different."

35

The Drive

MALCOLM GRIPS THE steering wheel tightly, his palms slick against the leather, his jaw clenched tight. His mind is racing, jumping from one thought to another in a way that he's not accustomed to. That room. Those books. That Black Warrior pencil, sharpened, lying atop the calculus homework, distracts him. But only for a moment. He forces himself to close that box and evaluate the scraps of his shredded plan. He assesses the damage and how to control it. He went into that trailer with an airtight plan for dealing with the Hoyers. He went in with just one loose end to worry about—Naomi—and a plan for dealing with her. Now he's going to have to deal with the Hoyers too. All because Henry and Tommy couldn't keep their fucking mouths shut. As he sorts through what they did, what they said, he can hear the rattle of the chains. Time seems to compress and expand and compress yet again, and he has no idea how long he's been driving, how much farther to Jacksonville. The silence in the car is funereal, and it's the silence that finally breaks him.

"What the fuck were you two thinking?" he spits at the windshield.

Tommy shifts in the seat next to him. Malcolm's eyes flick to the rearview mirror, and he finds Henry staring out the window.

"I took care of everything. I made the plan. I did all the talking. All you had to do was get up from that goddamn couch, keep your fucking mouths shut, and get back in the car. And you couldn't even do that."

Tommy puts his hands on his knees and stares straight ahead. Henry still doesn't look away from the window. Malcolm forces his eyes back to the asphalt. The white hash marks flicker past relentlessly. He sifts again through the words that Tommy and Henry surrendered in that bedroom. He shoves them against the words that he said before that, but he can't make them fit together. That look Mrs. Hoyer gave him as he squeezed past her on the way out of the trailer. Grief and confusion alongside accusation. He can't help but think that she's on the phone with the cops right now. He curses himself for using their real first names—and for trusting Tommy and Henry to stick to a simple, straightforward plan. He tugs at the scattered scraps of it, tries to shape them toward something that might keep the past where it belongs, but it's no use. His mind begins to drift toward Yuri.

"Did you see it, Malcolm?" Henry asks quietly.

"See what?" Malcolm demands.

"That room? Did you see that room?"

Malcolm takes a deep breath. He keeps his eyes on the road, and he counts the white slashes of paint. "I saw the two of you fuck up a perfectly good plan."

"She put his dirty clothes on the floor in front of the closet. Just like he left them all those years ago." Henry is quiet for a moment. "You saw that, right?"

Malcolm can't help but look in the mirror. Henry's still looking out the window. "Do you want to go to prison?"

Henry leans his temple against the window. Tommy rubs his thighs with his hands, as if he's trying to press wrinkles from his pants.

"Because that's where we're headed. All of us."

"And that Farrah poster," Henry says quietly. "You remember that Farrah poster?"

"Pri-son," Malcolm says again, enunciating each syllable. "Even if she doesn't call the cops, you can be damn sure that he will."

"It doesn't matter," Henry mutters.

Malcolm glares into the rearview mirror. "And why doesn't it matter, Henry?"

"I'm just saying. Compared to what—"

"You think you can pin it all on me?" Malcolm demands, glaring into the rearview mirror.

"What the hell are you talking about?" Henry says.

"You planning on turning state's evidence? Cop a plea?"

"Fuck you, Malcolm."

The rage and whatever it's wrapped around surges. "Fuck *you*, Henry."

"Jesus, Malcolm. You've forgotten all of it, haven't you?"

Malcolm sighs, checks the mirror, changes lanes to pass a truck. Like he could ever forget those three seconds of silence. He could only forget when he was drunk, so drunk that he could barely see, but he always woke up remembering. "I remember everything about that night."

"That's not what I'm talking about," Henry says in a voice that sounds like he's choking on something. "I'm talking about us."

"What the hell does that mean?"

Malcolm hears Henry turn from the window. He can feel his stare boring through the back of his head, but Malcolm keeps his own eyes on the road. Tommy shifts in his seat again.

"We were like brothers before that night," Henry says, his voice graveled with something. "And none of us questioned it. We would have done anything for each other." He swallows audibly. "Anything."

Malcolm squeezes the wheel tightly, and he wants to scream. He wants to steer the car into the ditch at eighty miles an hour, because with those few sentences, Henry opened a different box altogether, and for a moment Malcolm can't control the memories that leak from it. Cub Scouts and sledding and kick-the-can and football in Poplar Park and the tree fort near the quarry, and that night that they all got drunk together for the first time, down by the creek the summer before freshman year, struggling to swallow gulps from the bottle of vodka that Kevin had stolen from his mom, and that last time that they were all together, arguing in Tommy's basement on those filthy couches. Malcolm uses the sheer weight of that last memory to shove the lid of that box closed.

Tommy shifts in his seat again. "I'd still do anything," he says quietly. "For both of you."

Malcolm steals a glance at Tommy, but Tommy's staring straight out the windshield. They're all one phone call away from going to jail, and these two are reminiscing about high school. He remembers the set of Mr. Hoyer's jaw and the indictment in Mrs. Hoyer's glare, and he squeezes the wheel more tightly. That night *did* happen, and it changed *everything*. They can't go back and undo that night. They can't go back to how things were, no matter how much these two fools want that. He tries not to look in the mirror, but suddenly he can't not. Tears are streaming down Henry's cheeks, and he's staring right back at Malcolm. Malcolm's rage makes his mouth taste like pennies, and it forces his foot down on the accelerator. He wonders where exactly Yuri draws the line. It wouldn't surprise anyone to find two old people dead in that trailer. Carbon monoxide, probably.

"I'll fucking take care of this too," Malcolm says.

"What does that mean?" Tommy asks.

Malcolm says nothing.

"What did you mean by that?" Tommy demands.

Malcolm knows that Tommy doesn't want the answer to that question. Just like always, Tommy wants to act the part of the righteous and let Malcolm do the dirty work. He locks his eyes on the road and forces his mind back toward the task of sorting out the mess these two just made, because that's what he must do to ignore the core of shame around which his rage is so tightly wrapped.

36

Wrinkles

RODNEY WENT OUT to the shed after those men left. Helen can hear his bandsaw, but she knows he's not working on one of his projects. He's probably just cutting wood to settle himself, to keep himself from starting an argument that neither of them want. He's putting the argument off leastways. She's doing the same. Settling herself. She's standing at the ironing board, pressing wrinkles out of Rodney's shirts and trying to work through the wrinkles that those men left behind.

For so long she's been waiting to know what happened that night. For so long she's wanted to find the people that did what they did to Michael. Anyway, that's what she'd always thought. That social worker from the state of Wisconsin talked about closure way back then, as if Helen could close the door on what happened as easily as she closes Michael's bedroom door every morning after she dusts. Helen never bought into all that. She always thought that she'd attack whoever did that to Michael if she ever found them—give them just a little piece of what they gave to her son that night. But their visit left her confused and disoriented. She feels all opened up—like a fresh cut. Nothing closed about it.

Those men weren't what she expected. Not a day's gone by since Tyler Greavy picked Michael up in that car of his that she hasn't thought about that night. For thirty years she's been stewing on it. Long ago she stopped expecting to learn the truth, but she never stopped trying to imagine the people who had done what they did. It was all she could do to remember what Michael looked like, but she somehow had room left in her brain for the ones that killed him.

She didn't expect them to come to her house after so many years, and she certainly didn't expect to feel pulled in so many different ways. She couldn't help feeling sorry for Henry and Tommy—if that's what their real names were—but she hated the one that called himself Malcolm. Right from the start. Maybe it was his perfect hair and his expensive shoes. Or maybe it was the way that he smiled without showing his teeth. And once he started talking, once she heard what he came to tell her, none of it seemed to line up straight. The words seemed tilted. A little too convenient—just like Rodney said. And the way Malcolm said those words didn't seem right neither. He was so calm, so relaxed—not jittery like the other two. And they shoulda been jittery, considering what they came to talk about.

The growl of the saw stops for a beat, and Helen thinks that it might be time to argue with Rodney, but then the racket starts up again. She sets the iron on the board, hangs the shirt that she's been working on, and spreads a pair of Rodney's boxers. She used to think it ridiculous that her mom would iron her dad's underwear, but that was back when she had other things to keep her busy, other things to keep her mind away from the bad for just a little while. Rodney's gonna want to call the police. Helen's glad that the saw started back up, that he's decided to cut more wood into pieces that he doesn't need, because she still hasn't decided what *she* needs to do.

She could tell that Malcolm was lying from the very first word. The way he told that story, it was like he was trying to sell her cable TV. And then he clammed up tight when she made them look at Michael's bedroom. His smile disappeared, but nothing true spilled out. Michael's room seemed to squeeze some truth out of the other two at least.

It was all those years as a lunch lady at St. Catherine's that taught Helen how to sort out the truth from the lies. She learned right away that a lunch lady's job had as much to do with rapping knuckles with a wooden spoon as it did with serving up Tater Tots and applesauce. She also learned that those Catholic boys were chronic liars. She thinks it's because of the confession. Three Hail Mary's and every-thing's washed away clean. She had to learn to watch their eyes and their feet and the way that they breathed to make sure that the spoon landed on the right knuckles. So she knows that Malcolm's the liar, but she's still not sure what to do about it.

She folds the underwear and starts in on an apron. It's linen, and it's wrinkled up good, so she's gotta put a heavy dose of steam into it. Her memories of Michael have flat-tened out over the years in a way that was hard to notice while it was happening. He became faded photographs and scrawled handwriting in notebooks and clippings from the newspaper folded into the family Bible. When he first started to thin out in her mind, the first time she had trouble remembering what he smelled like, she knew she had to do something. That was when she set up his room like she did. Rodney didn't say anything. He just went real quiet in a way that told her exactly what he thought about that. At first the room helped, but the steady grind of keeping it clean eventually flattened it out, just like Michael. Until today. Hearing about that night made Michael thick and real in a way that she hadn't expected at all.

She wrote the men's names on an envelope that was lying on the counter as soon as they left. They're only first names, and she knows that they're probably fake, but she also wrote down the license plate of the car they drove. It was probably a rental, but the police will be able to figure out who rented it. She's gotta decide whether to make that call, though. She still doesn't have it squared away in her head. She still can't figure why those three came at all. She knows it wasn't Kevin McNamara that killed Michael, and she's pretty sure that Tommy and Henry didn't do the worst of it. Her mind is jumping around like a fly on the potato salad at a church picnic. That night ruined everything for her and Rodney—and for Michael, of course. Seems like it's about to ruin more lives after she decides.

The bandsaw goes quiet again and stays quiet. She hears the shed door slam shut in a way that tells her that Rodney has made up his mind, even if she hasn't quite. Rodney stomps up the stairs. The front door swings open, and the doorknob bounces off the paneling like it does when Rodney's worked up. She glances up, but the glare from the afternoon sun behind him makes his face hard to read. She looks back down at the apron and moves the iron carefully, chasing the last few wrinkles. The door closes. Rodney walks up close and crosses his arms across his chest like he does when he's made a decision and he doesn't want to change it.

"You still have that cop's number?"

"I do," she says, and manages not to smile. Obviously this day has put him into a spin, and he's not thinking straight. "But he was in in his fifties last time I talked to him. Almost thirty years ago. He's probably dead too."

Rodney shifts his weight and shoves his hands into his pocket like he does when he's not certain what to do next. "I guess I'll just call the station then."

But he doesn't move. Helen still hasn't looked up at his face, even though there are no more wrinkles on the apron. She's just running the iron over smooth cloth. She knows that his eyes are hard like they get when he thinks she might argue with him. She doesn't want to argue with him because suddenly she's exhausted by the whole afternoon. She knows that the day must have been hard on Rodney too, even if he doesn't show it the same. He can seem to go for days without thinking about Michael, and sometimes when she says Michael's name, he lurches, as if he just remembered that he had a son and that his son is dead. She wants to buy time, and it suddenly occurs to her how she'll do that. And when she decides on it, the easy way the decision comes tells her that it's an idea that's been lurking just out of sight for a while. She finally looks up at Rodney. His face is all screwed up with stubbornness.

"I want you to help me with something first."

"What's that?" Rodney demands suspiciously.

"You still have those empty boxes in the shed?"

"Yeah. Why?"

Even as the words make their way up her throat and past her lips, she knows them to be right and true and long overdue. And she knows that they'll melt Rodney's face toward something different, that they'll buy her some time to decide what comes next. "I want you to help me pack up Michael's room."

CHAPTER

37

The Knock

TOMMY WALKS THROUGH O'Hare surrounded by thousands of people, feeling light. Henry found a direct route to Denver, and Malcolm's platinum status earned him an earlier flight to Chicago. So Tommy was alone on the plane, and he couldn't stop thinking about that long awkward ride back to Jacksonville.

Brothers. They often used to call each other *brother*. Truth be told, before that night at Burger King, and before everything that flowed from that night, Kevin, Henry, and Malcolm had felt more like brothers than Tommy's real brother had. They finished each other's sentences. They could make each other laugh with just a look. They could truly count on each other for anything until that night, and Tommy never thought that would change. After that last day in the basement, their absence in his life felt like a hole in his stomach. The ache faded over time, although he never really did make new friends. There were people that he knew, people that he was friendly with, but nothing like those three. Coming out of that room, leaving that trailer, he felt awash in the shame of what they'd done, but he also felt that hole in his stomach again. It was probably that room, those trophies, those posters. That room transported him across the country and across decades. It could have been any of their rooms. Mike Hoyer could have been any one of *them*. Tommy thought that it had all ended in those weeks after Burger King, but driving back to Jacksonville in the seat next to Malcolm, he felt what Henry felt.

Tommy fingers the folded slip of paper in his pocket. Malcolm took a call during the drive. He murmured a few words, but mainly he just listened, and then he scribbled something down. When they reached the airport, Malcolm handed Tommy the folded piece of paper without a word before he disappeared into the crowd. Tommy knows that call was from Malcolm's guy. He knows what the note will tell him, even though he hasn't unfolded it yet.

He walks across the catwalk to the parking garage, and he feels like he's floating. Telling the Hoyers made him feel so light. Whenever he thought about telling the truth before, it was always Maggie who he imagined telling, and that always felt like sharing the burden rather than shedding it. Telling the Hoyers what he had done put the truth out into the world. The Hoyers will decide what happens next, not Kevin or Henry or Malcolm or Tommy.

Tommy stole a glance at Mrs. Hoyer before they filed silently from the trailer, and her face sagged, but not in a bad way. It was as if decades of clenching had begun to ease, and he wants desperately to think that they lightened the weight of her grief just a bit. Mr. Hoyer seemed angrier than when they arrived. He suspects that the two of them will argue about what to do next.

Henry didn't say anything else on the drive back to Jacksonville. Before he rushed off to catch his flight, he shook Tommy's hand, but the handshake shifted to an embrace. They promised to call each other. Malcolm just walked off without saying another word. There's no telling what the Hoyers will decide, but he and Henry surrendered control of the situation in that double-wide, and the freedom from deciding what to do next leaves Tommy almost giddy. They don't *get* to decide anymore—but they don't *have* to either.

Tommy climbs into his truck. He knows another decision still waits. As he pays for parking, he pushes it from his mind, because he's not ready to make it. But after he leaves the garage, he drives past the exit that heads north to Milwaukee. Instead, his truck turns west toward Rockford, as if it's making the decision for him. Forty minutes later, he stops at the oasis to get gas. Only then does he unfold the slip of paper and read what it says.

* * *

Tommy sits in his truck just down the street from the address that Malcolm scrawled on that folded scrap of paper. He's visited Madison often enough for football games to have a general sense of the city. The expensive mansions hug the curves of the lake. The tidy condos huddle around the capitol building. Student housing surrounds the university in concentric circles that grow seedier the farther one wanders from the center of the campus. The little bungalow that he finds at the address on the scrap of paper sags in the outermost ring. The grass hasn't been mowed since the previous fall. The house hasn't been painted since the previous decade.

Business is brisk. Every ten or fifteen minutes, another beater pulls to the curb, and someone climbs out and walks quickly to the house, eyes darting up and down the street. They climb the stairs and disappear inside only to reemerge moments later. The worn, rumpled clothing and the skittery look of the thin young men tell Tommy that Kyle's transition to selling heroin is further along than Emma led him to believe. Part of him wants to start the truck, drive back to Milwaukee, and give that folded scrap of paper to Maggie. Let her do this her way. It would be easier. In the short term, it would be more satisfying. But Tommy knows that if he lets Maggie do it her way, it might be a long time before he sees his daughter again, even longer before she forgives him.

Tommy climbs out of his truck and walks the half block to the house. The weeds growing from the cracks in the walk brush his ankles. The stairs groan under his weight. Tommy knocks on the unpainted door. Nobody answers, and he hears no movement inside. He wonders if there's a special knock, and when he sees the drapes flutter a bit, he decides that there must be. He wonders about a gun but decides that he can't care about that. He pounds on the door and waits some more. He's about to pound again when the door opens, spilling light out onto the porch.

Kyle stands in the doorway, wearing a Phish T-shirt, faded jeans, and his hair pulled back into a man bun. He stands as tall as his frame allows, but Tommy still looks down at him. For the first time in a long time, Tommy is glad of his size.

"Hello, Kyle," he says.

"Mr. Rizzo."

They stand there, sizing each other up over the threshold. Tommy can tell by the way that Kyle says his name that he's nervous. Kyle looks past Tommy toward the street, Probably checking for the cops or for Maggie.

"Are you going to invite me in?" Tommy asks.

Kyle squints at him, and Tommy can see him sorting through his options. It takes a moment, even though they both know that he has few.

"Now's not really a good time," he says, and he tries to stand taller.

All Tommy can see of the front room is the blue glow of a television. "I drove a long way, Kyle." And with that, Tommy pushes gently past Kyle, who shows the good sense—or the lack of initiative—to let him pass.

It takes Tommy's eyes a moment to adjust to the gloom of the front room, but his nose takes it in all at once. The pot, the mold, the dirty socks. Couches line three walls, and a flat-screen television leans against the fourth. On the couch under the front window, a bearded boy with close-cropped hair lies with his eyes closed and his mouth open. Tommy finds Emma curled into the corner of the couch opposite. She's wearing a baggy gray Marquette sweatshirt, and she's got it pulled over her knees. Greasy hair frames her face, and her eyes glitter with anger and fear and something that Tommy wants to believe is relief. He studies her closely, trying to decide whether his daughter has been sampling the product, but he doesn't really know what to look for, and he can't bear to accept that it's true anyway.

"Hey," he says tentatively.

"What are you doing here?"

Anger it is, then. But it's her voice, and she's right there in front of him.

"I came to talk," Tommy says. "That's all. Then I'll leave."

"Who the fuck is this guy?"

The beard has woken and is struggling to sit up. Tommy wants to respond but forces himself quiet.

"Cory," Kyle says from behind Tommy. "Why don't you split for a while?"

"But you said I could—"

"You need to leave," Kyle says, louder this time.

Cory's fully awake now. "Where the hell am I supposed to go?"

"Get out, Cory," Emma says, and Tommy hears Maggie in her tone.

Cory looks from Emma to Kyle to Tommy. He opens his mouth to argue and then closes it. Cory blinks at the TV and finally pushes himself up from the couch. Nobody says anything as he brushes past Tommy into the next room. Emma flinches when the back door slams.

Tommy looks around the room until his eyes fall on a floor lamp next to the TV. He turns the switch and is surprised when the bulb works, that there even *is* a bulb. He moves to the couch directly across from the TV and sinks into it. It smells of stale beer and incense. What looks like a documentary about penguins plays on the TV, the sound muted. He looks at Kyle because he finds it hard to look at Emma. The way his eyelids droop tell him that Kyle's stoned or worse. His jeans are dirty, and the neck of his T-shirt is stretched out, as if he's been wrestling with someone. Kyle's staring hard at Emma when he finally speaks.

"How did he find us?" he demands.

"She didn't tell me," Tommy says, but he feels the need to tell the whole truth. "She said you were in Madison, but that was it."

"How did you find us?" Emma asks.

"I know a guy that's good at finding people," Tommy says, and he leaves it at that.

"I'm not coming home," Emma says.

Tommy's gaze settles on Emma again. The harsh light casts shadows on her cheeks that make her look even more gaunt than at the diner. Her eyes seem clear, but it's hard to tell. He wants to gather her in his arms and squeeze her tight, keep her safe, but he knows she won't let him, and that she's too old for that anyway. "I can't make you do anything that you don't want to do," Tommy says. "I know that."

"Is Mom out there?" Emma demands.

"No," Tommy says. "I didn't tell her I was coming." He pauses. "I didn't tell her anything."

Emma swallows, and her hard edges soften a little. Just then, a loud knock on the front door, followed by three softer knocks. Emma goes still, and Tommy looks at Kyle. "You need to get that?"

Kyle looks at the door and then back at Tommy, his face twisted with indecision and defiance and fear. He doesn't answer the question, but he doesn't move to answer the door either. "What do you want?"

Tommy chooses his words carefully, but he knows his tone is as important as the words. "Why don't you sit down?"

Kyle glares at Tommy. "Why don't you say what you gotta say and then get the fuck out."

The knocks come again, and Kyle flinches.

"Either sit down," Tommy says. "Or *I'll* answer the door."

Kyle looks at the door and then at Emma. Their eyes meet, and something passes between them that Tommy can't read. Kyle finally perches on the edge of the couch across the room from Emma, his elbows on his knees. Emma curls more tightly into a ball.

"What do you want?" Emma demands.

Tommy looks at the television when he speaks. Penguins are diving one after the other into freezing cold water. "I want to offer Kyle a job."

Kyle snorts. Emma says nothing for a long time. The penguins in the back are shoving the ones in the front into the sea. "What kind of a job?" she asks more quietly.

"Working for me," Tommy says. "At the university. Apprentice to the building engineer."

"And why the hell would I want to do that?" Kyle demands.

Tommy shrugs. "You might not. But starting pay is thirty-five grand with a path toward a lot more. Benefits. And you can take classes for free."

"What are the strings?" Emma demands.

"What do you mean?"

"There are always strings," she says. Her voice has gone raspy, now, as if she's about to cry.

"Only one," Tommy says. "You can live where you want. You can talk to your mom. Or not. You can decide whether to go back to school. Or not. But Kyle would have to give up his current line of work."

They're all silent for a moment, and Emma and Kyle both shift in their seats. "Why would *you* do that?" Kyle blurts, more a challenge than a question. "Why would you offer me a job?"

Tommy wants to say that he knows what it means to screw up, that he knows what it means to keep a secret. But that would just make everything more complicated than it already is, and it isn't the real reason anyway. He works hard to keep his voice gentle so that Kyle might hear exactly what he's trying to say, so that Emma can hear it. "Because I trust Emma. If you take the job, I'll be really happy that I gave you the chance. If you don't, I trust her to see what *that* means."

Kyle's face twists, but Tommy can't tell whether he's sneering or trying not to cry. One last penguin remains on the cliff. Tommy turns to Emma and finds no ambiguity. Her mask of defiance has collapsed, and tears stream down her cheeks. When he speaks, he talks only to her. "I can't control you," Tommy says quietly. "But I can trust you."

A loud knock on the front door startles all three of them, followed by three softer knocks. The room is still and quiet. Both Tommy and Emma wait to see what Kyle will do next.

* * *

Tommy straddles a chair, backward, his chin resting on his forearms, watching Maggie's hands shape the spinning clay, waiting for her to say something. The house was quiet when he arrived home from Madison, and he expected to find Maggie asleep, but their bed was empty. It took him a few minutes to realize that she might be throwing clay, and the fact that he found her in the basement at one in the morning told him that she knew at least part of what he'd tell her. He told her all of it, though. Her hands remained steady when he told her about Gainesville and Burger King and Linden Glen, confirming that much of it wasn't news. When he described what he found in Madison, though, she ruined the piece that she was working on. She stopped the wheel, wadded the clay into a ball, and started over. He feels even lighter now that he's told her, but as he waits for her to say something, as the silence stretches, broken only by the hum of the wheel, he begins to feel more unmoored than free.

"I meant to tell you a thousand times," Tommy says. "I should have told you."

"But you didn't," Maggie says.

"No," Tommy says. "I didn't." Excuses and reasons and deflections filter through his mind, but he ignores all of them. "I was a coward."

She's quiet for a moment, and Tommy steals a look at her face. She's chewing on her lower lip, and her eyes are fixed on the wheel. "How did you find Emma?" she asks.

"We met for lunch," he says. "Last week. She told me she was in Madison, and Malcolm has a guy that finds people."

"You had lunch with her," she says. "And you didn't even tell me *that*."

Despite everything that he's told her, everything that he's confessed, anger surges through Tommy. She pushed their daughter away. She made it hard to bring Emma home. After everything he's done to overcome that, she complains that he didn't tell her about a lunch at Miss Katie's. But he says nothing. He can think of no words that would help her understand the destruction that *she's* caused, and if he *could* help her understand, he knows no words exist to balance the scales in Maggie's mind.

Maggie stops the wheel. She stands from her stool and turns to the sink against the wall. She washes her hands for a long time. Finally, she shuts the water off and tears paper towels from the roll. She turns back to him, her eyes locked on his, drying her hands thoroughly, like she's Pontius Pilate. Her lips squirm to a straight line like the they do when she's about to say something difficult. She opens her mouth to speak but stops at the sound of footsteps across the floor above. Her eyes dart to the ceiling and then back to Tommy.

"Is that—"

Tommy nods, and he can't help but smile. "Emma."

Her name comes out more like a sigh than a word.

"Thank you," Maggie finally whispers. For a long time that's all she says, and they've been married long enough that they both know that those two words come with *I'm sorry* embedded in them. But even as she says those words, her shoulders sag further, the creases around her mouth deepen, and Tommy knows that those footsteps change everything except the fundamental problem between them.

Her voice comes steady when she speaks, as if she's handing down a sentence. "So," she says. "Which one of us is going to move out of the house?"

38

Sabbatical

MALCOLM WALKS DOWN the long hallway toward his office, avoiding eye contact with everyone. He gulps his coffee, and it scalds, but he needs the caffeine desperately. He barely slept at all last night, and what little sleep he managed was riddled with unwanted dreams. He lay on his mattress, staring at the ceiling, trying to soothe himself with the fact that they hadn't told the Hoyers their last names. But he wondered if Naomi called them before or since, or whether she'll call them soon. He thought about the photos that Yuri sent to his office and considered when to drive north to Milwaukee. But then he fell asleep, and he was jumping off the cliff into the water at the bottom of the quarry with Tommy and Henry and Kevin, all of them screaming because they knew how cold the water was going to be when they hit the surface, but they never did hit the surface, they just kept falling and screaming, and then he lurched awake, and all he could think about was the Hoyers and what they would do next.

When Yuri called yesterday during the drive back to Jacksonville, Malcolm couldn't talk about the Hoyers with Tommy sitting next to him, and he couldn't quite make the decision to call him back last night. He woke up in the middle of the night with the decision made, and the thought of it comforted him enough to slip again toward something like sleep, and again he dreamed. This time, Tommy and Henry and Kevin were laughing without making any sound. Malcolm looked from one of them to the other, trying to figure out what could possibly be so funny. And then he looked down at those boys, so still, that puddle of blood leaking from Michael Hoyer's ear.

Malcolm swallows another slug of coffee as he makes his way through the maze of corridors. He'll call Naomi as soon as he gets to his desk. He'll tell her that he's coming to Milwaukee today, that they need to talk, and she'll probably wait to hear what he has to say. The photos are doctored, of course, but Yuri described the story that they tell, a story about Naomi's father and a prostitute. That narrative is bolstered by an affidavit from the woman. None of it will stand up to expert scrutiny, but it won't have to. It only has to convince Naomi that she doesn't want copies of the file sent to her mother and her brothers and her grandmother.

Malcolm pulls his phone from his pocket before he turns the corner, and he puts it to his ear so that he can walk past Claire without a conversation. He nods at her briskly, but instead of nodding back, she jumps up and stands in front of his closed door, looking alarmed. Why is his door closed?

"I'll call you back," he says into the phone to nobody, and then pretends to hang up. "What's up?"

"Breck Sneddon's in your office."

Malcolm's stomach clenches, and he forces all those thoughts back into the box where they belong so that he can take care of whatever *this* is. He looks at his watch. Seven thirty. Sneddon seldom leaves the twentieth floor and never arrives at the office before nine. "What's he doing here already?"

"I don't know," she says. "He arrived twenty minutes ago. I told him that I'd send you up to his office when you got in." Her eyes dart to the closed door. "But he insisted on waiting in there."

It's probably about ElekTek, but if it was good news, it would have kept until a more decent hour. Malcolm squares his shoulders and opens the door. He forces a wide smile as he walks in. Sneddon is sitting at Malcolm's conference table. He's leaning back in the chair, his legs crossed, intent on his phone, his thumbs tapping out a message. His gray hair is trimmed short, and his forehead, already tanned from afternoons at the country club, is furrowed.

"Breck!" Malcolm says heartily, trying his level best to sound pleasantly surprised. "Wasn't expecting you this morning."

"No," Sneddon says without looking up from his phone. His voice, as always, seems to come through his nose more than his mouth. "You weren't. Why don't you have a seat."

Sneddon's lack of eye contact confirms that the news is bad. Malcolm tries to think of something that he might have done that knocked ElekTek sideways, but he comes up with nothing. He sets his briefcase on his desk next to the FedEx envelope that must be from Yuri. He forces down another gulp of coffee, because he expects that he'll need it, and then he sits down across the table from Sneddon.

"So. What's up?"

Sneddon ignores the question as he finishes typing what must be the longest text message in history. Finally, he puts his phone on the table and looks up. His eyes match the startling blue of his silk tie, and they seem to look straight through Malcolm.

"I got a call last night." He studies Malcolm as if he were an insect pinned to a foam board. "From a reporter."

Malcolm's stomach turns to water, and he blinks, then blinks again. *That* box was never meant to be opened at *this* conference table. It's all he can do not to crush his coffee cup. He tries to look indifferent. "What did she want?" Malcolm asks.

Sneddon's eyebrows edge up. "How did you know it was a woman?"

Dammit. Dammit. Shit. Malcolm says nothing. There's nothing to say. He works hard to maintain eye contact.

"She wanted to tell me about a murder. It was a long, elaborate story that I won't bore you with because I think that you probably already know it."

"I have no idea what you're talking about," Malcolm says.

Sneddon shakes his head sadly. "You'll probably need to come up with a better response than that. Anyway. The firm doesn't need the distraction. We won't take the risk. You'll start your leave of absence—pending an investigation, of course—as soon as I walk out that door."

"Breck, I didn't—"

"Malcolm." Sneddon holds up a hand. His voice has gone hard. "You have the right to remain silent, and I have the right to fire you on the spot if that's what you'd prefer." He waits for Malcolm to speak again, eyebrows raised higher. "Good. A security guard will be by in a moment to take your keycard and your laptop. He'll escort you out."

Sneddon stands with a whisper of expensive wool and walks out of the office without another word. Bees swarm the inside of Malcolm's skull, along with thoughts of Elena and Naomi and Kinsey and Henry and Tommy and the Hoyers and even Kevin. He struggles to imagine a way to sort everything back into its proper box again, but of course it's too late for that. He stands and stares out the window, hoping to catch sight of a seagull, but the air between the buildings hangs empty. He's lost his family. He's lost his job. He's lost his friends. He feels hollow and light, as if *he* could float on the updraft. He thinks of that old Janis Joplin song, because he has absolutely nothing left to lose.

39

The Weakest One

NAOMI CLOSES THE door to her office, sets the Styro-foam coffee cup down on her small metal desk, and sits. She sips the coffee as she stares out the window at the half-full parking lot. She needs the caffeine. She didn't sleep well last night after calling Malcolm's boss. Her feet were ticklish, and she couldn't stop smelling Kevin, that mix of Right Guard and smelly feet and something like vanilla. Right after her call with Breck Sneddon, she felt exhilarated in a way that she hadn't expected. But she didn't expect the regret toward bedtime either. She hasn't felt this many conflicting emotions since she was a thirteen-year-old girl. Ruining lives is hard work, even if those lives deserve to be ruined.

She checks the clock. Nine thirty Mountain Time. She could wait, but she's waited long enough. And she wants to get this call out of the way. She wants to give them time to sit with it, to struggle with it—to wait for it like she waited for Kevin to die—before she makes that last call. She considers her cell phone but decides on the desk phone. She picks up the handset and carefully dials the number. The *Journal Sentinel* on caller ID will decrease the chances of voicemail, and this is definitely a message she wants to deliver live. The phone rings just once before it's answered.

"This is Alice."

Her voice is subdued, tentative. The caller ID had its intended effect.

"Hello, Alice, this is Naomi McNamara."

Silence.

"We met at the funeral. I'm Kevin's—"

"I know who you are."

Alice's voice has taken on a hard edge that Naomi wasn't expecting. It throws her, and for a moment she loses track of the words she rehearsed. "There's something that you should know about your husband," she finally says.

"Oh," Alice says. "And what's that?"

"There was an incident in a parking lot when he was eighteen."

Alice doesn't respond, so Naomi launches into her story, the condensed version, just the broad strokes. Naomi pauses a few times, but Alice doesn't ask any questions. When she reaches the end, a silence falls between them. The poor woman must be in shock, and a tiny slice of Naomi regrets dragging another innocent person into the muck.

"Are you still there?"

"Yes," Alice says in a voice steadier than Naomi expects. "I'm still here."

"Do you have any questions for me?"

"Why are you doing this?"

"I thought that you should know."

"Bullshit. Don't you dare act like you're doing this for me."

"I thought that you should know the truth before I take what I have to the authorities."

"Oh, Christ," Alice says, disgust dripping from the words. "You sound like Kevin."

Naomi's mind scrambles for purchase, and finally it grabs hold of the obvious. "You knew."

"Of course, I knew. I was there."

"That night?"

"No. For the rest of it. For the aftermath."

Naomi leans back in her chair. She tries to find a way to get back on top of the conversation, and she lunges at the first thing that comes to her mind. "That would make you an accessory."

"Oh please. By that logic, you'd be an accessory too."

"But—"

"But nothing. How long have you known about this? Did you learn about this *after* Kevin died?"

Naomi opens her mouth to respond, but no words come.

"That's what I thought. You *are* just like Kevin. Always blaming others while claiming your own innocence."

Naomi leans forward again, her face hot. Somehow, she manages to keep her voice calm. "You know nothing about Kevin."

"I knew him long before you did, sister. I gotta ask. If Kevin thought it was so important to share the truth, why didn't he do it while he was alive?"

Naomi blinks, and her lips tighten. "Kevin's motivations really aren't any of your business."

Alice laughs a short, brittle laugh. "I guess you just made it my business, didn't you? Henry always said that Kevin was a coward. I'm inclined to agree with him."

"He was anything but a coward," Naomi says thickly.

"Really?" Alice demands. "How would you explain it, then? All these years he could have said something. Instead, he sends his wife after them when he's dead."

Naomi's lip curls. "Maybe his wife went after them on her own," she growls.

"And why would his wife do that?"

Her eyes narrow, and her free hand gathers into a fist. "Have you ever lived with a junkie?"

It's Alice's turn for silence.

"Let me tell you what it's like. I watched him swallow his cravings every day except when he couldn't, and then I cleaned up his vomit and monitored his breathing and his pulse when he was sleeping, and I lied to his boss when he was able to keep a job, and I always had my car keys in my pocket because I never knew when we'd have to race to the hospital, and I always answered my phone because I never knew when I'd get the call telling me that my husband was dead." She takes a breath and then continues. "He held that night bottled up inside of him because of Henry and the others. It ate at the center of him even as he tried to numb it with the drugs. And you know the worst part of it?"

More silence.

"I asked you a fucking question," Naomi says more loudly. "Do you know what the worst of it was?"

"I don't," Alice says quietly.

"He never said a bad thing about the three of them. Never once. He never stopped loving them, and I find it impossible to forgive him for that."

More silence. Louder this time. When Alice speaks, her voice has gone soft. "I'm sorry. I really am. You're probably the only innocent one in this whole mess. But I think you should know the whole story."

"What does that mean?"

"Did he tell you that he started the whole thing? Did he tell you that none of it would have happened if he'd just kept his mouth shut?"

Now is not the time to share Kevin's regrets, so Naomi says nothing.

"I didn't think so. And he couldn't have told you how that night affected the rest of them."

Naomi wants to tell Alice to shut the hell up, that she doesn't want to hear a sob story about how those other three "suffered," but something in Alice's voice forces her quiet.

"Did Kevin have friends?"

"What do you mean?"

"Besides you. Besides *your* friends. Did Kevin have any friends of his own?"

Naomi doesn't want to answer that question, but Alice holds the silence, and she's forced to say something. "He—it wasn't really—because of the—he—"

"That's what I thought," Alice says. Naomi can hear her swallow. "Henry doesn't have a single friend that wasn't my friend first. From what I can tell, same goes for Malcolm and Tommy."

"That's hardly—"

"Did you know that Tommy abandoned a football scholarship to Madison after that night? Did Kevin tell you how Malcolm buried himself so far under a mountain of work that his family never could find him again? And did you know that my husband's life jumped so far off the tracks that he's spent it renting body parts?"

Naomi says nothing. Alice fills the void.

"I'm sorry that Kevin died," she says in a softer, rounder voice. "I'm sorry for everything that you've gone through.

And I'm sorry for what happened to those boys and to their families. But from what I can tell, although there are different degrees of guilt, nobody in that parking lot that night was innocent. And that includes Hoyer and Greavy. You're going to do what you're going to do, and I won't try to stop you. But you should know that every one of them has suffered in their own way. I knew all four of those boys. I knew Kevin. And he may have suffered the most simply because he was the weakest."

40

The Blue Room

MALCOLM STANDS AT the window in the dark. There's no point in turning on the lights because there's nothing in his condo, nothing in his life to see or even bump into. Turning on the lights just makes it more difficult to see outside.

The perp walk from the office was terrible. Word spread fast somehow, and the associates and the paralegals and even a few of the partners filled the hallways. Nobody made eye contact. They carried files or legal pads, and they all pretended to be hurrying toward a meeting, but there just aren't that many meetings scheduled for seven forty-five in the morning. Malcolm knew that they emerged from their offices to see him with his cardboard box tucked under his arm and a security guard at his side. He doesn't blame them, really. The stink of humiliation is irresistible.

Malcolm stumbled from the building, blinked into the morning sun slanting between two buildings, and dumped the cardboard box in the first trash can that he found, because even though he couldn't remember what he'd packed in it, he was certain that he would never need it again. And then he walked.

He remembers just bits of the day. He remembers walking along the lake and through the renovated warehouses of River North and past the bars in Wicker Park and the murals in Pilsen, but his mind was a jumbled mess. Usually walking helps him sort things out when life gets difficult. It helps him to separate the things that matter from the distractions. But today, everything matters. It usually helps him to sift the things he can control from the things that he can't, but today he found nothing to do about any of it. At some point he pulled off his tie and threw that in a garbage can too. Walking usually helps him compartmentalize his problems so that he can address them one at a time, but today, as his shoes pounded the sidewalks, his problems churned together into one swirling, steaming mess, and the best he could manage was to itemize everything that he had lost. His job is gone. His wife and daughter both hate him and want nothing more than to put distance between themselves and him. The home that he no longer lives in and the condo that he's yet to make a home will both be sold, and the proceeds will be divided between Elena and Linden Glen and legal fees. He was tired by the time he trudged back into the Loop, but he knew that his next walk might be around the perimeter of a prison yard. And as he tallied all those losses, his thoughts inevitably drifted back to those terrible three seconds of silence.

He ignores the Willis Tower and the cars and the lake tonight. He scans the apartment building across from his. Some of the blinds are drawn, but he sees the woman a few floors below his, cooking a late dinner for herself again—looks like stir fry. The man a few floors up is jogging on his treadmill like he does every night. He looks straight out his window, but his lights are on, so he probably only sees a reflection of himself. A few floors above that, three people are sitting on a balcony. The red ember of a cigarette or a joint flares, and Malcolm can't help but think about Tommy and Henry and Kevin.

He thinks again about what they said in the car yesterday. It's been such a long time since he thought of their friendship as anything but dead, so their words made no sense to him—nonsense syllables spoken by men under stress. But looking at those three friends passing a joint back and forth—it must be a joint because nobody passes cigarettes—he can't help thinking about the first time they got high together and the first time they met and the first time they played ding-dong ditch and the first time they shot bottle rockets at each other out of Wiffle ball bats and, of course, the last time that they were all together down in Tommy's basement. But that friendship is gone. Tommy and Henry's words in the car yesterday amount to pointless chest compressions on a long-dead carcass. But if that's the case, why does he keep replaying those words in his mind? Why does the word *brothers* keep ringing in his ears like a car alarm?

Malcolm forces his gaze from the pot smokers, and his eyes settle on the apartment straight across, where the newlyweds live. He thinks of them as the newlyweds, but he has no idea if they're even married. Their television sits in a corner near the window, the only evidence of its existence the warm blue glow cast over the couple. They lie sprawled across the couch, their bodies twined. Her head is tucked against his shoulder, and his chin rests in her hair.

Malcolm tries to remember how he and Elena used to
be, back before the Cellutec deal, back before the applesauce. He remembers the way that they'd watch TV,
spooned on the couch in that apartment in Wicker Park
and on the slightly bigger couch in that house in Lakeview. They kept the volume low so that they could talk as
much as watch, and he remembers the way her hair smelled,
like basil and lilacs. She would finish his sentences when he
paused to find the right word to describe something that
happened to him at work. And he laughed, from deep in his
belly, when Elena told him funny stories about what happened in the classroom or about something stupid one of
her brothers had said. Mostly, though, he remembers how
they fit together back then, not just their bodies on that
couch, but how their thoughts and their goals and their lives
used to fit together—like spoons—before he pried himself
away from her.

He remembers the intensity of his anger when Elena
started in that night—that night he fled to the guest bedroom. He remembers how his mind unspooled the argument like it always does, how he lay in bed considering the
inevitable conclusion of that argument, that old familiar
rage swelling in his chest. He didn't know what he'd say or
what he'd do if he engaged. He knows that he can't blame
his father or his job or even that night in the Burger King
parking lot. He knows who to blame. In the end, the proxi-
mate cause of their divorce is his own cowardice.

In the end. He knows that he's reached the end. He's
spent his day considering his options, and he knows that
he's run out of them. He thought about calling Naomi,
but then remembered that the FedEx envelope was in that
box that he threw out. He thought about walking back to

find it, but he couldn't remember where he was when he dumped it. He thought about calling Yuri, but his mouth filled with bile when he considered what he was going to ask him to do. When he was walking across the bridge over the river, he decided that if someone else was going to die because of that night, it certainly wouldn't be the Hoyers. He still doesn't know why he didn't climb over the railing and let himself fall into the ice-cold water. Maybe later tonight. Maybe tomorrow. Maybe he's too much of a coward for even that.

When Malcolm's phone vibrates, he lets it go to voice-mail. It's probably Henry or Tommy calling about an article that just appeared on the *Journal Sentinel* website, and he's not yet ready for that and all that will follow. The phone vibrates again, so he tugs it from his pocket. He sees that it's Security downstairs, and he feels the hot breath of the inevitable. He didn't expect the next thing to happen so quickly, and he wonders whether they're Chicago cops or federal marshals. It doesn't really matter in the end, so he answers.

"Hello, sir. You have a visitor."

Singular, not plural. Malcolm forces himself not to hope. "Who is it?"

"Elena O'Donnell."

Malcolm's eyes lock on the couple snuggled into the couch washed with blue light, and he wills himself not to hope for that either. "Send her up," he says.

While he waits for the elevator, he wonders why she's come. He wonders if Naomi has already called her, seeking comment. He wonders what she'll make of his dark empty condo. And for a moment, when the elevator opens and he sees her face, he wonders how he could have let her go, how he could have let things fall apart. But before he can get a read on her mood, she steps out of the elevator, the doors close, and she too is shrouded by the gloom.

She walks across the room and stands next to him, taking in the view. Malcolm turns back to the window, tries to see what she sees, wonders what her eyes have locked on. He waits for her to say something, but she remains mute.

"Hey," he finally says.

"You couldn't even call her yourself," she says.

The ripple in her voice tells him how upset she is. Why would he call Naomi? "Call who?" he asks.

Elena snorts in disgust. "You're pathetic, Malcolm. Do you have any idea how important that concert is to Kinsey?" Malcolm's mind skids as it shifts directions. "You send me a goddamn text to tell her you can't make it? Because it's *my* job to tell her yet again that you don't give a shit about her?"

Kinsey. Of course. He remembers the way his daughter's face turned to stone at Sienna Grill when he called her mandolin a banjo. He feels again the stiffness in his fingers when he sent that text to cancel. "I'm sorry," Malcolm whispers toward the window, toward that young couple on the couch.

"Damn right you're sorry. You're a sorry excuse for a dad." She pauses for a long moment. "And you were a worse husband."

No arguments present themselves, and he doesn't go searching for any. She's right. About all of it. He feels settled, still, and he doesn't have to strain for it. "I know," he says to the window.

"And look at this place!" she growls. She turns to peer into the gloom. "There's nothing here! You want Kinsey two weekends a month when you can't even make the time to buy a goddamn couch? Is she supposed to bring a fucking sleeping bag with her?"

Malcolm wants to tell her why he hasn't bought the furniture yet, the indecision, the regret, the hope that keeps him from signing off on the designs that Evelyn sent. He wants to tell her that he means to change, that he thinks maybe he *can* change. He wants to point to the couple on the couch across the street and remind Elena of when that was them lying together, touching each other, breathing each other's scent. But he knows she's probably looking past that building, out at the dark expanse of the lake. And there's two layers of thick, shatterproof glass and a thirty-nine-story drop between them and that blue room. He knows there's no way to get to that apartment, no way to claw their way back to that couch. And he hasn't earned the right to say any of those things. "I know," he says instead. "You're right."

Malcolm can tell by the way that Elena goes still that she was expecting an argument. She's quiet for a beat, and then he can feel her gather herself, even as he searches for the words to tell her that he'll no longer stand in her way.

"But that's not why I came," she says, steel in her voice. "Maybe you can explain Burger King to me."

Malcolm goes still. He wants to ask how much she knows. He wants to explain it to her, tell her it's not what she thinks, but it's really much worse than she thinks. So instead of telling her what he wants to tell her, he tells her what she really wants to hear.

"You can move to Milwaukee," he says. "With Kinsey. I'm sorry that I made that hard."

She blinks at him.

"And you can have the money," he says. "I'll fix Vanguard tomorrow."

She looks back out the window, and he wills her not to press about Burger King. "Why?" she asks quietly. "Why did you make it so hard?"

"I guess I thought if we spent some time together that I could—" He has trouble finding the words for what he thought might happen if Kinsey slept in that room overlooking the Ferris wheel. What would they do together? What would they say to each other? What else could he do but watch her while she slept? All the images, all the words that flicker through his mind seem unlikely and naive to the point of absurd, and he can't force himself to say them. How to explain that Milwaukee felt so far away? How to explain that Kinsey moving there felt like a door closing, like the loss of a last chance that both of them know that he doesn't deserve? "I didn't want to give up," he finally says as his eyes settle again on the newlyweds on their couch. "I didn't want to fail her too."

They stand next to each other for what seems like a very long time. He wants to point out that flickering blue square and tell her what he sees in it, what he remembers. He wants to reach out to her, to say something, to say everything that he's failed to say for so many years, but his throat is closed up, making it hard to breathe, much less speak. And where would he start anyway?

"Goodbye, Malcolm," she says.

She says it with a heaviness, a weariness that he's never heard from her. It's another long moment before she turns and walks toward the elevator. Malcolm is overwhelmed with the urgency to say something, to do something, to make her stop, but he knows the time for those words has passed. When the elevator doors slide open, the window glares with the reflection of the elevator's lights, but the image is refracted through Malcolm's tears, and he can only glimpse Elena's shape. He tries to blink the tears away, tries squeezing his eyes shut, but when he opens them, the doors are closing, and then she's gone.

Malcolm refuses to look at the newlyweds, because he knows that if he does, he'll bawl. He looks toward those friends getting stoned on the balcony, but there's only two of them now. He knows that his friendship with Tommy and Henry will never be the same, but it strikes him that it might be all that he's got left. He thinks about what they said in that bedroom in Gainesville, and instead of getting angry all over again, he's afraid for them, protective in a way that he's not used to. For the first time since he was ejected from his office, he's able to focus on something. For a long time, he stares at those men as he sorts through options and scenarios and terribly rash actions. By the time the men finally stand up and go inside, Malcolm's decided what he'll do. He walks straight to the elevator and hits the down button before he can change his mind.

41

Viral Load

HENRY DRIVES UP the serpentine road from the city without paying much attention to the sharp turns and sheer drops. They've lived on Ridgeline Drive almost seventeen years, and he's driven the route so many thousands of times that muscle memory navigates the curves, allowing Henry to try to navigate what he'll say to Alice when he gets home.

He won't tell her about his doctor appointment. She won't want to hear that his viral load ticked down just a bit. That would just piss her off and make it difficult for her to hear what he really wants to say. He will tell her what he's decided about work, because although he can't put his finger on exactly why, it seems related in a curvy, hairpin way to the rest of what he wants to tell her. He won't say any more about Gainesville because he's been talking about that since he arrived home from the airport the day before yesterday, and he can tell that she's tired of hearing about it. He talked about it so much because he hasn't yet found the right words to describe how his time in that trailer made him feel. It left his mind quieter and his body more settled than he can ever remember. Although he really wants to make Alice understand what happened in that bedroom, he has more important words to assemble—the answers that he owes Alice above all else.

The phone rings as he rounds the switchback just past Silver Fork Road, and his dashboard display tells him that it's Tommy. Before Gainesville he would have let Tommy's call drop to voicemail, but ever since he arrived home, Henry's felt an urge to call him, so instead he answers.

"Hey."

"Hey," Tommy says. "How are you doing?"

The pensive way Tommy asks the question tells Henry that it's not a casual, throwaway question, that Tommy really wants to know, so he considers his answer carefully. "Better," he says. "It felt good to tell the truth for once."

"Yeah," Tommy says in a voice that sounds more tired than Henry expects. "Me too."

"How are *you* doing?" Henry asks.

A heavy silence rests on the line until Tommy finally answers. "It's complicated." Before Henry can ask what that means, Tommy asks, "Have you talked to Malcolm?"

"No. Why?"

"I'm worried about what he said in the car about fixing things. I've been calling him. He doesn't answer."

"I can't say that I'm surprised."

"I called him at work. They said he doesn't work there anymore."

Henry squeezes the steering wheel. "Malcolm wouldn't just quit."

"His assistant said extended leave of absence, but the way she said it seemed wonky. Like she was about to start crying."

Henry thinks back to that drive to Jacksonville. "What do you think that he meant by that?" he asks. "When he said that he'd take care of things."

"I don't know," Tommy says. "But I can't stop thinking that he'll do something that he'll regret. Something that we'll all regret."

Henry turns onto Ridgeline Drive, the steering wheel spinning through his fingers, the possibilities tumbling through his mind. Regret. The last thing that any of them need is more regret. "I'll call him," he finally says.

"Let me know if you talk to him," Tommy says.

Henry pulls into the driveway and shifts into park. He stares at the garage door, sorting through the possibilities, listening to the silence.

"Take care of yourself, Henry," Tommy finally says.

Henry can tell that these, too, are real words, freighted with anxiety and concern and—although it takes him a long moment to even think the word much less say it—with love. "You take care of yourself too. I'll call you when I talk to Malcolm."

He says *when*, because he refuses to say *if*.

* * *

Alice finishes chopping the onions, ginger, and garlic and scrapes it all into the butter chicken with her knife. She stirs the sauce, puts the lid on the pan, and turns the flame down until it barely flickers. You can't cook butter chicken on high heat. You can't rush it. You have to let it simmer. Alice glances at the clock, and she knows that Henry will be home soon. She's let that decision simmer too long.

She has to decide. What happened in Gainesville, along with the call from Naomi, tells Alice that everything is about to get very complicated for Henry. And that flight to New Zealand for a trip that she'd rather take alone than with Henry leaves in five days. But neither New Zealand nor Burger King explains the urgency that's making her fingers tingle. And it has nothing to do with Mark. Every day of distance from that night it becomes more clear that Mark is just a stand-in for what might be next if she leaves Henry. She'll decide today because she can't continue to live like this, her emotions jangling, her mood shifting like the spring mountain wind. She's already decided today—three different times, three different ways—but once she declares a decision, once she's said it out loud to Henry, it will stick, and she'll be done with it.

The day Henry was gone in Gainesville, she started taping closed the boxes on the bedroom floor. If he didn't make it home that night, if he didn't tell her what he'd said in that trailer home in Florida, she would have moved out yesterday morning. She always thought it would be Tommy who would crack, that he'd be the one to come clean. She was surprised to learn that Henry was still capable of digging the truth from under the decades of rationalization and repression. But the Henry who told Mrs. Hoyer what he had done, simply so that she could have some peace, was the man Alice had fallen in love with. Still, he hasn't been able to explain why he did what he did to *her*. So it's come down to this: Does she still want the *we* without the *why*?

When Henry opens the front door, Alice turns back to the stove, takes the lid off the pan, and starts to stir again. She hears him sit down at the island behind her.

"Indian," he says, stating the obvious.

"Indian," she agrees without turning.

They're quiet for what seems like a long time. "I'm thinking about taking the realtor's exam," he says. "I was wondering if you could help me."

Alice turns and glares at him. She knows that he thinks that what she does is easy, that anybody can do it. His words insult her, and they amount to a colossal lack of imagination. "Really."

"Yeah," he says. "I don't want to rent dead bodies anymore."

Alice licks sauce from the wooden spoon as she studies him. The heavy cream tries to cut the bite of the chili peppers but fails. She thinks about that long-ago drive up the Pacific Coast Highway. "You mean cadavers?"

Henry's lips flicker. "No," he says firmly. "I mean dead bodies."

Alice turns back to the stove. "I'll send you some links," she says. Whether she stays with him or not, she can't imagine committing to more than that. She wants to ask him why, but he'll inevitably talk about an epiphany in Gainesville, and she just can't stomach that.

"And I want to talk about why I cheated on you."

Alice stops stirring and stares at the gurgling yellow sauce. Hot flecks of it splatter on her hand, but she barely feels them. Impatient bubbles of air, making a mess as they escape. Finally, she sets the spoon on the counter and turns. She crosses her arms across her chest and looks at him hard. "I thought the answer to that was *'I don't know.'*"

"I know that I have to do better than that." He picks up a pen from the counter. He takes off the cap, scribbles on a takeout menu, puts the cap back on. "When Lyla came on to me that first time, I was flattered."

"You fucked her because you were flattered."

"I hadn't felt that way since freshman year of high school. When you, when we—"

"Don't you ever compare her to me."

Henry shakes his head but doesn't look up from the pen in his hands. "That's not what I'm saying at all. I was fifteen the last time that somebody wanted me like that. I know it sounds pathetic—"

"It's beyond pathetic."

Finally, Henry looks up, and his eyes are red-rimmed and needy. "I know," he whispers.

"How many times did you fuck her?"

Henry looks back down at his hands. "Eleven."

"You fucked her eleven times because you were flattered."

He shakes his head. "After that first time it was the thrill of the forbidden, I think." He's quiet for a long moment. "The fact that it was so wrong made it exciting."

"That is so messed up."

Henry nods slowly. "I know," he whispers as if he's baffled by what he just told her.

"Is this supposed to make me feel better?"

Henry shakes his head again. "No. It's not." He stares hard at the pen, as if it might hold answers. "But it's the truth. I guess that seems more important right now than making you feel better."

The truth. Alice feels hard, like her entire body has turned to stone. And that hardness feels brittle, as if she might shatter if he says anything more. Dinner is boiling behind her now, but she ignores it. She wanted the truth. But did she? When she speaks, her own voice comes as flinty as she feels. "Are you done?"

"No," he says. "One more thing."

One more thing. Alice wants to tell him to shut up and get out of her house. She wants to leave the house herself, but that hardness makes her heavy, and it keeps her from speaking or moving.

"I didn't tell you for a month. About the virus. I went to bed every night thinking that I'd tell you the next day. Every morning, I woke up and told myself that would be the day I would tell you. But every time I started to form the words, I choked on them. I didn't tell you, because I didn't want to see that look on your face, the look of disgust that I see right now. I was terrified that you'd leave me, and you're the best thing that ever happened to me." He looks out the window at the city for a long moment, and then back at Alice. "I'm so sorry for all of it. I love you more than anything in the world. There's nothing more true than that."

* * *

Henry sits on the couch in the dark and waits. After Alice walked out onto the deck, he turned down the flame and stirred the butter chicken, but after a while he turned the stove off entirely. An hour after that, when it had cooled, he poured it into a Tupperware bowl and put it in the fridge, because Alice might want it tomorrow or the day after that. She hugs herself at the railing, looking at the lights below. He wants to bring her a sweatshirt, but her stillness tells him that she wants to be left alone, that she's probably deciding right now. When she comes back through that door, she'll tell him what's next. The fact that she's stood there for so long tells him that he probably won't be around to share the butter chicken.

He decided not to tell Alice why he kicked Greavy and Hoyer, even though he's finally arrived at a reason for that too. Since he left Michael Hoyer's bedroom, he hasn't been able to stop reliving those moments. He kicked Greavy that first time because Greavy was about to jump Tommy, but he kept kicking because it felt so good. He can't say those words out loud—it feels terrible even to think them. He knew it was terrible even while he was doing it—evil is probably more accurate—but he kept kicking because it gave him a rush of something that he can't quite wrap words around. He won't tell Alice. He can't tell her that he kept screwing Lyla for essentially the same reason that he broke those boys' ribs. Even Alice doesn't want that much truth.

Henry tries Malcolm twice while he waits, but the calls go straight to voicemail. He hadn't given much thought to what Malcolm said in the car until Tommy called, but now he's worried. A few days ago, he'd mainly be worried about what might happen to him. But telling the Hoyers the truth felt like the first right thing he'd done in decades. It felt like such sweet surrender. Surrender. *That's* the word to describe what he felt in that bedroom. He's no longer worried about what Naomi will do. He's no longer worried about what will happen to him. Now, he's mainly worried about Malcolm.

Alice finally sits down in one of the deck chairs. She crosses one leg over the other and then resumes her staring. Henry wonders if he should start packing his things instead of watching the back of her head, but he decides it would be cowardly to spill his guts and then go hide in the bedroom.

When Alice stands, Henry almost expects her to drift back to the railing, but instead she turns toward the house. Her face tells him nothing as she comes through the sliding glass door. She doesn't look at him as she walks to where he's sitting, and he thinks about what they always say about juries on *Law & Order*. She turns on a lamp, and Henry blinks against the sudden glare. She settles on the chair across from him, leans forward, her elbows on her knees and her eyes on the floor. All that stillness has softened the shape of her face, and Henry allows hope to wriggle in next to the inevitable.

When she looks up at him, her eyes are wide, and the animosity seems to have drained from her expression. But he sees no forgiveness there either. It's all he can do to keep from looking away. He surrenders to this too.

"You should probably start packing," she says, her voice ragged.

Henry releases the breath that he's been holding. His chin drops to his chest. The room falls so, so quiet, and his whole body goes slack. So that's it, then. Five words and it's over. All of it. Done.

"And don't forget blister pads," she says.

Henry looks up at her, tilts his head, puzzled. Her gaze remains steady, and her expression still tells him nothing. "What—?"

"And your rain pants. The Gore-Tex. I don't want to listen to your complaining this time."

42

Boxes

RODNEY'S TAKING A box of Michael's clothes out to the shed. Helen pulls the packing tape across the bottom seam of the last box with a loud screech. She flips it over on the bare mattress of what used to be Michael's bed and starts packing Michael's books. Some are textbooks he was using when he died, but the rest are novels. Some he read for school, but others he checked out from the library, and still others he bought at the used bookstore down on Harrison. One time she asked him why he liked reading stories so much, and he said that they helped him see how other people lived. That hurt her feelings a little bit because it made her think that he didn't like how *they* lived. After he died, she read a few of his books, starting with *Of Mice and Men*. After that, she felt a lot better about his stories.

They've been packing Michael's things on and off for the last few days. They've been taking a lot of breaks because Rodney's too old to be carrying a bunch of boxes in the heat, but also because she doesn't want to rush it. She knew

as soon as they started that she'd made the right decision.
She could see Rodney's shoulders loosen up almost as soon
as she told him what she wanted. And he talked a bit while
they packed, which he doesn't do much anymore. He talked
about wrestling meets, and building models, and the way
Michael refused to let any of the food on his plate touch.
She didn't say anything back—she just listened. Mostly, she
talked to Michael.

She still hasn't decided what to do about those men who
came to visit, so she's been asking her son what he thinks.
She often talks to Michael when she's cleaning his room,
and he sometimes talks back to her. She doesn't hear his
voice or anything weird like that, but sometimes, when she's
really quiet, and usually when she needs it the most, she
can feel what he's thinking. She never tells Rodney about
talking with Michael because she knows how *that* conversation would go. She doesn't believe in God anymore—that
stopped in the weeks and months after Michael died. She
knows that heaven isn't a real place, but she feels what she
feels, and she knows that what she feels is real, because it is.

Helen knows that Rodney will start asking questions
out loud as soon as they finish packing up the room. He'll
ask about calling the cops, but his questions will really be
statements—demands, even—and she still doesn't know
what she wants to do about that. She knows that Rodney
made up his mind even before those men left the trailer. He
wants to hurt them. He wants to make them pay.

Maybe it's Michael telling her, but she's become certain that the one that called himself Malcolm was the one
that killed Michael. She believes that the other two told the
truth once they started talking, and she knows from the
coroner's report that the truth they told wasn't the worst of

what happened. And as she thinks about how they acted, she can't help but imagine what they were like back when they were eighteen, and she can't help thinking that maybe they weren't that much different from Michael.

Helen seals that last box with another screech of tape, but she still hasn't made up her mind. She wants to hurt the one who called himself Malcolm, but how can she do that without hurting the other two? That's the question that she's been puzzling over, the question that she's been asking Michael. She still hasn't told Rodney that she wrote down the license plate number of the car they drove. She can let him call the cops about a thirty-year-old murder with just three first names, and she knows that would probably go nowhere. But the hollow place that opens up in her gut tells her that Michael doesn't like that idea. Michael wants to hurt someone too.

Helen hears Rodney come through the front door, and he appears in the doorway of the room that will soon be her sewing room again.

"Last one?" he asks.

"Yep. Last one." She suddenly realizes how heavy the box must be. She should have packed the books into two boxes. She wants to tell him to bring the dolly from the shed or to wait for someone to help him, but she knows how stubborn he is, so instead she just says, "Be careful. It's heavy."

Rodney picks up the box, but then sets it back down on the bed to get a better grip. He picks it up again and staggers from the room under the weight of it, and Helen follows him out. She opens the front door for him, and she watches to make sure he makes it down the steps before closing the door to keep the heat out. She makes her way to the kitchen and sorts through the pile of bills near the phone until she finds the envelope with the names and the license plate number. She tries to listen, tries to feel, but Michael tells her nothing. She knows that the fate of those three men is scrawled on that envelope, but also the fate of their wives and their children and *their* parents, and for a moment she softens. But those three men kept Michael from finding a wife, they kept *him* from having children, and they kept her and Rodney from having grandchildren. A wave of determined rage washes through her once again, and she steadies herself for what she must do. She's standing so still and staring so hard at those numbers that she startles when the phone rings. She picks up the handset and sees that it's a Milwaukee number. She wonders if one of those men is calling. She's glad that Rodney's out at the shed. Finally, she answers.

"Hello?" she says, her voice a greasy whisper.

"Can I speak to Helen or Rodney Hoyer, please?"

It's a man's voice, but it's high-pitched. Not one of those three. "This is Helen."

"This is Officer Driscoll with the Waukesha County Sheriff's Office. Is now a good time?"

Helen lowers herself into a chair at the kitchen table. "I'm here," she says.

"Your son was Michael Hoyer?"

"My son *is* Michael Hoyer," she says.

A long pause. Officer Driscoll clears his throat. "There's been a development in the investigation of his death."

Investigation? She called them every six months in the years after Michael died, and it always took them fifteen minutes to even remember who Michael Hoyer was, and now, thirty years later, he has the gall to call it an investigation? "What kind of development?"

"The man who killed Michael came forward." Driscoll waits for a reaction, but when he gets none, he continues. "He confessed to the murder. We have him in custody now."

"You said *man*," Helen says. Her hands are shaking, and she's gone cold. "Just one of them confessed?"

Another long silence. "Yes. His name is Malcolm O'Donnell. He said that he acted alone."

Helen has gone completely numb. She can't feel her arms or her legs or her face. She feels nothing. She hears Rodney come back inside, but she doesn't turn. All these years she's imagined what this moment would be like, how she would act, how she would feel, but she never expected that she'd feel nothing. She didn't think those names that they gave were their real names, and she certainly didn't expect that the short one, the liar, the one who called himself Malcolm, would be the one who confessed. She thinks of the envelope in her hand—she can't feel that either—and she asks Michael what she should say about those other names, but she feels nothing. She can't help thinking about all the suffering that has flowed from that parking lot over the last thirty years, and she knows that more suffering won't bring Michael back, and it won't help with the numbness, and it won't help with the waves of grief that she knows are coming next. She crumples the envelope into a ball as she looks up at Rodney. He stares at her intently—he must see something in here face. "Thank you for calling," she finally says and hangs up the phone.

"Who was that?" Rodney demands.

"The police," she says. "From Waukesha."

Rodney stiffens and blinks. He steadies himself against the table and then sinks onto the other chair. "What did they say?"

Helen reaches across the table and takes his hand in hers. This is the first time in a long time that she's touched him like that. It startles him, but he doesn't move his hand. She tries to figure what's best. What's best for those other two men, but most important what's best for her and what's best for Rodney. She looks him straight in the eye and keeps her voice gentle. She tells him the truth, twisted around a partial lie, because she knows it will bring him peace. "Those men that came to see us. They turned themselves in. They confessed to killing Michael."

43

Old Town

ELENA AND DOM find two open seats about ten rows up. It's a larger crowd than Elena expected. She knows that the String Masters are a big draw for a bluegrass band, but more than five hundred people pack the auditorium. Six stools are staggered across the bare stage, and Elena finds it hard to believe that her daughter will sit atop one of them. Kinsey can't seem to believe it either. She's been practicing long and late every night for the last week. She's talked about nothing else—the songs they'll play, the quirks of the band members, the ticket sales. It seems to help keep her mind off her father.

Dom turns in his seat and surveys the crowd. "There's a shitload of people here," he says. "I thought I was coming to a recital."

Elena smiles. She doesn't tell him that the String Masters are *the* Chicago bluegrass band, because she knows how that will sound. "Her teacher plays for them, but he's at a wedding, so they asked her to sit in."

"She must be good."

"Yeah," Elena says. "She's good."

"Dad says that you guys are moving soon," Dom says.

"Yep. First of the month." Elena finally talked to her dad about the move, about the divorce. It went better than she'd expected. He listened to her, and he didn't ask those two questions. Maybe Dom gave him a heads-up, but maybe he was actually listening to Elena's mom back when they shouted at each other about other people's divorces. She didn't say anything about Malcolm's arrest, because it only warranted a few paragraphs on the fourth page of the Metro section in the *Journal Sentinel*—under Naomi McNamara's byline. She's hoping nobody else noticed.

"I heard that what's-his-name is out on bail."

Elena shifts in her seat. So much for nobody noticing. Of course people noticed. If Dom knows, her dad knows, and she wonders if everyone that she knows knows. Juicy gossip has a way of splashing about. "He is," she says, her eyes on the stage. "Seems that rich people don't wait in jail for their court dates."

"How long have you known?"

"He texted me right after he got out. He said he didn't want Kinsey to worry."

Dom looks at her, but Elena studies the stools. "That's not what I mean," he says. "How long did you know about— how long did you know about all of it?"

Elena turns on him. "Really, Dom? Is that what you think of me?"

"I was just—"

"You were just suggesting that I was helping Malcolm cover up a murder," she spits at him. "I found out the day after he turned himself in."

Dom looks back at the stage. Neither of them speak for a long time. Elena wonders if her dad thinks the same of her. She'll call him tomorrow, pull the Band-Aid off. Get all this out in the open.

"How's Kinsey doing?" he asks.

She doesn't answer right away because she's still pissed about Dom's insinuation and because she's really not sure how Kinsey's doing. She told Kinsey as soon as she heard Malcolm was in jail. Luther called to tell her—divorce attorneys seem to be the first to learn everything. Elena tried to explain things in the broadest possible terms and with the smallest dose of judgment that she could manage, but Kinsey has a way of asking questions that dig right to the heart of things. Her face went hard as Elena shared the details that she knew. Her last question was the same as Dom's, and Elena told her, a bit too sharply, that no, she didn't know all along that her father had murdered someone. After that, Kinsey climbed the stairs to her room. She played the mandolin for hours, the same hard-edged, angry song over and over. "To be honest," Elena tells Dom, "I have no idea how she's doing."

Elena watches the door to the right of the stage as hipsters wearing boots and beards and flannel shirts file in and climb the stairs, looking for seats.

"How are *you* doing?" Dom asks quietly.

How is she doing? Ever since Luther called, her emotions have been whirling like a salad spinner. That night in Chicago, Malcolm seemed so vulnerable, like a turtle without its shell. And he was so cooperative that she was starting to second-guess everything. But then Luther called, and denial and disbelief spun toward anger and betrayal until she couldn't quite tell any of them apart. For almost half a day she wondered whether she had pushed him toward his confession by asking about Burger King, and she began to feel guilty, but then she reminded herself that *Malcolm* was guilty, guilty of so much worse, and she grew angry all over again. She's still not certain why Malcolm confessed, but undoubtedly, he's playing some angle, because with Malcolm there's always an angle. "I'm relieved," she says.

"How so?"

Elena takes a moment to sort out how to say it because she knows that she isn't just telling Dom but also Dom's wife and Tony and Tony's wife and her dad, because that's just how her family works.

"My marriage was broken for so long," she says. "For years I've been asking myself what I did or didn't do to make things worse. For a long time, I blamed myself as much as I blamed him." Elena licks her lips and searches for the exact right words, but she knows she doesn't have time to tell Dom everything she feels about Malcolm, and she knows that Dom doesn't really care. So she tells him what she's certain of. "I know that it sounds weird, but it's a relief to learn that he was broken from the very start."

Dom takes that in. When he speaks next, thankfully, it's to change the subject. "Kinsey plays banjo, right?"

"No. Mandolin."

"What the hell is a mandolin?"

"It's a cross between a guitar and a banjo," she says, not because that's really true, but because Dom doesn't really care about that either. Besides, he'll see Kinsey play soon enough.

More hipsters straggle through the door. The seats are full, and latecomers begin to line the wall up the stairs. The house lights dim, and an usher closes the door. When the band strolls onto the stage with their instruments, the crowd breaks into applause. The regular members of the band bow at the front of the stage while Kinsey, who is the last to emerge from the wings, simply climbs onto the stool farthest from the center. She props her mandolin against her thigh and scans the audience with that remarkable composure that always amazes Elena. When she spots Elena and Dom, a smile flickers, but then she continues to scan.

The first song is a scorching all-hands-on-deck bluegrass number that Kinsey told her belonged to Ralph Stanley. Kinsey bends over her instrument and plays with an intensity and precision that makes Elena swell up inside. Her fingers blur, and the mandolin sings. When the crowd erupts after that first song, some of the band members stand up from their stools to acknowledge the applause while Kinsey and the banjo player tune their instruments.

Dom leans toward Elena. "Holy shit," he says over the noise of the crowd. "She's good."

Elena just smiles and nods.

The second song starts slow and quiet, just a guitar, the banjo, and bit of fiddle. Kinsey sits with her heels on the bar of the stool, the mandolin across her knees. Watching. Listening. When she looks back out at the crowd, her eyes wander until they lock onto something. Her lips pucker but then settle toward a smile. Elena follows the line of Kinsey's gaze and standing halfway up the stairs, leaning against the wall, she finds Malcolm. He wears jeans and a sweater, garments Elena didn't know that he owned. His arms are folded across his chest, and a smile not unlike Kinsey's dusts his lips. Elena hears the mandolin join the song, but she keeps her eyes pinned on Malcolm.

Dom leans in again to whisper. "Is that what's-his-name?"

Elena considers the man leaning against the wall smiling at their daughter, the man she's still married to, the man she'll divorce just before or soon after he goes to jail. He's taken so much from her, and he never had the common decency to tell her why. For so long, he was absent from their lives, an occasional visitor, and *now* he finally has the audacity to show up? She hates him, but it's a complicated, multilayered hatred. The sound of the mandolin comes louder, more insistent, and Malcolm's head bobs almost imperceptibly, and that, too, makes her angry. She wants Kinsey to hate him as much as she does, but even that's complicated. Because Elena sees him now. It suddenly feels like she sees him more clearly than she's ever seen him before. And just as suddenly she recognizes the rhythm giving structure to the melody of her hatred—pity.

"No," she finally whispers back. "That's Malcolm."

44

Pepsi. No Coke.

ON THE WAY up to Malcolm's condo, Tommy holds the cardboard tray of sodas and watches the numbers flash by. He marvels at the elevator's speed. It's a Mitsubishi, of course. The smell of the Billy Goat burgers leaking from the sack that Henry clutches makes it hard to focus on the words that he's been arranging in his head.

Henry can't stop thinking about how much condos in this building must go for. Ever since he became a real estate agent, every home is a price tag. And Malcolm must own the penthouse, because the security guard inserted his keycard into the slot before pushing the button for the top floor. He's about to make a crack to Tommy about lawyers and their billing rates when the doors slide open to reveal the largest and most empty condo that he's ever seen. Malcolm is staring out the floor-to-ceiling windows at the city.

Malcolm turns when he hears the elevator open. He would have been embarrassed by the enormous emptiness of the condo, but a few days in jail and losing his job and reading his name in the paper and several months of wearing an ankle bracelet have all raised the bar on what it takes to embarrass Malcolm.

"Come on in, fellas."

Henry and Tommy walk across what would have become the living room to join Malcolm at the window. Henry shakes Malcolm's hand. Tommy embraces him.

"It's big," Tommy says.

"It's fucking enormous," Henry says looking around. "And empty. You have the whole floor?"

Malcolm nods. "Until the first of the month."

"Who's buying it? An oligarch?"

Malcolm's forced smile and the reality of Malcolm's likely next address wedges an awkward silence between them. Henry, who was never comfortable with awkward silences, holds up the bag. "Cheeseborger, cheeseborger."

"Pepsi," Tommy says, holding up the cardboard tray.

Malcolm grabs a drink from the tray. "No Coke."

Those magic words from their childhood make all three men smile. For just a split second, it's the summer that Henry first got his license, and they're stopping at the Billy Goat Tavern on the way to Comiskey for a Brewers game. And of course, their thoughts slide toward Kevin, because that whole day he couldn't stop channeling Belushi.

"Sit," Malcolm says, and slides to the floor with his back to the window.

The other two sit down on either side of him, and they unpack the burgers. While they eat, they talk about their families, because that's what middle-aged men talk about, but also because they're not ready to talk about thirty years ago—or about tomorrow for that matter. Tommy speaks of the unbridled joy when Emma came home, and the paralyzing fear that she'll disappear yet again. Henry tells them about the virus and about how Alice reacted to *that*. He talks about how long it might take to fully regain Alice's trust and how he tells her absolutely everything, to the point that last week she'd said, *"Henry, I don't need to hear about it every time you take a shit or rub one out."* Malcolm doesn't talk about Elena, because he feels like he's lost the right to talk about Elena. And he doesn't talk about Naomi. Nobody's heard from her except for that brief article about Malcolm's confession. Henry thinks it's because of what Alice said to her. Malcolm thinks that it was always him she was after. Tommy doesn't know what to think.

Malcolm describes trying to rebuild his relationship with Kinsey because there's almost nothing left. He tells them about how he writes down a list of things to talk about before he calls her, because he knows that it will fall to him to fill every silence. But he also tells them about the gratitude that washes over him every time that she answers the phone. After everything. Those two words bring another silence, but it's a comfortable silence, and even Henry can sit with it. And in the quiet, they all feel it. They feel the not-so-subtle shift away from their stilted conversation at Kevin's funeral toward how it used to feel when they were together in Tommy's basement. *Before* everything. When they were brothers.

Tommy wads the wax paper from his burger into a tight ball. "What time does it start tomorrow?"

"Ten o'clock," Malcolm says.

"What do you think they'll—What do you think will happen?" Henry asks. He doesn't really want to hear the answer, but he feels like he can't not ask.

Malcolm's lawyer was able to plea the murder charge down to manslaughter, which Malcolm knows is the best he could hope for given that he confessed. His lawyer hopes that the judge might take extenuating circumstances into account—the money Malcolm paid to Linden Glen, his youth the night of the crime, the decades of good behavior since, but Malcolm knows the sentencing guidelines, and he knows that hope is not a plan. "Three to five years," he says.

Malcolm's words fall heavy between them. Henry wishes he hadn't asked. He wants to say, *"Thank you"* and *"I'm sorry."* He wants to yell at Malcolm and hug him and tell him a joke to make him smile, but instead he says nothing.

"I'll be there," Tommy says. "Tomorrow. At the sentencing."

"No," Malcolm snaps, his lawyer voice suddenly flaring. "That's a very bad idea."

A very, very bad idea, Henry thinks.

"It's the least I can do," Tommy says, even though he thinks that going to the sentencing falls far short of the least that he can do. "After what you did for us."

"And what if the Hoyers show up?" Malcolm demands. "Or Naomi? What then?"

Tommy shrugs. None of this sits right with him. "We were all there that night."

Henry closes his eyes. *Here we go again. Shut up, Tommy. Shut the fuck up.*

Malcolm stands and turns to look out the window. He watches a single boat sail out into the otherwise empty lake. A dozen arguments stand ready, but the most relevant springs to his lips. "We *were* all there that night. And we all know what I did."

"None of us were innocent," Tommy says.

"True," Malcolm says. "But Henry was right. I was the most guilty."

Henry opens his eyes. He blinks, his mind scrambling and then landing on those words he said in that diner. "Malcolm, that's not what I—"

Malcolm attempts a smile, but he can't quite manage it. "For the last thirty years, I've known it, even though I did everything I could to avoid it. In the meantime, I made a mess of everything."

Tommy opens his mouth to argue, but Malcolm waves him quiet. He wants to tell them that he hollowed out his life long before Kevin died, that what's left is completely meaningless, emptier than the condo they sit in. He wants to tell them how he ruined everything bit by bit and that all he has left are two friends that he thought he'd lost decades ago. He wants to tell them that it would break him to see those friends do something stupid, something that will ruin *their* lives and *their* families. He looks down at Henry where he's slumped against the glass. "And you were right about what you said in the car on the way back from Gainesville. We'll always be brothers."

Henry looks up at Malcolm and blinks away what might be a tear. Tommy swallows audibly and stares at his boots. A few months ago, Malcolm would have appealed to their self-interest, and it would have worked, but everything has shifted back toward how it was. Before everything.

"Please," Malcolm says. "For me. Please. Just let me do this one right thing."

45

The Truth

TOMMY PARKS AT the curb outside Miss Katie's. He checks his watch and sees that he's a few minutes early. When Maggie suggested that they meet for coffee, he texted back right away. When she suggested that they meet at Miss Katie's, it took him a few minutes to text back *Sure*. He's never been to Miss Katie's with Maggie before, and he can't help but think that her suggestion is a not-so-subtle jab, a reminder of that surreptitious lunch with Emma.

Maggie's been so hard to read. She said nothing to him in the days that it took him to pack and move out. The first few times they spoke on the phone, she used the fewest possible words to discuss the kids and the visits and the money. Over the summer, she became civil, then cordial, then friendly even, but Tommy has no idea whether it's the kind of friendly that signals forgiveness or the sort that comes from the relief of living apart.

He climbs out of the car and makes his way across the parking lot and through the door of the diner. He scans the dining room until he finds Maggie. She sits in the booth right next to where he and Emma had lunch, but that part *must* be a coincidence. He eases onto the bench across from her. "Hey," he says.

She smiles, but it's an indeterminate, in-between kind of smile. "Hey."

She's wearing earrings and a navy suit that he's never seen before. She had to step up her game for the new firm, evidently. She's got her hands around a mug of coffee, and a second mug sits in front of him. A glance tells him that she already poured two creams into it. A sip tells him she didn't forget the sugar. "You look nice," he says. "How's the new job?"

Maggie shrugs. Her lips flicker between a frown and a smile, like they do when she's nervous. "I'm still getting used to tracking my day in fifteen-minute increments," she says. "The pay's better, which will be good if—" She takes her glasses off and rubs a smudge away with her napkin. "Well, it's better. And it's easy not to care when you're just negotiating contracts." She sips from her coffee. "How's your friend Malcolm doing?"

Tommy sets his own mug on the table. It's still hard for him to think about Malcolm, much less talk about him, without feeling heavy with guilt. "Henry and I went to visit a couple weeks ago. He's in a minimum-security place up in Oxford. He seems to be doing okay, but it's hard to tell. He's lost weight, and he seems, I don't know, skittish. He says he's playing a lot of chess. He laughed at Henry's jokes, which is something, I guess."

"How's Henry?"

It's strange to hear Maggie ask about his friends that she's never met. It's stranger still to find Henry in his life again. He and Henry talk at least once a week, and they text each other in between. In so many ways, it's like they picked up exactly where they left off, but how to tell Maggie *that*?

"He's fine. He's a real estate agent now," he says, because he's not sure what else to tell her. "How're the kids?" he asks, because he doesn't want to keep talking about Malcolm and Henry and because he can't not ask about the kids. They stay with him on weekends, but usually one or two at time, and they come and go from his crappy little apartment, because they're teenagers and they've got friends and their own lives. He's fallen back into the weekly rhythm of lunches with Emma, but even so, it feels like he's seeing the shadows of his children through a pinhole—like he's watching a solar eclipse.

Maggie puts her glasses back on. "We need to talk about Jeremy."

"Uh-oh."

"Yeah. Somebody got him into DraftKings. I saw it on his phone when he was asleep. He's been betting a lot."

"How much did he lose?"

"That's the thing," she says. "He's up almost two hundred dollars."

"Have you told him you know?"

"Not yet. I wanted to talk to you first."

A collaboration. Tommy's embarrassed by how good it feels. "Maybe you should wait," he says.

"Wait for what?"

"Wait for him to lose. Everybody loses eventually. If we talk to him about it when he's *down* two hundred bucks, he'll hear us better." *We.* Tommy uses that word on purpose, and that, too, feels good.

Maggie's lips settle into a smile, and she nods. "I'll keep an eye on it for now."

"How's Sophie?"

"She's good. She and Ben seem to be getting along."

"That helps," Tommy says.

They both take a sip of coffee. Tommy's about to ask the obvious next question, but Maggie beats him to it.

"How's Emma?"

Tommy blinks at her, confused. When Tommy moved out of the house, Emma wanted to come with him, and truth be told, that would have made the transition easier for Tommy. But he and Maggie both agreed that Emma should stay at home for the summer—until it was time to move back into the dorm. They decided that the familiarity and stability would help her regain her footing. More importantly, it would allow Maggie to start spackling the cracks in their relationship. "I was about to ask you the same question."

Maggie sets the mug down and looks out the window. She chews her lip and then looks back at Tommy. "See, that's the thing. Just because she lives with me, doesn't mean that she talks to me."

Tommy sits with that for a long moment, and for the first time in the last few months, he feels more pity for Maggie than for himself.

"Does she tell you anything?" she asks. "During your lunches?"

Emma does him tell him things. Quite a bit, actually. If anything, her time in Madison has made them closer. He lives for their lunches. "She seems to be doing okay," he says. "All things considered. She says that she's not in touch with Kyle, and I believe her. She's thinking about changing her major to accounting in the fall, but I'm not sure she really means that. I don't think there's another boy." He pauses. "She blamed herself for our separation." He calls it a separation, because Maggie hasn't yet brought up the next step, and the D word makes Tommy's stomach hurt. "But I made it clear that was my fault."

"What does she say about me?"

There it is—the reason Maggie asked him here, the question that will test his resolve. If he tells the truth, he'll tell Maggie exactly what she doesn't want to hear. And he knows that Maggie might say something to Emma, something that will tell Emma he broke her confidence. Emma will stop meeting him for lunch, stop telling him things. But every night as he lies awake, piecing together everything that he did wrong and making bargains with a God that he doesn't quite believe in anymore, he tells himself that if he gets another chance with Maggie, he'll tell her nothing but the truth. No matter what.

"She said that she finds it difficult to talk to you."

Maggie swallows hard, and Tommy wants to stop there. He wants to think this is enough, but he knows that it isn't. "She says that every conversation feels like an interrogation."

The color drains from Maggie's face. "An interrogation?" she whispers.

"Actually, I think she said deposition." Tommy licks his lips, tries to find gentler words, but he knows that some of the truth will leak away if he tries to be gentle. "She says that it feels like you'll never trust her. She can't wait to get back to the dorms."

He watches Maggie take this in. She looks down at her coffee cup. Her mouth opens and then closes several times, but she says nothing. He prepares himself for her rant, her defense, her attack. She'll point out that Emma hasn't exactly earned her trust. She'll remind him that she's the parent, that Emma's the child. She'll say that she just wants to keep Emma safe, and she wouldn't have to ask so goddamn many questions if Emma would just talk to her. He knows that all of that is true. And he's heard Maggie run across these well-worn ruts so many times that he could probably say the words for her. And then, after she's done with Emma, she'll demand to know what Tommy said back to her, she'll express her deep dissatisfaction with his answer, and he'll leave Miss Katie's feeling shittier than when he arrived. But when she looks up at him, she blinks and forces a smile.

"Thank you," she finally says. "For telling me the truth."

Tommy leans forward and he wants to take her hand, but of course, the new boundaries in their life don't allow for that. He scours what Emma has said for something true that Maggie *does* want to hear. "For what it's worth, last week she said that she could tell that you were trying."

Maggie rubs her eyes with the heels of her hands, and she smiles wanly. Her voice hitches when she speaks. "How are *you* doing?"

It's Tommy's turn to look down at his mug. He wants to say that he's doing okay. It was like he lost fifty pounds in Gainesville, another fifty in the basement that night. Shedding those lies still makes him feel light, and he wants to tell her that lightness is enough. But he works late every night in order to delay his return to that tiny apartment. He heats up something in the microwave for dinner and listens to the heels on hardwood in the apartment above, the bass of the death metal from the apartment below, and the television that he always keeps on in order to hear human voices.

When he's not texting the kids or worrying about whether Naomi or the Hoyers are going to drop another shoe, he thinks about Maggie. Constantly. He imagines how he might be able to make it up to her, fantasizes about forgiveness. But regret is the last emotion that he feels before he finally falls asleep each night. It washes over him again every morning, when he blinks awake to the paint peeling from the unfamiliar bedroom ceiling. He doesn't want to lie to Maggie, but he can't find the words for all that, so he just says, "Not so good."

Maggie's face tightens in a way that Tommy finds hard to read. She looks like she's going to say something, and he's afraid of what she'll say, so he blurts, "What about you?"

As soon as he asks, he knows that he should have kept quiet. She won't cut her response with compassion because that's not how Maggie answers important questions. He doesn't want to hear that she's doing better than she expected, that she's reinventing herself for the next chapter in her life. He doesn't want to hear about the new friends that she's made at her new job, and he doesn't want to hear that subtle inflection in her voice that will tell him, without her saying it, that she's relieved that he's gone. He looks out the window so that he doesn't have to see the expression on her face. It takes her a long time to answer, and before she does, her hands wrap around his on the mug. Her voice, when she speaks, feels like an embrace.

"I know that I'm not perfect. I know that it's my fault— what happened with Emma. And I know how angry that must make you."

Tommy doesn't say anything. He stares hard at a car across the street, careful to keep his expression neutral.

"But you lied to me, and I'm not talking about lunch with Emma. You lied to me about something enormous."

Her hands squeeze his, and he forces himself still.

"I'm not sure that I can ever forgive you for that, but I miss you," she says. "Desperately. More than I ever thought that I could. Both of those things are true at the same time, and I just don't know what to do about that."

Tommy tears his gaze from the window but only manages to look down at Maggie's hands squeezing his. Her words make him want to smile and laugh. They make him want to shout. They make him want to sing. Never have uncertainty and confusion infused him with so much hope, so much gratitude. Her wedding band gleams on her finger, and he wonders if it's been there all along. He finally looks Maggie in the face. Her expression tells him nothing, but her eyes glisten behind the lenses of her glasses. He wants to say something, something that will tip the balance, something that might help her decide, but words seem far too dangerous for now. She doesn't look away. Her words echo in his ears. Her hands grow warm on his. He knows that it's all more than he deserves, and for now, it will have to be enough.

ACKNOWLEDGMENTS

THIS STORY WOULD have remained just a jumble of words without the help of all who read it, including Matt Turkot, Carolyn Boykin, Sara Hoffmann, Bob Hoffmann, Jean Hoffmann, Sandy McGrath, Cathy Knott, Dan Fouts, Mark Splitstone, and Ed Short. It would still be just a file on my computer without the tireless efforts, unbounded optimism, and insightful feedback of Harvey Klinger, my agent. And it would have sagged in embarrassing places without the badass editing of Sara J. Henry.

The team at Crooked Lane sanded the edges and make a book out of it all. The team in Junction City, Kansas, as always, pushed me relentlessly. My children, Roshan and Grace, were generous enough to make excuses for their layabout father while he "worked." My wife, Sara, never lost faith, and she read it again and again. And I never would have dared to write at all if my father, Bob Hoffmann, hadn't taught me to love the smell of books and the melody of words on paper. I'm grateful that he lived to see my first book published, but I miss him.